A killer took aim, and now one disliked doxie owner is dead on the sidelines at Laguna Beach's Dachshund Derby Races. Naturally, Mel is ankles-deep in dachshund drama.

I WAS LOOKING for a sweaty rock star with a dog tattoo and smeared eyeliner carrying Betty's stolen gun and an oversized camera. "You take the east side of the field and I'll take the west. If either of us sees Darby, we fill her in. We need all the help we can get."

Betty hiked her handbag onto her shoulder. "What about our booth? Who's gonna sell our stuff? Who's going to keep people from stealing it?"

"That's the least of our problems."

I had no idea how true those words were. But I was about to find out.

D1412365

The Pampered Pets Mysteries from Bell Bridge Books

The Girl with the Dachshund Tattoo

by

Sparkle Abbey

Bell Bridge Books

This is a work of fiction. Names, characters, places and incidents are either the products of the author's imagination or are used fictitiously. Any resemblance to actual persons (living or dead), events or locations is entirely coincidental.

Bell Bridge Books
PO BOX 300921
Memphis, TN 38130
Print ISBN: 978-1-61194-466-2

Bell Bridge Books is an Imprint of BelleBooks, Inc.

We at BelleBooks enjoy hearing from readers.
Visit our websites
BelleBooks.com
BellBridgeBooks.com
ImaJinnBooks.com

10 9 8 7 6 5 4 3 2 1

Cover design: Debra Dixon
Interior design: Hank Smith
Photo/Art credits:
Girl walking dogs (manipulated) © Caroll | www.Fotolia.com
Street (manipulated) © Canaris | Dreamstime.com
Collar © Roughcollie | Dreamstime.com
Paw Print © Booka1 | Dreamstime.com
Magnifying glass © Yudesign | Dreamstime.com
Bag logo (manipulated) © Kydriashka | Dreamstime.com

:Ldgt:01:

Dedication

For all the doxie lovers and the wiener racing fans

Chapter One

WE WERE ABOUT to experience more waving, cheering, and crying than a TV audience during the crowning of Miss America.

Doxie Dash. Wiener Race. The Great Dachshund Derby. The name wasn't important. The crux of all the events was the same: running dogs, excited families, squeaky rubber toys, frantically waved treats, and a mega trophy for the winner. True, a trophy is not as glamorous as a tiara, but we can't all be beauty queens.

"Are you Team Zippy or Team Pickles?" Betty Foxx raised her grape- colored eyebrows expectantly. "I bet it's going to be a real smack-down. Their bitter rivalry has been all over the news."

Yes, you heard that correctly. Grape eyebrows. My eighty-something assistant had yet to explain the occasional lipstick-painted eyebrows, and I've wisely refrained from questioning her makeup application process. I have my own hang-ups. Who am I to judge her eyebrows?

Our race, the Laguna Beach Dachshund Dash, was an outdoor event at the local dog park. With a smattering of food booths and a slew of pet-related vendors, playful contestants and pumped-up fans had plenty to do throughout the day. The aromas of funnel cake, chili, and deep-fried mac and cheese collided in the air. My stomach rumbled, craving for a sample of everything.

Betty had nagged me to donate the official doxie jersey, which is how Bow Wow Boutique ended up with a vendor booth for the first time since the race had arrived in Laguna three years ago. What can I say? I'm a sucker for an assistant in silk pajamas, pearls, and lipstick eyebrows.

She had insisted the event organizers promise to pitch our booth, a shelter canopy with three sidewalls to display merchandise, adjacent to the racing lanes. They weren't as easily persuaded by Betty's pleas as I was. We were nowhere near the track.

I stepped around my sleeping bulldog, Missy. She looked dead, stretched out on a small patch of grass, bathing in the morning sun. Don't worry—she was alive and well, with a puddle of drool watering the grass. That dog could sleep through an earthquake.

I tossed a stack of lime canine jerseys on the display table and quickly separated them by size. The material felt a little thinner than I'd have liked, but, overall, the uniforms were darling.

"You do realize the feud is all media hype? Their rivalry is about ticket sales and money." I tried to hide my amusement at her insistence that the two dogs were enemies.

Of all people, Betty understood the power of the almighty dollar. Her retail background and quirky personality had boosted sales for my pet boutique since I'd hired her last Christmas. The success had gone to her head. Now she was convinced she was the Rainmaker of pet accessories. She concocted outlandish plans almost weekly, "guaranteed" to generate more sales. I adored her, but she was a handful to manage.

"Not true," she said. "The new reporter from *Channel 5 News,* Callum MacAvoy"—Betty took a breath long enough to shoot me her "hubba-hubba" face before she continued—"well, he's been talking about the bad blood between them for weeks. At the last race, Pickles almost closed the gap, but Moby bumped Pickles out of bounds before they crossed the finish line. Pickles was disqualified, and Zippy was declared the winner." Betty danced in place, about to burst the seams of her tiger-print silk pajamas any second.

I laughed at her outdated dance moves. "Are you done?"

She snagged a stack of size-small jerseys and stacked them at the far end of the table. "Who are you backing, Cookie?"

My name wasn't Cookie. I'm Melinda Langston. Mel, to my friends. For reasons only known to Betty, she refused to call me by my name.

Unlike my spry assistant, I'm not as well versed in the drama of wiener racing. What few rules I knew would fit on a sticky note.

No running alongside your dog.

No loud horns or laser pointers.

The dog must cross the finish line within the boundaries and without help.

If Betty had the story straight, Pickles had a difficult time staying in bounds. Sounded like someone else I knew. I eyed my assistant, who stood with a hand on her hip, white sneaker firmly planted in the freshly mowed grass, waiting for an answer.

Oh, I almost forgot the most important rule. *You have to pick up after your racer.* I'm amazed at the number of people who "forget" that last one.

"If I have to choose, I guess I'm Team Pickles."

Betty wrinkled her nose in disapproval. "You would pick the dog named after food. I'm Team Zippy. He's the favorite. If I were a bettin' gal, I'd put my money on him. A win today would be his fourth title in less than a year." Betty scurried behind me to rearrange the display rack of collars hanging on the sidewall.

"What can I say—I love an underdog."

Wiener racing was a little different than, say, horse racing or even greyhound racing. Wiener enthusiasts adorn themselves in over-the-top doxie-themed outfits, with an occasional superhero cape for added dramatic flair. Winners break into victory dances, while geeked-out fans storm the grassy area to demand a photo op with their favorite racer. That's the humans.

Then there are the dogs. Adorable low-riders with long, wiggly bodies, who race fifty yards toward their beloved human or favorite toy. As they sprint down the track, doggie tongues hang from their mouths, like Miley Cyrus mugging for the camera.

The majority of the pack has absolutely no idea what they're doing and ends up plowing into one another, reenacting the Puppy Bowl. But there are a few true competitors who can concentrate on the finish line for more than eight seconds. They're the ones who sprint down the field, all heart, for a photo finish.

That's where my best friend, Darby Beckett, comes in. As the official Dachshund Dash photographer, her job was to document the winner of each race. The number of prima donnas who dispute the final results, certain their pup had won by a nose, would surprise you.

By the end of the day's events, there will have been five heats, in three different weight classes, with one winner in each category: miniature, lightweight, and heavyweight.

Betty shoved an empty box under the table. "It's almost nine. The contestants will arrive any minute."

"Great. We're ready for them." I pushed a stack of extra-large jerseys to the front of the table.

"Oh, make sure you're here at ten o'clock."

I stared at the faux innocent expression on Betty's face. "Why?"

"We have an interview."

Unpleasant memories of my last year in the beauty pageant world sprang to mind. I shook my head. "No. Not going to happen."

Her grape eyebrows shot upward. "What do you mean 'no'?"

"I don't like reporters."

In my experience, reporters were neither balanced nor impartial.

Their goal was to tell a titillating story. Facts and truth were not necessary. To be fair, Betty didn't know that my mama had "persuaded" a male judge to vote for me during my Miss America run. Nor did she know about the wacky publicity that had resulted from my melodramatic disqualification. If she had, she'd understand my distrust of reporters.

"She's a filmmaker, Cookie. She's shooting a movie. Besides, it's free publicity."

Bless Betty's naïve soul. "Nothing's free. We don't even know what the film's about."

"What's there to know? It's a dogumentary. A wiener racing biopic. *The Long and the Short of It.*" Betty barked out a laugh and slapped her thin thigh in amusement. "That's the best title."

I groaned. "That's an awful title."

"When she comes around, I'll do the talking," Betty announced. "And don't stare at her."

"Why in the world would I stare?"

Betty tossed a sassy smile over her shoulder. "She's not sexy like us."

"Is that so?"

"She's a behind-the-camera kinda person. Smeared eyeliner, ratty short hair, ripped jeans. You know, I should offer the poor girl pointers on her eyeliner."

I ignored the comment about eyeliner. "Sounds like any eighties glam band after a long concert."

Betty nodded excitedly as she moved the treat jars from the top shelf to a shelf at eye level. "So you've seen her?"

"How often have you talked to this *filmmaker*?" I resisted using air quotes, my skepticism obvious.

Betty patted my arm reassuringly. "Don't you worry, Cookie. I've got it all under control."

I'd experienced Betty's version of control. Lord help us all. We were in trouble.

"HEY, MEL. THE booth looks great." Darby's blond curls brushed her shoulders. Her normally pale skin already sported a SoCal tan. We were dressed alike—jeans and the event T-shirt Betty and I had designed. The shirts had turned out great—a sunshine yellow material with the words "Wiener Takes All" in brown above a smooth-haired dachshund. All the vendors had agreed to sell the shirts, the profits to be donated to the rescue group, Doxie Lovers of OC.

As my best friend, Darby knew my drink of choice and handed me a chai tea latte from the Koffee Klatch.

"You are a lifesaver." I inhaled deeply, savoring the aroma of cardamom, cinnamon, and vanilla. "Where's Fluffy?" Fluffy was Darby's Afghan hound who has a superiority complex. I imagine she thought a doxie race was beneath her.

Darby slipped the strap of her soft leather messenger bag over her head, then laid the bag on the table. "I left her at home. This isn't exactly her idea of a good time. Where'd Betty run off to?"

"She took Missy to check out the other vendors. Ensuring we can beat the competition. You know how she gets. The boutique never sells enough of anything."

Darby sipped her favorite drink, a white chocolate mocha latte. "When are you going to tell her you don't need the money?"

She referred to my "Texas money." Montgomery family money I rarely touched, much to my mama's displeasure. Mama would prefer I attended charity balls and wasted my days "stimulating" the economy by buying junk I didn't need nor want. I preferred to work for a living.

I shrugged. "Not today. What have you been up to?"

She pulled her camera from her messenger bag. "Snapping candid photos. I got some great shots of the protesters. I found Zippy and Richard out front signing autographs. I thought I'd grab Betty and see if she'd like to join me."

"Wait. Did you say 'protesters'?"

She nodded, brows furrowed. "A dozen people with picket signs. One woman had a poster-sized photo of a dachshund racing in a wheelchair. To be honest, at first I found the idea inspirational, but the longer I looked at the picture, it became a little . . . disturbing."

"This is the first I've heard about any opposition to the race."

"They're part of a local animal activist group concerned about the possibility of back injuries. As the popularity of racing grows, they think the dachshunds may have the same overbreeding issues as greyhounds."

We sipped our drinks in silence. Darby took a couple of random photos. I felt a little uncomfortable. I'd never given any of those concerns a second thought. Could that controversy be the impetus behind the dogumentary? I was about to ask Darby if she'd seen the filmmaker when I caught a glimpse of my trusted assistant.

"Here comes Betty," I said.

We watched her stroll up the vendor aisle as she cast sly glances toward the other merchants. Missy waddled behind. With her short nose and bulky frame, she looked completely out of place around all the wiener dogs. The second Betty caught sight of Darby, she transformed into The Prancing Grandma.

"Darby, you're slacking," she announced. "As the official photographer, you should be taking pictures of the booths. Start with ours." She shoved Missy's leash in my hand, then scooted around the table. She struck a pose in front of a rack of merchandise. "Make sure you get the sweaters. They're on sale."

Darby snapped pictures as Betty acted out her interpretation of a supermodel photo shoot. I watched, amused, as I drank my breakfast.

"I saw Zippy," Betty said. "I don't like his owner. He tugged on Zippy's leash and made the poor dog walk in circles, backwards. I think Zippy hurt his leg. I saw him limping. Instead of Ricky-Dicky being concerned, he yelled at him to stop whining. He made me so mad. I've switched teams."

Ricky-Dicky? Since when had she started calling Richard Eriksen Ricky-Dicky? Betty suddenly struck an awkward wide-legged stance and threw a punch.

"He's lucky I didn't show him my new moves. You girls should have seen me in that self-defense class I took a few months ago. I was a rock star." Betty acted out what could have been a scene from a Jackie Chan movie. Birdlike arms flailed in front of her face; her right knee jabbed the air.

"Boom." Step. "Boom," she shouted.

"Settle down, girlfriend, before you attack the rack of dog collars." I guided her away from the merchandise.

"You don't get it. If anyone pulls a gun on us again, I'm ready for them." Betty struck a Charlie's Angel stance, complete with clasped hands imitating a gun.

Last Christmas, Betty and I had been held at gunpoint, a life-changing moment for both of us. Apparently, she'd gone on the defensive, whereas I had decided to cross a line without thought about the repercussions. More on my poor decision later.

"That was a fluke," I said.

"You don't know that," she insisted.

For everyone's benefit, I'd better be right. "Let's finish the pictures."

"Stand next to the sign," Darby ordered. "I want the boutique's name in a couple of shots."

"Good idea. Cookie, get over here."

Betty's previous kung-fu impersonation over, Missy and I reluctantly obeyed. I set my half-empty cup on the table.

Darby slowly lowered her camera. "Mel, where's your engagement ring?"

Was the undertone of concern in her voice real, or had my own insecurities surrounding my personal life made me oversensitive? That line I'd just mentioned? Well it involved my fiancé, Grey Donovan, and he couldn't seem to get past my impulsive decision. He had every reason to be angry. I'd messed up. But that wasn't the real problem. The real issue was that, presented with the exact set of circumstances, I'm pretty sure I'd make the same decision. Yeah, not good.

By the look on their faces, you'd think a hairy wart had bloomed on my finger. I resisted the urge to cover my bare left hand so they'd stop staring at it. If I were an accomplished liar, I'd claim wearing a six-carat sapphire heirloom to a wiener race wasn't practical. But Darby knew I didn't possess one ounce of practicality.

I settled for a half truth and prayed she would drop the subject. "I accidently left it on the bathroom counter this morning."

Darby placed her camera next to my chai. "There's only been one other time you've been without your ring. Last year when you two 'took a break.' Is everything okay?"

I swallowed hard. "There is nothing for you to worry about."

"Where is that sexy man of yours?" Betty yanked on the elastic waistband of her pants, hiking them higher up. "I wore my new outfit for him. I got it off of that all-night shopping TV channel."

I rubbed my ringless finger. "Grey flew to New York."

Grey's secret life as an undercover FBI agent had, by default, become my secret life too. What my friends and family believed to be gallery business trips were a cover for his real job.

He was actually in DC, preparing for a new white-collar case involving counterfeit wine. By definition, white-collar crime (lying, cheating, and stealing) was considered nonviolent. In Grey's case it was the undercover aspect that created the danger—raids, arrests, and, frankly, desperate criminals who didn't want to go to prison, and who had a tendency to act out in violent ways.

He'd promised me the most dangerous situation he'd come across while in New York was a hangover. I was holding him to it.

"He'll miss the race. He sounded like he was looking forward to it," Darby said.

He had been, until my little stunt. After that he looked forward to time apart to clear his head.

Thank the good Lord, Luis and his long-haired doxie, Barney, walked up to our table, saving me from further discussion about Grey and my missing engagement ring. Barney's tail wagged double time when he noticed Betty.

"You're the first to arrive." I blinded them with my brightest smile.

Betty grabbed her orange clipboard from under the table and checked them off our list. Darby snapped a photo, and I handed Luis a jersey for Barney—an extra-large.

"Mel, the uniforms are great." Luis was your average guy. He wore an event T-shirt with a pair of cargo shorts and sneakers. Nice, unassuming, and he loved his dog. Bless his heart. He didn't hold Betty's nagging about Barney's need to drop a few pounds against either of us.

Betty bent over and patted Barney's head. "You're looking good." She straightened and eyed Luis. "You still use too much of that dog cologne. He smells like a fifteen-year-old boy going out on his first date."

Luis face reddened. "He likes it."

"He stinks."

She was right. Barney's cologne overpowered any smell within twenty yards. My eyes watered a bit. "He looks like he's lost a little weight. Has he been training?"

Luis rubbed his chin as he studied his dog. "A little. He has a lot of energy. He really likes to socialize with the other dogs. Running at the park seemed like a good idea."

"Which heavyweight heat is Barney in?" I asked.

"The first one. We're on our way there now. To check it out. Are you going to watch us race?"

"Absolutely," Betty and Darby said in unison.

"Wouldn't miss it," I said. "Did you bring the fried chicken? He's definitely motivated by food." A character trait I could relate to.

Luis nodded, a huge smile split his thick lips. He patted the fanny pack hidden under his belly. "Right here. So, I guess we'll see you there." After a quick wave, Luis ducked his head, and the two made their way toward the west end of the field.

Betty shook her head in pity. "The minute Barney takes his eyes off that chicken he'll forget all about the race and meander out of bounds."

I wanted to disagree, but she was right on the money. Barney possessed only one speed—distracted. The big guy wasn't a natural competitor. He liked to roam, explore, and hang out with his pals. Fried chicken was his only chance at victory.

Within minutes, a line of contestants stood in front of our table. Happy chatter blended with excited barking as we processed the racers. Darby disappeared into the noisy crowd of humans and dogs to photograph the day. An hour quickly passed, and we'd handed out over half the jerseys. Presently, the line was only a half-dozen people deep.

Betty held her clipboard in front of her tiny body like a drill sergeant. "Name?" she barked out.

"Pickles." The man's voice was as thick as his bulging biceps. I looked at the black-and-tan wire-haired dachshund he cradled gently.

I won't lie; inappropriate jokes sprang to mind, one right after another. I pinched off the natural impulse to verbalize them.

"I got two dogs named Pickles," Betty said. "One's racing with the miniatures. The other must be you. You Lenny Santucci?"

Lenny looked like an angry frat boy who was minutes away from discovering his "brothers" were about to expel him due to anger mismanagement. I changed my opinion about Lenny and Pickles being the underdog.

"That's right." He adjusted Pickles so the dog rested on one gigantic forearm.

Betty scoffed as she checked his name off her list. She mumbled something inappropriate under her breath about a man naming his dog "Pickles."

"Size?" I asked.

"Medium." It was a dare, not a statement.

"There's no way he's a medium." Betty pointed a boney finger at Pickles. "A large."

"You tellin' me my dog is fat?" Lenny leaned closer. His hips bumped the table, and his upper lip curled with intimidation.

Betty inched up on her toes, meeting him halfway, undeterred by his surliness. "I've seen fat dogs. Pickles is knocking on the door of tubby. Doesn't matter, these things run small." She grabbed the large uniform I handed her and held it toward him. "Here. If he can't fit into a large, tell Cookie here. She'll hook you up with a bigger size."

I hid an amused smile. Betty always spoke her mind, unconcerned with what someone might think. And at her age, who wanted to stop her? Frankly, I was thankful she was finally comfortable pushing something other than paw-lish. Even if it was free jerseys.

"Aren't you the sweetest little guy?" Betty held out her hand for Pickles to sniff. "You've got winner written all over you."

He squirmed to get closer to Betty as she tried her darnedest to pet the little bugger, but Lenny wasn't cooperating. He kept his pooch just out of Betty's reach.

Lenny jutted his chin. "That's right. This time those pesky Eriksens and their juiced dog, Zippy, are going down."

As Betty had mentioned earlier, Zippy was the three-time champ. I'd heard some scuttlebutt about a group of contestants who'd filed a lawsuit against the race organizers in an effort to force the judges to declare Zippy ineligible to give the other dogs a fair shake at the championship. I'd dismissed the talk as pure gossip. Seriously, who sues over a wiener race? But Lenny presented a whole new level of crazy.

"What do you mean 'juiced'?" I asked.

"Exactly what it sounds like. The Eriksens dope Zippy."

Betty gasped, then quickly gathered herself and gave him the stink eye. "You got any proof?"

A million years ago, I'd come from the beauty pageant world. I understood true competition, and how the need to win could drive even the most honest person to color outside the lines. Even today, the desire to compete pumped through my veins.

But doping? Really? Well, that was one allegation I never thought I'd hear in conjunction with dachshund dashes. What did he think the Eriksens were doing? Slipping the dogs creatine shakes? Shooting them up with steroids?

Had our fun event turned into a bad reality show?

"I got plenty of proof. In fact, I sent the dogumentary filmmaker after those cheaters." His eyes gleamed with satisfaction.

Lenny Santucci didn't seem like a guy above unleashing a little controversy in order to secure a first-place win. It was time to pick a new team.

Chapter Two

"YOU'RE A LIAR!" A tall curvy brunette shouted it from the back of the line.

Talk about a facelift gone awry. At one time she had probably been very beautiful woman. Today, she looked like ten miles of Texas back roads.

Gia Eriksen. One of Zippy's owners. I recognized her from the program. She sliced through the mini-crowd in a preposterous peacock-colored jumpsuit. With each angry step, her spike heels stabbed the lawn. It sounded like she took exception to Lenny's claim that she drugged her dog.

"No one believes your ridiculous lies," she bit out, stroking her long mud-colored hair. She pursed her lips and tsked. "Speaking of ridiculous, Pickles looks a little sad."

I looked at the tail-wagging pup gently cradled in the crook of Lenny's arm. His brown eyes sparkled and his ears perked up at the sound of his name. The dog. Not the owner. Pickles looked particularly joyful. Lenny, on the other hand, radiated frenetic energy.

He pulled Pickles back in a protective move. "Shut. Up."

Going out on a limb here, but I got the feeling these two didn't like each other.

Gia smiled wickedly. "Oh, I'm sorry. Is he still depressed about second place? Again. For the fifth time?"

"I'm warning you, lady."

"You wouldn't be interested in a friendly wager on the race would you? No, I guess you wouldn't. When are you going to learn? Your dog's a loser."

Lenny's pooch suddenly yelped. Missy, who'd been snoozing under the table, lifted her head and barked.

"You're squeezing your Pickles." Betty lunged across the table. I quickly grabbed her by the waist and held her back as she wiggled to get free.

What the heck? "Put down the dog," I ordered.

Lenny snapped out of his dark thoughts, and set Pickles on the grass.

"I'm watching you." Betty wagged a finger at Lenny.

"Will you behave?" I asked my assistant.

She grunted something unintelligible under her breath. I took it for an agreement to calm down. Assured she wasn't about to start a riot, I released her. Missy ambled out from under the table to view the action. I shooed her back to her resting spot.

Gia's pouty lips turned in Lenny's direction. "Poor Lenny. Have you thought about therapy?"

"You rabid porcupine." His menacing voice made the hairs on the back of my neck stand on end. "You know we'd have won that last race if Pickles hadn't been pushed out of bounds. We'll see who's crying at the end of the day."

Gia scoffed, completely unaffected by Lenny's wrath. "The same person who cries after every race. You. And your little dog." She tossed an artificial smile over her shoulder, then slinked away.

The veins on Lenny's forehead popped. "I hate her."

I couldn't blame him. Lordy, I was exhausted. It wasn't even noon, and there had already been way too much drama. Everyone needed to take a deep breath and relax. This was supposed to be a fun day.

An announcement over the loudspeaker informed the crowd the first race was about to begin. Lenny stomped off, muttering about how much he despised the Eriksens. Betty and I channeled our energy to work our way through the line of folks who still needed to pick up their jerseys.

Surely, the day could only get better.

WITH A SHOT, The Dachshund Dash started.

Instantly, the park filled with triumphant cheers mish-mashed with cries of disappointment. We couldn't see the race, but we were close enough that we could hear the rhythmic squeaking of the toys at the finish line. The closer the dogs drew to the white line, the faster the cadence of excited clapping, and the louder the cheers and whistles from the fans.

As the morning passed, people swapped shopping at the vendor booths for watching the wiener races. Since foot traffic was dead, Betty had rearranged our entire stock of merchandise to pass the time. My mind was still on Lenny and Gia's public dogfight. Pickles and Zippy were sweet, adorable pooches, but after their owners' immature squabble, I wanted any other contestant to outrun them today. I had a low tolerance for bad sportsmanship.

"I like the water bowls and treats up front." Betty rested her hands on her hips and scrutinized her handiwork.

"Do you realize the filmmaker never showed?" I asked.

She spun around. "Oh, yeah. Do you think she heard about the fight? Maybe she secretly filmed it. That would make great TV."

I pulled a couple bottles of water out of the cooler and handed one to Betty. "You never mentioned her name."

Betty shrugged. "She didn't tell me."

I wiped a dollop of water from my chin. "You didn't ask her?"

"It never came up. She wanted us to be in her movie. That was all that mattered to me."

"Did she give you a business card?"

"Sure." Betty rummaged through her Michael Kors straw handbag and pulled out a bright orange camera-shaped card. "Bright Eyes Films."

I grabbed it and looked for a clue about the filmmaker. No name, no phone number, no street address. Just a generic email address that could belong to anyone. I didn't have a good feeling about this woman.

"If you see her again, let me know." In the meantime, I'd dig around on my own to find out if this was a legit operation. I pulled out my smartphone and launched the Internet.

"I'm checking on Zippy and Pickles," Betty said.

"I'm sure they're fine," I muttered, distracted by what I'd found online. Or more accurately, the lack of what I'd found.

"I'll be back."

My head snapped up. "What are you up to?"

"Ricky-Dicky mistreats Zippy. I'm going to make sure someone's there to protect that pup." The determination in her voice rang in my ears.

Could this really be the same woman who'd walked into my shop last December and declared she didn't want a canine and only barely tolerated cats? Something had turned her into a pet activist. Or at least a dachshund activist.

"Look, I'm not sure what you think you saw, but if he had truly hurt Zippy, his nightmarish wife would have taken him down."

Betty stared at me, her gray eyes unblinking. "I know what I saw. I'm not blind. I don't even wear glasses. He dragged that poor helpless dog around by his leash."

Now that she pointed out her lack of eyeglasses, I wondered when she'd had her eyes checked last. Sidetracked by Betty's eyesight, I missed what she'd said.

"What'd you say?"

"I'll be back," she announced.

I sighed. She was like a dog with a bone. "Do I need to come?"

Betty huffed, offended. "I don't need a babysitter."

I held up my hand. "I was just asking. Do us all a favor and keep a low profile."

"What does that mean?"

"You know exactly what it means. Stay out of trouble."

I don't know what I was thinking, but I should have known better. Betty Foxx and trouble were joined at the geriatric hip.

IT WAS ONE O'CLOCK, and Missy and I had been alone for over an hour. As much as I didn't want to act like the overly concerned employer, I was troubled that Betty hadn't returned. The miniature and lightweight races had wrapped up, and the emcee had recently announced over the loud speaker that the heavyweight races would start in an hour.

"Do you want to go for a walk, girl?"

Missy lifted her head and grunted. She stood up, stretched, then shook off her boredom.

Bark. Lick, lick.

Missy-speak for "Let's hit the road."

I snapped on her leash with a loud click. We ambled around the park. Missy relieved herself, and I people-watched. It was a great turnout. The warmth of the sun was like a promise of good things to come. The energy in the air, palpable. I grabbed a gyro, eating lunch as we threaded ourselves through the crowd.

"Hey, there's Zippy," a young boy yelled out in excitement.

I looked in the direction he pointed and caught a glimpse of what looked like Betty jumping around like a toad on hot Texas pavement. The concentration on her face suggested there was more to her determination to see Zippy than fandom.

Zippy and his human, Richard Eriksen, were immediately surrounded by demanding fans. They were far enough away that I could only hear bits and pieces of the conversations over the chatter of the crowd. The longer they stayed, the more people appeared. Missy and I moved closer.

Richard, or as Betty liked to call him, Ricky-Dicky, was a tall lanky man with a forced smile and a rigid stance.

"Get back," he shouted.

"Don't be an ass. They want his autograph." Gia's bossy voice sliced through the commotion.

The crowd parted enough for me to see a young boy, no more than ten years old, reach out to pet Zippy. Richard yanked on the leash, dragging Zippy backwards. The dog's feet slipped on the grass, dropping him to a sit position.

"They can stop by the winner's circle after the race. Right now, we have to get to the waiting area," Richard argued.

"It's bad luck to celebrate before a win." I heard Betty's reedy voice drift through the crowd.

Please behave. Please behave.

"Not when you know you'll come out on top." Gia shoved her way into the middle of the group. She reached for Zippy's leash, but Richard refused to relinquish it. Directly behind Gia stood a woman of average height and build with a video camera. Our missing filmmaker? Missy and I slowly inched closer. Her face was obstructed, but I could see her bad haircut clear as day. For once, Betty hadn't exaggerated.

"How would you know that unless you've stacked the deck in your favor?" someone from the crowd shouted.

"Who said that?" Gia shrieked.

"We don't need to stack the deck." Richard's chest puffed with inflated confidence. "Champions are built. Zippy loves to train. Right boy?"

Zippy, who'd been obediently sitting during this entire exchange, barked on cue.

Everyone cheered, and the circle tightened as people rushed to get closer to the dog.

"Back away," Richard growled. "He needs air. He must stretch."

"Your stupid ritual can wait. His fans want to meet him," Gia screeched.

Husband and wife squared off like two tomcats ready to defend their territory. Not exactly the picture of a healthy relationship.

The reigning champion wiggled his long body between a young admirer's legs eager for some well-deserved attention. Richard mumbled a mouthful of colorful language, then tugged on the leash, dragging the pooch beside him.

"Hey," Betty yelled. "You're hurting him."

"He's fine. Mind your own business."

Betty shot Ricky-Dicky a hateful look. "I've seen how you tug on the leash and yank him around. Just because he doesn't whimper doesn't mean he's not hurt. You're choking him."

Missy and I moved faster trying to reach Betty before she said something she'd regret, but the crowd blocked us from any forward progress. A couple of young surfers tossed me a disgusted look. What was their problem? It wasn't as if I was trying to cut to the front of the Taco Bell line.

"Did I ask for your opinion?" Ricky-Dicky's face turned a dark shade of red. His cold brown eyes bored into Betty. "That's right, I didn't."

"I've been watching you. You're mean to that sweet dog. You don't deserve him. Either of you." Her voice grew more agitated.

I'd never heard her so angry. My stomach knotted. She's wasn't a spring chick. Someone his size could easily hurt her.

I picked up Missy, worried she'd be stepped on, and elbowed my way into the crowd. "Excuse me, I need to get through."

A handful of people let us through, but the majority refused to let us get closer.

"Are you the one who's been following us today?" Gia's unkind laugh filled the stunned silence.

I hoped Gia was mistaken, and Betty hadn't followed anyone.

"He took away his food. When Zippy wanted a drink, you took away his water bowl," Betty yelled.

She was too short for me to see if she was in physical danger, but I imagined her balled fists at her side, ready to defend herself or the dog. I continued to shove my way through the crowd, praying I'd reach Betty before one of the Eriksens hurt her.

"You need to get your eyes checked, you pajama-wearing wacko. Have you looked in the mirror?" Ricky-Dicky bellowed.

Betty sucked in a breath. "You two are the crazy ones."

"Stay out of my business. You don't know what you're talking about." He pushed past the group of gawkers.

I got a quick peek of Betty as she stepped directly into his path. "You don't deserve that dog."

He muttered something as he pushed Betty aside. She stumbled backward and fumbled for her handbag.

"Hey," I yelled, propelling myself forward. "Don't touch her."

"You're insane, lady. Put away the gun." Ricky-Dicky's tone was no longer angry, but scared.

Gun?

Chaos erupted. People screamed and ran directly into my path. Crap. Protecting Missy the best I could, I took off toward the crazy lady in silk pajamas, who pointed a handgun at a perfectly normal-looking man and his dog.

I half expected to hear gunshots over the frightened screeching any second. But by the time I reached Betty, she was alone. Everyone was gone.

And Betty's gun along with them.

Chapter Three

SO MUCH FOR keeping a low profile.

I pulled Betty behind the corn dog trailer. It smelled like fear and hot grease.

"Where in all of Texas did *you* get a gun?" I bellowed, sounding like a mixture of Grey and my Grandma Tillie.

Betty blinked. "My son-in-law, Duane. After that crazy broad tried to kill us at Christmas."

An older couple stared at us as they walked past. I flashed a smile, as I pulled Betty further away from the pathway.

I lowered my voice. "So he thought the answer was to give you a firearm? Do you have a permit?" Forgive me for my ageism, but what I really wanted know was if it was legal for someone her age to carry a weapon.

She tilted her head. "Of course. Weren't you listening to me? I took a class."

"A self-defense class. Not target practice to carry a concealed weapon."

She sighed dramatically. "Cookie, you need to pay more attention. I took that self-defense course months ago. The same one your sneaky cousin, Caro, took. By the way, she was pretty good. You better not let her get the drop on you. Anyway, after I learned all those self-defense moves, I signed up for a gun safety class. Once I passed that, I applied for my permit. It arrived in the mail a few days ago."

"That's it? You get a piece of paper and suddenly you're allowed to carry a gun?"

"It's America," Betty stated, as if that explained everything.

I took a deep calming breath, and pushed the bangs from my eyes. "Why did you aim it at Richard like a hoodlum?"

"He attacked me."

"No, darlin'. He wasn't attacking you. He wanted to get away from you." Not that anyone would blame him.

She pondered that for a minute. Her narrow fingers tapped the outside of her purse in what sounded like an SOS signal. Any other time, I might have found her antics amusing. Not today.

"Where's the gun?" I asked.

"She took it."

"Who's she?"

"The girl with the dachshund tattoo. The one making the dogumentary. She recorded everything."

I rubbed my eyes. Bad, bad, bad. "I don't understand. Why in Sam Hill did you give her your gun?"

She reached up to pat my shoulder. "Cookie, are you okay? You're not keeping up with the conversation. It's not mine. Remember, the gun belongs to my son-in-law? Um, you wouldn't mind telling him *you* lost it, would you?"

"Hell, no. You've got to find, that girl—the girl with the dachshund tattoo—and get that gun back."

I've been known to be impulsive and make some decisions that have turned out less than spectacular, but I would never let someone, especially a stranger, take my firearm.

When had I become the responsible one?

"Betty, you don't know what she'll do with it. We have to get it back."

"What do you think she'd do? Hold up a group of doxies and demand their prize money?" She rolled her eyes.

I didn't want to think about the ramifications of that whole episode being filmed by someone with an unknown agenda. And I certainly didn't want to dwell on the possibilities of what a dishonest person might do with someone else's firearm.

The look on my face must have communicated my seriousness.

Betty held up her hands in surrender. "Okay. Okay. She can't be that hard to find. She's got a camera. And a dachshund tattoo on the back of her neck."

That did narrow it down. "Describe her. In detail," I ordered.

"You aren't paying attention today. I already told you what she looked like."

Wonderful. I was looking for a sweaty rock star with a dog tattoo and smeared eyeliner, carrying a gun and an oversized camera. "You take the east side of the field and I'll take the west. If either of us sees Darby, we fill her in. We need all the help we can get."

Betty hiked her handbag onto her shoulder. "What about our booth?

Who's gonna sell our stuff? Who's going to keep people from stealing it?"

"That's the least of our problems."

I had no idea how true those words were. But I was about to find out.

THE FIRST HEAT for the heavyweight category was scheduled to start in thirty minutes. I hadn't found anyone I was searching for. It was as if they'd disappeared into thin air.

I finally spotted Darby snapping photos of a trio of Doxies—a couple of long hairs, and one short hair. The pups were young, maybe ten or twelve months, full of energy and playfulness. Their handler, a gray-haired older gentleman with a wide grin, asked if the photos would be available to purchase.

Darby looked up and caught my eye. I waved her over.

"Have you seen Betty?" I asked.

"Not since her fight with Richard." She reached down and patted Missy on her head.

I looked at her questioningly. "You were there?"

She shook her head no. "Everyone's talking about it. Did she really pull out a gun and threaten to shoot Richard Eriksen and his dog?"

"She had a gun. She would never hurt Zippy." Notice I didn't mention Ricky-Dicky. I quickly filled in Darby on the situation and Betty's missing gun.

"Oh, no," she exclaimed, wide-eyed. "Where do you think the girl with the dachshund tattoo went?"

I shook my head. "Your guess is as good as mine. She has to be here somewhere."

"Would you like me to check out the racing area? If she's there I can text you."

"Please. If you see Betty, send her back to the booth."

Darby hung her camera around her neck and scurried off. Missy and I backtracked through the vendor area and made our way toward the spectator section next to the racetrack.

"Fifteen minutes until the heat number two. All competitors report to the starting gate," a garbled voice rumbled over the PA system.

Although she had offered to help find Betty, Darby was still the official photographer, and her first priority would be to photo document the race. I weaved my way through the group of yammering teenagers and made a beeline toward the track—a roped-off area with spray-painted white lines on the grass.

I could see the racers and their humans lined up at the starting gate, while their favorite person waited at the finish line. I imagined last minute instructions whispered into each racer's ears. Everyone was eager for the race to begin. I noticed Darby speaking to a group of judges huddled together watching the lineup. One judge checked her wristwatch, then said something to the group.

"All competitors must report to the gate," the emcee announced again. "This is the last call." His tone held a strong sense of urgency.

Sounded like someone other than Betty was missing.

I joined Darby at the grassy edge. "Any sign of Betty?"

She shook her head, worried. "Mel." She took a breath. "Zippy's not at the gate. He's supposed to run in this heat."

I felt my face blanch. "What?"

"Apparently Gia has been looking for Richard and Zippy. She's frantic. No one has seen him since his argument with Betty."

I had a bad feeling. "We've got to find Betty."

BETTY WAS AWOL.

So were Richard and Zippy.

I rubbed my temples in an effort to ward off the throbbing pain behind my eyes. I had a feeling Betty was behind Zippy and Richard's disappearance. If she'd seen them, she wouldn't have been able to stop herself from confronting him again. And that concerned me. I didn't know what Richard was capable of if pushed too far. Judging by the show of temper he'd displayed earlier, it was possible he might try to intimidate Betty if she crossed the line.

Bless her heart—Betty hadn't met a line she didn't want to cross.

Darby agreed to keep Missy while I continued my search. I took a turn around the track again, checked out the vendor area, and did a quick scan in the spectator section, but didn't see Betty. Either my timing was terrible or she wasn't with Richard after all.

I stopped walking and concentrated. It was possible she'd taken off in her Mini Cooper. Where she might have gone, I didn't have a clue, but her car was one of the few places I hadn't looked yet. And I was out of options. I ignored the pit in my stomach.

The dog park had a tiny parking lot, with limited space, so most of us took the trolley from downtown or we parked along the canyon road. Since Betty and I had arrived about the same time, I knew she had driven herself and left her car along the street.

As I exited the park, a slight breeze rustled my hair. Goosebumps rose on my arms. Directly across the street from the entrance stood the group of protesters waving their signs and marching in one continuous circle. I picked up the pace until I was practically jogging. I ran across the street. A car horn honked as my foot hit the sidewalk. The driver slowed to a crawl and flipped me off as he passed by.

I'd run past a half-dozen vehicles when I saw a man leaning against a white sedan. Focused on finding Betty, I didn't think much about him, until his body slid off the car, and with a dull thump, landed on the road.

Bright red blood oozed down the car's snowy-white side panel where his body had been seconds ago. My first thought was that a car, probably the same person who'd honked at me minutes ago, had hit him. I ran toward him, yelling for help, digging my cell out of my back pocket to call 911.

"Sir! Sir, are you all right?"

Cars whizzed past us, oblivious to the man who lay face first on the ground. I dropped to my knees next to him. I rolled him over, praying he wasn't seriously injured.

I gasped; my cell slipped from my fingers.

It was Richard Eriksen. And he hadn't been hit by a car.

He'd been shot in his black heart.

Chapter Four

BETTY FOUND ME. Right after I found Richard Eriksen's dead body. And if you're paying attention, you know who found the two of us next. Homicide Detective Judd Malone.

Betty and I waited on the sidewalk as Detective Malone moved in our direction with a heaviness that suggested the last place he wanted to be was here. With us. I felt the same way. I sighed in dread knowing what was about to happen.

Betty, on the other hand, gasped in wide-eyed excitement. "That's *my* kind of man."

She sprinted across the gravel parking lot straight for Malone as if reuniting with her lover after a long separation. He immediately held out his arms in warning. A warning Betty blithely ignored as she threw her pint-sized body against him. "You're here. I knew you'd come."

Of course he'd come. It was his job.

Malone unhooked Betty's arms from around his neck, and peeled her off his chest like a fruit roll-up. "Mrs. Foxx, don't do that again."

Yes, the three of us have a history. During our brief, but action-packed time together, Betty had developed a major schoolgirl crush on the good-looking detective.

"You're all dusty." As she brushed herself off, the bottom of her straw handbag repeatedly slapped Malone's arm. With a resigned sigh, he stepped to the side.

"I've been at the shooting range." He stared at me with reserved restraint. "It's my day off."

My stomach sank. Not good. I gathered my hair into a ponytail and lifted its weight off the back of my neck, unsure if I was sweaty from the heat of the sun or Malone's glare.

He motioned to where I stood on the sidewalk, separated from the crowd of gawkers. "Let's talk over here."

Because Malone possessed the perfect poker face, pinpointing the exact emotion he was feeling was difficult. Based on personal experience, I would wager happiness and excitement were not options for today. I was one of the last two people he'd want to see at a crime scene. The other person would be my cousin, Caro. The two of us seem to possess an internal dead-body-detector.

Speaking of Caro. Normally, she would also attend a local pet event. Instead, she was championing the Orange County Greyhound fostering program in L.A. I'd heard through the grapevine she was teaching a class on how to read and understand a dog's body language to a new group of foster parents. Caro was sort of a big deal in the pet behaviorist world. Not that I'd ever admit it to her, but I was proud of what she'd accomplished. In my humble opinion, kicking her cheating husband to the curb was her greatest achievement.

Not surprisingly, Malone wore dark jeans and a T-shirt, sans the leather jacket, even on his day off. Traffic slowed to a crawl as they passed us. Malone ordered a uniformed officer to direct the cars to move along.

"Melinda."

I shoved my hands inside the back pockets of my jeans, and rocked on the heels of my Stuart Weitzman motorcycle boots. "Detective."

"What happened?"

"I found him slumped against that white four-door sedan." I pointed toward the car surrounded by yellow police tape. "I thought he'd been hit by a car, but when I rolled him over to see if he was conscious, it was obvious he'd been shot." I kept my story free of whimsy and speculation, and full of facts. Malone wasn't always interested in entertaining my theories.

Typical Malone didn't bother to take notes; he listened intently. That sense of foreboding that I had thirty minutes earlier, while searching for Betty, exploded into heavy dread. Betty had waved a gun at the dead man. At some point Malone would find out. I mentally plotted a way to relate the facts in the least damaging way possible.

"Do you know anyone who'd want to hurt him?" Malone asked.

I shook my head. "It would be an assumption on my part to name anyone. I didn't know him."

He crossed his tanned arms. "Is that so?"

I waited for him to ask another question. I'd learned from experience his silence was a tactic to make me uncomfortable in hopes that I'd spill my guts. Well, believe it or not, I was perfectly comfortable waiting for him to make the next move.

The three of us stood together. Malone's eyes darted back and forth between Betty and me. Only the noise of light traffic filled the lull of his barrage of questions.

"Cookie, what about Lenny. Or Ricky-Dicky's bonkers wife, Gia?" Betty broke under the pressure.

I glared at my overly helpful assistant, warning her to keep her lips sealed. I knew how this worked. We'd point the finger at them. In return, they'd point a finger at her. And since she was the only one who'd publicly threatened the dead guy with a gun, she had the most to lose.

I swallowed hard, knowing it was time to spill the beans about Betty's Dirty Harry impersonation. "Earlier, Richard, Mr. Eriksen—"

Suddenly, a microphone whizzed past my shoulder and stopped a few inches from Malone's nose. "Detective, can you confirm Richard Eriksen has been murdered?" A deep male voice boomed in my ear.

Annoyance flickered across Malone's stone face for a second. "No comment."

What? Someone annoyed Detective Judd Malone as much as I did? I stepped aside and turned to face Callum MacAvoy, TV reporter for the local news. The newest pain-in-Malone's-backside easily met the Hollywood standard of sexy scene-stealer. I wondered if the station's owner had brought the new reporter on board for his good looks or because of his reporting abilities.

Alert green eyes zeroed in on Malone. "Do you know what happened?"

"We're investigating."

The reporter turned in my direction and sized me up. He flashed a camera-ready smile; his white teeth gleamed against his sun-kissed skin. I bet he spent more on his facial moisturizer than I did.

He lowered his voice as if he were sharing a secret with me and asked, "Would you like to be on TV?"

I felt like a young girl who'd been offered candy by a stranger.

"I would, handsome." Betty raised her hand and bounced excitedly.

Good grief, that's all we needed. A loose-lipped chatterbox talking to the town's newest TV reporter, who was eager to make his mark in the community.

MacAvoy turned his body square with mine, blocking Malone and game-show-contestant Betty. "You wouldn't mind answering a few questions on camera, would you, Miss . . . ?"

Seriously? He'd sized me up and deduced I was a girlish doormat he could seduce with a practiced smile, intimate body language, and a cocky promise of fifteen seconds on the twelve o'clock news? Mr. TV wasn't even primetime.

I stepped closer. I wet my lips and stared dreamily into his green eyes. Calling up the soft Texas accent that I'd worked so hard to drop over the past few years, I spoke into his microphone. "Anderson Cooper already called, sugar. We have an interview date at nine."

Malone coughed in an attempt to cover his laugh. I turned my head and winked at him.

"Nice one, Cookie," Betty cackled.

The reporter studied me intently. I'm sure he was reassessing his snap-judgment opinion, backtracking to the moment when he'd drawn the wrong conclusion. Better luck next time, buddy.

"Salinas." Malone waved over a uniformed officer. "Escort Mr. MacAvoy and his cameraman away from my crime scene. They can wait with the rest of the press."

Once MacAvoy was out of earshot, Malone offered a piece of advice. "Don't make an enemy out of the media."

"Obviously, you don't know my history as well as I thought you did," I said dryly. "I don't appreciate being underestimated because of how I look."

My entire life people have made assumptions about my aspirations and intelligence based on my appearance. That included my mother. I no longer tolerated that shortsightedness. And I wasn't about to apologize for it.

Malone nodded. "I won't ever make that mistake."

"You never have."

I sighed. It was time to confess about Betty's poor judgment. "Here's the deal. Betty and Richard got into a rather loud and public argument earlier this morning."

He shifted a questioning gaze toward Betty, who immediately clutched her chest dramatically. "He came after me. I was defending myself."

Malone rubbed his unshaved face. "What happened?"

"That stupid man mistreated Zippy, and I told him so. He burst into a rage and lunged at me. I didn't have time to use my self-defense moves. I thought he was going to kill me, so I pulled out my gun to protect myself. It's nice one too. A 9mm Beretta Nano. Fits perfectly in my hand. That's important, you know."

I squeezed my eyes shut for a second, replaying Betty's words. It sounded just as awful in my head as when she'd spoken the words out loud.

Malone was all business. "Do you have a license for your gun?"

"Of course. I'm a law-abiding citizen."

"I need your handgun, Mrs. Foxx."

"That's going to be a problem," I muttered.

Malone's cheek muscle twitched. "Why?"

"The girl with the dachshund tattoo took it," Betty explained, edging closer to the detective.

He stopped her with a look. She batted her eyes and smiled. He shook his head, not willing to entertain her flirtatious behavior.

"Who?" he asked me.

I shrugged. "I don't have a name. She's filming a dogumentary, *The Long and the Short of It*. I don't suppose you've seen her?" For a crazy second I allowed myself to believe he knew where to find the missing woman, along with Betty's missing gun.

"No." He was annoyed. The one-word sentences were a dead giveaway.

I pulled out the business card she'd given to Betty and handed it to him. "We've been looking for her. That's what we were doing when Richard was killed."

"You were together?"

"Yes."

"No," I said at the same time as Betty lied.

"You want to answer that again?" he asked Betty.

A nervous smile toyed with the corners of her mouth. "I was right behind Cookie; she just didn't see me."

Oh. My Gosh. She was making this a hundred times worse. "Can we have a minute?" I grabbed Betty's elbow and started to drag her toward the dog park for a one-on-one chat to explain, again, why she had to keep her lips zipped.

"No."

We froze.

"I want you both to stand over there by the trees with Officer Salinas and give him a description of this . . . woman. And you,"—he pointed at Betty—"you will behave yourself until I get back. When I do, we will have a private discussion. Understood?"

Betty's grey eyes sparkled with romantic interest. She tossed Malone an exaggerated wink. "I'm saving all my lovin' for you, big fella."

Awkward silence hung in the air. His mouth opened, then it snapped shut. He closed his eyes for a second. I swear he looked like he was praying for patience. He turned his frustration in my direction. "Watch her."

He bellowed for Salinas, and they chatted discreetly for a couple of seconds. Once Malone had finished with his instructions, he stalked off toward the crime scene while we followed Officer Salinas in the opposite direction toward the dog park. We ended up waiting near the food tents. My stomach rumbled as the aroma of fried foods filled my nose.

Betty opened her purse and pulled out her designer lip gloss. "I knew he liked me. It was only a matter of time before he recognized my animal magnetism."

I pulled her a few feet away from where Salinas stood. He never turned his head, but I knew he was watching us.

"This isn't a joke. You're in trouble. And the only activity Malone is interested in is arresting you."

"I know my way around a pair of handcuffs, Cookie." Betty wiggled her smeared lipstick eyebrows.

I didn't doubt her for a second. "Where were you? Really."

"I told you. I was right behind you."

I wanted to believe her, but she was acting cagier than usual. "What about before then? We were apart for over thirty minutes."

She snapped her purse shut. "Melinda, I didn't kill anyone."

I am far from a hand-wringer, but cold apprehension rooted itself in my gut. That was the first time Betty had ever called me by my name. I didn't believe for one minute she'd hurt anyone, but she was hiding something. And I knew from experience that never ended well.

Betty stared over my shoulder toward the park entrance. "Hey, Cookie. I thought you said your man was in New York."

"He is."

"Well, he's back."

It felt like my knees would buckle under the weight of anxiety that rippled through my body. What was Grey doing here?

There was zero time to formulate a plan. Not that it mattered. I worked best shooting from the hip. I sucked in the fresh air and pulled myself together.

As Grandma Tillie told me the night before I left for my freshman year at Stanford, "You gotta risk it, to get the biscuit."

Chapter Five

I HESITATED, AND I hated it. That wasn't me. I was an all-in-and-never-look-back kind of woman. Grey and I have an on-again-off-again history. During the "off" times, I had never doubted we'd end up together. Until now. I felt insecure and unsure. The worst part was that I had no one to blame but myself.

I took a couple of tentative steps toward him, then stopped. "Hey."

"Hey, yourself," he said.

No one could pull off a tailored Tom Ford suit like Grey. My pulse raced as I waited for him to make the first move. I counted my heartbeats: one . . . two . . . three . . . four . . . five . . . six. Finally, he bent down and brushed his lips against mine. I closed my eyes and breathed in his woodsy aftershave scent.

"What are you doing here?" I asked as I opened my eyes.

"I've been reassigned," he said softly.

I looked around making sure no could hear us. "You don't look happy about that. I'm sorry." The weight of those last two words hung so heavy between us it felt like I could pluck them out of air.

I reached out to caress his rugged face. My breath caught as he pulled back, and I glimpsed the hurt in his blue eyes. We still had unfinished business to discuss.

He trapped my hand and held it against his chest. I felt his strong heartbeat under my palm.

"Where's your ring?" he asked.

This wasn't the time or the place to confess I wasn't sure he wanted me wearing it. Heck, I didn't know if we were "on" or "off" at this point.

"I set it on the bathroom counter this morning getting ready. I forgot to put it back on."

We searched each other's face for some type of reassurance. I wasn't sure if he found what he was looking for. I know I didn't, and it scared me. He released my hand. It shook as I tucked a lock of hair behind my ear.

"What's going on?" he asked. "Why are the police here?"

I cleared my throat, thankful for a change in topics. "Richard Eriksen, one of the owners, was shot on the canyon road. He's dead."

"Are you okay?"

I nodded. After a quick glance over my shoulder, I said, "But I'm afraid Betty might be in trouble." I quickly filled him in from the beginning, up to the last conversation with Malone.

"What do you think she was doing?" he asked.

I shook my head. "I don't know. She's not saying. You know, she has a thing for you. Maybe if you asked her . . ."

He placed his palm on the small of my back. "Let's go talk to her."

As we made our way back to my assistant, I savored the feel of his hand. I missed the natural connection we shared.

"Hey, good-lookin'," Betty cooed. "Cookie said you were in New York. I guess you couldn't stay away."

Grey bent down and kissed her wrinkled cheek. "You're looking good yourself. Melinda tells me you're in a bit of trouble."

She waved her hand. "You know Cookie. She's exaggerating."

"Hardly." I rolled my eyes in exasperation at her insistence on making light of the situation.

Grey unbuttoned his suit jacket. "The police do not play games. If you can tell them exactly where you were, and who you were with, that helps them rule you out, and concentrate on finding the person who did this."

Betty scrutinized him. "You seem to know an awful lot about how the police work."

Grey shoved his hands in his pockets. "And you're changing the subject."

"You think the police believe I shot that idiot?" Betty huffed.

"You've got to stop calling him that." I looked over my shoulder double-checking Salinas wasn't close enough to overhear Betty's rant.

"Even if it's true?" she asked.

"Yes."

"From what Mel's said, I'd be surprised if you weren't a suspect." Grey, the voice of reason, leveled a stern look her way.

"I didn't shoot anyone. Isn't there some kind of test they can run? I thought these coppers were smart now, with their new technology."

Grey studied a group of crime-scene techs walking toward their van. "We could ask them to run a test for gunshot residue."

I groaned. "No good. Betty glommed onto Malone like a leach when he first arrived. He'd been at the firing range. Chances are Betty's got residue all over her."

She examined her top. "I don't see anything."

Grey shook his head. "You won't."

Betty crossed her arms. "Well, I didn't do anything wrong. I don't care how crazy sexy that Malone is, he can't make me confess to a crime I didn't commit."

GREY STEPPED AWAY to take a call while Betty and I waited for Malone, who was taking an extra-long time to return. Lenny and Pickles hung off to the side. Smart, since he'd publicly argued with the dead guy's wife.

I spotted Darby surreptitiously snapping pictures of the crowd standing behind the crime scene tape. She still had Missy with her. I waved for her to join us. She rushed over, Missy bumbling behind her.

"I've been looking for you two," Darby blurted. "What's going on?"

"Cookie's hunk-of-burning-love is back."

Darby's eyebrows disappeared beneath her blond bangs. "Grey's here?"

"Surprise," I sang out. I bent down and hugged Missy's stocky body, hiding my unease at Grey's unexpected appearance. After a few kisses on her head, I rubbed her behind the ears. She happily licked my face. With a quick shake, she showered me with bulldog drool. I wiped the back of my hand on my jeans.

"Thanks for taking care of her." I stood and accepted the leash from Darby.

"Anytime. Sooo . . . we're not talking about Grey right now?"

I shook my head. "No. I, uh . . . I stumbled over another dead body."

Darby and I had discovered Laguna's celebrated plastic surgeon Dr. O'Doggle, who'd been strangled and left for dead, outside my boutique not too long ago.

Darby gasped. "What? Who?"

"Ricky-Dicky," Betty spat out. She pulled a dog biscuit from her handbag and slipped it to Missy who eagerly chomped the treat.

"What happened?"

"When I was looking for Betty, I found him instead. He's been shot."

"Was Zippy with him?"

"No. Hopefully Malone's crew is looking for him."

"Did you find Betty's gun?" Darby whispered.

Betty waved her hands in front of our faces. "Hello. I'm standing right here."

"Sorry," Darby said, sheepishly.

"Not yet. Did you find the filmmaker?"

Darby shook her head. "Do you think they'll postpone the last few races?"

"If they do, Lenny Santucci will blow a gasket. There's nothing more frustrating than being mentally ready for a competition and then the contest being postponed. He probably thinks Pickles is guaranteed the win if Zippy doesn't race."

"Lenny's intense," Darby mused.

"Here comes dreamboat." Betty made kissing noises.

Grey approached us with a confident swagger that had been missing minutes earlier. I smiled. He must have received good news. He'd ditched his suit jacket and had rolled up his sleeves.

"Welcome back." Darby's gaze swung between Grey and me, obviously unsure of what to make of his unexpected appearance. "I thought you were out of town."

"The seller changed his mind."

"I'm sorry."

He shrugged it off. "That happens. I'm going to take a look around. Betty, describe the woman who has your gun."

"She's a mess," she said without missing a beat. "A walking fashion disaster."

This coming from the woman whose purple eyebrows looked like smeared grape jelly.

Grey smiled. And this time his smile reached his eyes. "Let's start with the basics. How tall is she?"

"Tall. Like Cookie."

"Okay, that's good. So, about five-eleven. What color are her eyes? What about her hair?"

Betty tapped her top lip with her finger. "Well, she's got ratty black hair. Short, like a boy—or one of them punk rockers. I think she's got brown eyes. No, green. Definitely black. Black eyes."

Betty would make a horrible eyewitness.

"Grey, she has a dachshund tattoo on the back of her neck."

"And she's got that movie camera," Betty piped up. "Don't forget about that. We were going to be in her dogumentary."

"A what?" he asked me.

"A dogumentary. The film is about wiener racing, so . . . ," I trailed off with a shrug.

He rubbed his chin. "I see. Well, the camera she can ditch. The tattoo is a little harder to get rid of." He pointed at Darby's camera. "What about you? You've had that all day?"

She held the camera toward him. "Do you want to borrow it?"

"No, I want a copy of the memory stick before Malone confiscates it."

"Do you think he'd do that?" She pulled the camera back, resting it against her chest.

"I would," he said.

I shot Grey a confused look. I wasn't sure why he was being so helpful. I wasn't complaining, mind you. Just confused. Normally, he was the first one to let the police do their job while demanding I stay as far from the action as possible.

"Can we make a copy?" I asked.

"We won't. But no one will think twice if Darby's downloaded her photos throughout the day as a precaution."

"I have online storage. I've already uploaded them, just in case."

Grey smiled. "Perfect. I'll be back." And without a goodbye kiss, hug, or a slap on the back, he was off.

"Is he really going to look for the girl with the dachshund tattoo?" Darby looked as confused as I felt.

"I guess so. No offense, but I'm really tired of calling her 'the girl with the dachshund tattoo'."

"What do you want to call her?" Darby tucked her camera in her messenger bag.

"Stephanie," Betty stated.

What? "Where did that come from?"

She shrugged. "She reminds me of my youngest daughter's college roommate. The poor girl looked like she slept in a garbage can. She dropped out of school and managed to get herself into a girl band."

"Was she any good?" Darby asked.

"Horrible. Stephanie got booted from the group eventually. Right after that, the band made it pretty big. Even got a couple records on the radio."

Man, she knew how to drag out a story. "What was the name of the band?"

"I don't remember. I think it was the Bye-Byes."
Darby and I stared at each other. Yeah, I didn't think so.

Chapter Six

MALONE HAD BEEN gone for over thirty minutes. Darby and I sat cross-legged on the lawn and watched the police. Missy stretched out next to me, her head in my lap. The longer Malone kept Betty waiting, the harder she stomped the grass as she paced, smashing the thick green blades into a blanketed pathway between a eucalyptus tree and me.

"If he doesn't hurry up and get back here, I might have to turn him down for dinner."

"He'll come back when he can." I stroked Missy's head.

Betty continued to mutter as she paced. Finally, we noticed Malone heading in our direction. He wasn't alone. Darby immediately stood and announced she needed to talk to the event director, Hagan Stone, and split. Wise move on her part.

Malone introduced Officer Shughart to Betty.

"I have to go with her?" Betty pointed to the grim-faced female officer with the sleek ponytail, whose eyes were a little too close together to be considered beautiful.

"Yes." If at all possible, Malone looked more stoic than usual. Or maybe, Betty had just worn him down. She had that effect on some people.

Betty slung her purse strap over her arm and huffed. "No offense, cupcake, but I was kinda hoping Officer Hottie would be the one to frisk me."

"No one is frisking anyone." The edge to Malone's voice indicated he didn't find Betty's antics amusing. "Officer Shughart is going to ask you a few more questions. That's it. Go."

She gave Shughart the once-over. "You got a pet?" she asked, as they walked toward a group of police cars in the parking lot.

"Betty doesn't mean to be difficult," I started to explain.

Malone shot me an exasperated look. "Yes, she does."

I tried again. "She's lived a long life and doesn't want to be over-looked. Can you blame her?"

Without bothering to acknowledge my defense of Betty, he walked away toward the vendor booths, cutting a path through a flock of Zippy worshipers. "I've been able to corroborate that the filmmaker exists," he said, over his shoulder.

I grabbed Missy, and we ran to catch up. "That's good, right?"

"Unfortunately, no one knows her name."

"Did you find her? Does she still have Betty's handgun?"

"We're looking for her."

His monotone answer made me a little nervous. "You can't seriously believe Betty did this?"

"What I believe is immaterial. My job is to ask questions and follow the evidence."

"No offense, but let's think back to the last time you told me that. You arrested Darby. And she was *innocent.*"

"She was guilty of keeping secrets. That's what got her into trouble."

I opened my mouth to rebut, but couldn't come up with a reasonable argument. He spoke the truth. And judging from Betty's recent disappearing act, she was taking a page out of Darby's playbook.

"When are you going to fill in your cousin on your boyfriend's real job?"

I stumbled. Certainly, he didn't know about Grey's undercover work. "What do you mean?" I hedged.

Malone stopped and faced me. "I have connections. You didn't think I'd turn a blind eye when I found out evidence that *I* had turned over to the FBI had been returned to someone other than the person I took it from? That someone being the girlfriend—"

"Fiancée."

"Fiancée, of a well-respected FBI agent."

I swallowed my unease. A couple months back, in a rather unusual turn of events, a dying man had torn Grandma Tillie's brooch right off Caro's beautiful Jenny Packman gown in the middle of a fundraiser. Turned out he'd been murdered, which was why Malone had taken the pin from Caro as evidence. Somehow, the Feds had gotten involved, and once they had taken over the case, they'd taken custody of the brooch too.

"What did you tell Caro?"

"I haven't said anything. And I won't. But you know your cousin better than I do. She won't give up until she gets her brooch back."

"*My* brooch, detective."

The vintage pin was a family heirloom that had belonged to our

Grandma Tillie. She'd left it to her "favorite granddaughter." Caro mistakenly believed that meant her. I knew Grandma Tillie meant me. Over the years, Caro and I have been . . . how should I put it? Repossessing the pin from each other.

To outsiders, the ugly, multi-jeweled basket of fruit wasn't worth the effort Caro and I exerted. Maybe if we were on speaking terms we could come to some type of joint-custody agreement. But we weren't speaking. That was a whole other story.

The hard planes of Malone's face and set jaw didn't convey an ounce of understanding for my situation.

"That's for the two of you to figure out," he said. "I didn't peg your boyfriend, fiancé, as someone who'd get involved in whatever it is you and Caro have going on."

I bristled in annoyance. "He's not. I called Grey's partner for help. Grey didn't have a clue I had the brooch until after it was all over."

Malone raised a brow. "Wow."

I shoved my hand in my pocket and walked toward the Bow Wow Boutique booth. Missy snorted her displeasure at the fast pace. I took a deep breath and slowed down. I sensed Malone had followed.

"Not my finest moment. Grey's not exactly over my little stunt." Or the fact that he'd found out from his partner, and not from me, that I'd managed to retrieve the brooch. "We'll work it out. We always do." Let's be honest, I was reassuring myself, not the detective by my side.

Malone declined to comment. A smart man. We walked in silence until we reached my booth. I got the feeling there was more he wanted to say. After the bombshell he'd dropped on me, I couldn't imagine what it could be.

He took a deep breath and said, "Against my better judgment, I want you to keep an eye on Betty."

Okay, you can imagine my shock. For the past year, all I'd heard was, "Butt out. Keep your nose out of my investigation, or I'll toss you in jail." This was unchartered territory. I was so stunned, I barely heard what he said next.

"Let me make it clear, I'm not giving you license to conduct your own investigation. You're to keep Betty out of police business. That's all. Got it?"

I bit back the relieved smile that tickled the corners of my mouth and nodded once. If he wanted me to keep Betty out from underfoot, he had to believe she wasn't involved in Richard's death. "I understand."

He pinned me with his intense dark eyes. "Do you?"

"Absolutely. I swear. You know, I never intend to get involved. It just sort of happens."

"Make sure it doesn't 'happen' this time." He looked unimpressed.

"Understood." I changed the subject before he changed his mind about my babysitting Betty. "Do you know if Zippy's been found?"

"One of my men discovered him hiding under a food truck. He seems fine, but I've asked Dr. Darling to check him over to make sure."

"That's good news. We've been worried. Betty's taken a liking to the guy; she'll be relieved to know he's safe."

"Keep her away from him. If she gets in my way, I'll throw you both in jail."

I watched Malone stalk off toward the racing area with a smile on my face. Some things will never change.

SHORTLY AFTER MALONE left, Hagan Stone announced over the PA system that the remaining heavyweight heats, and championship race, would resume tomorrow at two o'clock. It couldn't have been a surprise to anyone that after a two-hour delay the race would be rescheduled. A dead body would dampen any party.

With the competition over for the day, I decided to pack up and return to the boutique. If Betty were with me, she'd throw a fit about deserting the booth when there were still potential customers within reach of the cash register. My smiled faded. Where was Betty? How many questions could Officer Shughart have?

I was wrapping the doggie IDs, when a cold shadow fell over me. "There you are. What have you been doing?"

"Where's the crazy bat who killed Richard?" Gia Eriksen demanded. Her voice squeaked like an ill-tempered Chihuahua.

I looked up and cringed. Egad. She looked like she'd crawled out from the wreckage of nasty breakup. Death did not become her.

Gia wasn't exactly who I'd expected to see next to me. "I'm sorry for your loss. But we don't know who killed your husband."

"Where is she? That old woman in the ugly pajamas." She peered around me. Did she think I was hiding Betty in my back pocket?

I didn't appreciate her attitude or comment about Betty. My mama had taught me to be polite, even when the other person was off her rocker, but *this* woman could make me forget all about my upbringing.

I narrowed my eyes. "Is there something I can do for you, Gia? Would you like to make a purchase?"

She shoved her hands on her curvy hips. "I want my dog. Where's Zippy? He competes tomorrow."

It struck me a little suspicious that she suddenly seemed more concerned about her dog than her recently deceased husband.

"Why in the world would I have your dog?"

"Because that senile woman was spying on us. She tried to lure Zippy away with a corn dog."

I bit my bottom lip, fighting back an amused smile. That sounded like Betty. I quickly composed myself. After all, missing dogs and murder were serious business.

"I believe the police found him and took him to the vet to be looked over."

Gia's amber eyes glazed over with anger. Or was that fear? Hard to tell with mascara smeared around her eyes. Were her possible tears for her deceased husband or her missing pooch?

"They had no right," she ground out. "Zippy's a champion. He's not to be treated by just any doctor."

Now she was making me mad. "Dr. Darling is an amazing veterinarian. Zippy couldn't be in more capable or loving hands."

Dr. Daniel Darling was a friend and Missy's doctor. He not only ran a successful practice, but he donated more time to the local shelter than any other veterinarian in our ocean-side town. In my humble opinion, he was not just *any* doctor.

"He doesn't have *my* permission to treat Zippy. Where can I find this Dr. Darling?"

There was something about her reaction that didn't ring true. Why wouldn't she want her beloved pet examined? I remembered what Lenny had said about Ricky-Dicky doping his dog. At the time, I'd pegged Lenny as a sore loser. Could he have been telling the truth?

I moved to the other side of the table, directly in front of Gia. "What are you afraid of?"

"Nothing."

"Not even the accusations about drugging Zippy?"

She blanched. "You can't possibly believe what that lunatic Lenny Santucci said. He's a troublemaker. He was our biggest fan, until Zippy beat his loser dog, race after race. Since then, he's made it his life's mission to take us down. Including spreading those horrible, horrible lies."

"The rumor is simple enough to refute. Allow Zippy to take a blood test," I suggested.

Gia tossed her dark hair over her shoulder in a huff. "If the judges decide to require tests, I'm happy to oblige." She shoved a razor finger in my direction. "She won't get away with it."

I stepped back. I assumed she was referring to Betty. I sighed. "She didn't kill him."

"Everyone saw her threaten him with a gun."

"And everyone saw them both walk away . . . alive." The word "alive" hung in the air between as she thought about the possibility.

"Well, if it wasn't her, then who?"

I shook my head. "You'll need to talk to the police."

I'm not going to lie. That's the same question I'd been mulling over the last couple of hours. I've heard that if the deceased was married, the spouse was always a person of interest until proven otherwise. For all I knew, I was looking at Richard Eriksen's killer.

His wife.

Chapter Seven

GRANDMA TILLIE USED to say, "I'd rather die from exhaustion than expire from boredom." Today had been many things, boring was not one of them.

First Betty had pulled a gun on abrasive Richard Eriksen. Then I'd stumbled over Richard's dead body. Grey had unexpectedly hightailed it home from DC after being reassigned. On the positive side, Malone had begrudgingly asked me for a favor.

As sunset approached, a chill clung to the salty air. I grabbed a hoodie from my day bag and slipped it on. Since I'd spent the majority of the afternoon away from the booth, I decided to take a quick inventory as I packed the merchandise in a plastic totes.

I sorted through the leftover stock. I was only short one water bowl and one box of Bowser dog treats. Not bad. I quickly recounted and came up with the same total. For as long as we'd left our merchandise unattended, I was pleasantly surprised more items weren't missing.

I lined up the four large storage bins on the table. I felt comfortable leaving the cooler of water bottles behind. That meant only four separate trips to the Jeep. Or I could call Grey and ask for help.

I ran my hands through my hair as I contemplated my options. My head hurt anticipating another argument with Grey where neither of us ended up a winner. I doubted my handsome fiancé was ready to rehash our relationship status either. But I missed him more than my desire to avoid a heated discussion.

There was still a number of people milling around the park; certainly Grey had to be around somewhere. I pulled out my cell and called him before I changed my mind. Straight to voicemail. I sighed. He either was on a call or had shut off his phone. I decided to wait a few minutes before trying again.

I grabbed a couple of water bottles from the cooler, then sat on the grass next to Missy. I patted my lap for her to join me. She snorted excitedly as she waddled over.

"Hey there, sweet girl. How are you holding up?" I scratched behind her ear. "Do you need a drink?"

I cracked open a bottle and poured water into her collapsible bowl. She eagerly slurped the cold liquid, splashing both of us in the process. I laughed as I brushed water droplets off my jeans.

"I guess you were thirsty."

Determined not to dwell on Grey, I thought about Richard Eriksen. Who hated him enough that they'd shoot him? Gia was an obvious suspect. There was also Lenny. He had a grudge against both Eriksens.

Like it or not, Betty was also a likely suspect.

Speaking of my errant assistant, where the heck was she? The longer she was gone, the more worried I grew.

"I pegged you more of a Jack Russell Terrier-type," a male voice spoke from behind me.

I looked up to see that hack TV reporter standing over me. Ok, "hack" was a strong word to describe someone whose work I'd never seen. I'd reserve further judgment until I watched one of his reports on the Internet.

Jack Russells were known for their intellect, spirited personalities, and strong will. If not trained with a firm hand, the dog would walk all over a passive owner. Since I didn't know anything about Laguna's new reporter, I didn't know if he was implying I was intelligent or assertive. Both were accurate, but he didn't know that.

After one last love pat for Missy, I grabbed my water bottle and stood. Mr. TV wasn't as tall as Grey or Malone, but he still had at least a couple inches on me. Dressed in blue jeans and hunter green T-shirt, he should have blended in with the rest of us, but his gray blazer gave him a business edge that managed to set him apart from the average Joe.

I could see why he had a reputation as the heartthrob reporter. His eyes sparkled with a mischievous glint, which immediately put me on alert. Malone's earlier advice echoed in my ears.

I brushed grass clippings off my jeans. "What can I do for you?"

"I think we got off on the wrong foot. I'm Callum MacAvoy; my friends call me Mac." He extended a hand, along with a smug smile that I guessed he thought was charming and meant to disarm me.

I ignored the smile, but accepted his hand. Smooth, no calluses, firm grip. "Is that an invitation to call you Mac?"

He lifted his eyebrows. "Can I call you Mel?"

I pulled my hand back. "Melinda. You've been busy since I saw you last."

I didn't trust him. And not only because he was a reporter. Maybe it was the way his eyes continued to assess the area. Or maybe it was that he wanted to call me by a nickname without knowing me.

"I'm good at research."

That remained to be seen. He could have read my bio in the vendor pamphlet. Easy to find with little effort.

"Is that your dog?" He pointed at Missy who'd returned to her worn spot under the table where she'd spent the majority of the day.

"I call her Missy, but her papered name is Miss Congeniality. Although, being good at research, you probably already knew that."

He held my gaze for a second, then bent down and extended his hand. Missy stretched her thick neck inviting him to pet her. "I don't know much about bulldogs," he confessed.

He was good. He'd picked up on my weakness. I was always willing to educate people on how wonderful bulldogs were. "Don't let her looks deceive you. Bullies are extremely gentle and affectionate. Definitely stubborn, especially when they're bored or really want something. She snores, drools continually, and is prone to skin infections if I don't keep her skin folds dry." I left out her flatulence problem. "All in all, bulldogs make great companions."

Once he finished greeting Missy, he stood and motioned toward the table. "Leaving?"

"Eventually. Where's your shadow?"

"Who?"

"Your camera guy."

"Oh. That's Ryan. He's gathering B-roll."

"B-roll?" I asked.

"Sorry. Supplemental footage we can use later." He rubbed the back of his head. "Look, I've been kicking around an idea about a piece to spotlight local businesses. Are you interested?"

I set my bottle of water on the table. "Depends."

"On?"

"What you really want."

My directness managed to surprise a genuine smile out of him.

"You're not what I expected," he said.

"That's not a good trait in a reporter, forming a conclusion before you have the facts."

"Fair enough."

I shoved my hair behind my ear. "Are you going to tell me what you really want or make me guess?"

He sat on the table. He propped his elbow on the lid of a plastic tote. "I want an exclusive on the Richard Eriksen case. On the record, off the record, whatever you're comfortable with. I'll make it work."

"Why me? Why do you think I know anything? And if I did, why would I tell you?"

The smug smile returned. "Because I have what you want."

"I doubt that." I shoved my hands in my hoodie pockets. Mostly to warm them up, but also to keep from smacking Mr. TV upside the head. Let's be honest here. Half the time I didn't even know what I wanted. How could someone who'd known me all of two minutes know what I wanted?

"I can help you find the person you're looking for," he claimed.

"Who said I'm looking for anyone?"

"Betty Foxx, your fascinating assistant."

Good grief. Why couldn't she keep her mouth shut? She wasn't helping her situation by talking to everyone who asked her a question. Where was Betty? With the police? Or wandering the park looking for more trouble?

"When did you talk to her?" The last person I wanted help from was Mr. TV. Unfortunately for me, the reporter had more answers than I did at the moment.

He shrugged. "I ran into her earlier."

I waited for him to elaborate. The distant chatter of reckless speculation about Richard's death and Missy's heavy snores were the only sounds.

I narrowed my eyes. "Okay, Mr. Evasive, spill it. What did she say to you?"

"I should find the girl with the dachshund tattoo."

Of course she did. "Did Betty tell you why?"

He slipped a hand into the pocket of his blazer. "I'd like to hear from you. Do you think she can clear your friend?"

I didn't like that he used "clear." That didn't bode well. I also found it dodgy that he'd chosen now to shove his hand into his jacket pocket. Call me suspicious, but I'd wager a year's salary he had a recorder hidden in there.

"I thought you were more daytime talk show fluff pieces than hard news."

His broad shoulders tensed. "It seems you also draw conclusions without all the facts. I'm a serious journalist. I follow the news."

Well, give the man an Emmy for his journalism excellence.

He followed the news. Malone followed the evidence. I followed my gut.

"You said you had something I want. So far all you've done is ask questions."

"In my line of business you don't give away information."

Finally, the truth. I picked up the collapsible bowl I'd left in the grass and dumped the small amount of water Missy hadn't finished. "Don't let Detective Malone hear you say that."

"Why?"

I folded the bowl and dropped it on the closest storage container. "I'm going to do you a huge favor and give you a heads up." I pointed at his blazer pocket. "Make sure your little voice recorder is on so you get every word." His eyes widened, and I knew I'd been right. I continued, "Malone hates it when people butt into his investigation or withhold information. If you're going to follow the news on his turf, make sure you stay out if his way."

"Sounds like you speak from experience."

I shrugged, not willing to confirm or deny his assumption. "Keep in mind, you may both have the same goal, but he has the badge."

He was about to say something when Darby appeared. God bless her. She had perfect timing.

"Hey, Mel." She strolled up to Mr. TV and me. Her gaze darted between us. She cocked her head and asked, "Am I interrupting?"

He jumped off the table and shot Darby a boyish grin. "Not at all."

If he thought I was going to introduce him to Darby, he was barking up the wrong tree. "Actually, Mr. MacAvoy was just leaving."

His green eyes flashed with a promise that he'd be back. "I'm sure we'll see each other again." I had to give him credit. He didn't attempt to outstay his welcome.

I refrained from rolling my eyes. "No doubt." My delivery was as dry as the dirty martini I'd downed last week at a charity event for pet health awareness.

As soon as he turned his back, Darby spoke, "Mel—"

I cut her off with a look.

Once Mr. TV was out of earshot I said, "He's as crooked as a dog's hind leg. Don't trust him."

Her eyebrows shot up. "Your Texas doesn't come out often, but when it does, it means you're mad. What happened?"

Darby knew me well. She was right about my Texas side.

"Mr. TV Reporter was *clearly* pumping me for info on Betty and

Stephanie. He claimed he has something I want, but he made it crystal clear he wasn't willing to tell me anything without some type of deal."

"Do you have any idea what he meant?" She pulled her electronic tablet from her messenger bag.

"None. He had a voice recorder in his pocket. I called him out on it. He wasn't expecting that." I replayed the surprise on his handsome face in my head. "Oh, he may show up around the store. He mentioned doing a segment on local businesses. I have no idea if that was a legitimate idea or a flimsy ploy." I leaned toward a tactical move.

"If that's a sincere offer, that would be great exposure."

I shook my head. Sweet Darby. Even after the dire circumstances she'd endured since she'd arrived in town, she was still a trusting soul. You can take the girl out of the Midwest, but you couldn't squash the natural instinct to believe the best in people.

I reached out and gave Darby a quick hug.

She laughed. "What was that for?"

"I'm lucky to have you in my life."

She squeezed my hand. "I feel the same about you."

I tugged the hem of my hoodie back into place at my waist. "Enough of the sappy love fest. What's up?"

Darby's face lit up with excitement. "I've been thinking about what Grey had said. You know, about my pictures. If they could be that important, I thought I should review them now. I'm only halfway through the five hundred photos, but when I saw this I couldn't wait. You'll never believe what I found. Look." Darby shoved her tablet at me.

On the screen was a photo of Richard arguing with a female protester. The woman was at least six inches shorter than he was. Her long, brown hair flared around a beautiful heart-shaped face. Her mouth curled in anger. She looked primed to whack Richard over the head with her "Save the Doxies" sign. The right corner of the photo was time-stamped—two thirty.

A smile as wide as the Pacific Ocean spread across my mouth. "Looks like we've got a new suspect!"

Chapter Eight

"DO YOU KNOW her," I asked Darby, flipping through the other photos.

"No, but I asked around. Her name is Fallon Keller. She's the head of Rights for Doxies, an animal rights organization that's known to protest all the dachshund races in southern California."

Darby had taken a handful of pictures of the protesters, but there was only one perfect shot capturing Fallon Keller, arms raised, poised to beat Richard with her peace-love-and-save-the-doggies sign.

"Is Malone still here?" she asked.

"I haven't seen him since his stock comment about throwing me in jail if I didn't stay out of his way. It takes a while to process the scene and talk to everyone. Certainly, he's around here somewhere." I handed her the tablet. "Will you email me a copy of that?"

"Sure." After closing the cover, she tucked it safely in her bag. "I saw Grey talking to Hagan Stone. I didn't realize they knew each other."

That was news to me too. However, Grey had been looking for Betty's gun, so he would have talked to everyone. It was part of his training. You never knew what small detail could break a case wide open.

"He meets a lot of people through the gallery. Have you talked to Hagan since he decided to postpone the rest of the event?"

She nodded. "He's worried people won't come back."

That was a possibility. I pushed out a long breath. I couldn't believe what I was about to suggest, but I wasn't the type of person to hamper the success of the race because I didn't like or trust someone.

"If we see MacAvoy again, let's make sure he knows about tomorrow. He can at least get that on the evening news."

Darby grinned. "That hurt."

"More than you know."

She grabbed my arm and tugged. "Hey, there's Hagan." Darby waved him over with gusto.

Somehow, I managed to keep my mouth shut and my expression neutral. This was my first face-to-face with Hagan Stone. Up until this moment, all of our interaction had been over the phone or by email.

He didn't look at all like I had imagined. He was fortyish, with thick dark hair in need of a trim, a high forehead, hawkish nose, and the voice of Cary Grant. I half expected him to air-kiss my cheeks or the back of my hand. He barreled over and introduced himself.

"Melinda, you'll be here Sunday, correct? We really need you. Your Bow Wow Boutique is widely respected and enormously popular. It's been a huge draw for the event."

Normally, I was immune to flattery, but I couldn't deny the warmth of satisfaction that washed over me. "Sure, I can do that. Not a problem."

He squeezed my shoulder gently. "Wonderful. I believe I've talked to almost everyone now, and they've all agreed to come back." He nodded, satisfied with his accomplishment. "I think we'll do okay. I may be short a judge. Would you mind filling in if that proves to be the case?"

"Whatever you need." I had no idea what I'd agreed to, but his enthusiasm was contagious.

He smiled broadly. "That's what I wanted to hear."

"Any news on Zippy? Will he race?" Darby asked.

Hagan's brows furrowed. "That's not up to me. That's for Gia, Mrs. Eriksen, to decide. But I don't see why he wouldn't. He's our big name, you know."

"Did you know Richard well?" I asked.

He smiled sheepishly. "This is my first year as Chairman of the Board, but he seemed like a decent chap."

"We should have a moment of silence for him," Darby suggested.

Hagan nodded in agreement. "That's very thoughtful. I'll make sure to take care of it myself."

"Did Richard have a lot of enemies?" I asked.

He pushed his thin lips together and pondered my question. "There's always a variety of rivalry; that's the nature of competition, correct? No, I wouldn't call them enemies, but there was definitely tension between him and a number of other owners. Not to speak ill of the dead, but he could be difficult."

I'd noticed. His wife was equally difficult. "What about the protesters?"

He waved his hand dismissively. "Don't pay them any attention. They're a nuisance, nothing more."

Interesting. Darby and I exchanged a questioning look but refrained from commenting. We had proof it was possible the head protester was more than a nuisance.

"Are they here every year?" I asked.

"From what I understand, yes. Last year there was an altercation between the animal activists' organizer and a couple of doxie owners. I'm terribly sorry, but I wasn't informed about the specifics."

Well, maybe Darby and I need to find out. My phone chirped, interrupting our enlightening talkfest. A quick glance at my cell showed it was Grey. I looked at Darby and said, "Excuse me."

I walked toward a couple of locust trees for privacy before I answered. I released the breath I'd been holding and managed a half smile. "Hi."

"Hey. I saw I missed your call."

I looked around the grounds for a glimpse of Grey making his way toward me. I didn't see him. "I thought you'd be back before now."

He hesitated then said, "Something came up. I had to leave."

I recognized the indifferent tone. He used it anytime he worked on a case I couldn't know about. I started to pace. Was he on his way out of town already? Was that why he seemed happier after his call this afternoon?

Good grief. *Pull yourself together.* "Will I see you tonight?"

"I'm not sure. I have a couple of things to take care of." The tension crackled across the phone.

"Are you blowing me off?" I leaned against a tree, the rough bark pressed against my back.

He sighed so hard I was amazed I didn't feel his breath on my ear. "No. I have people waiting for me."

I rubbed my chest, pushing back the ache building inside. I was waiting for him too. I'd been waiting for him for weeks. "It's just as well. I wasn't expecting you for a couple of days so I made plans." My face warmed at my blatant lie.

"Melinda, we're not finished." His voice softened, but it still sounded detached. "We have a lot to discuss. Just not tonight."

"I don't really want to talk tonight either," I muttered. I squeezed my eyes shut. "I love you."

He didn't respond immediately. I felt sick to my stomach.

"I love you too," he finally said.

I ended the call hurt and frustrated, and in no way reassured. What a horrible day.

IT WAS DUSK by the time Darby left to find Malone and update him on the photos. I'd managed to load three of the storage containers in the Jeep fairly quickly. Frustration could be a terrific motivator. Bless Missy's sweet bulldog heart, she didn't complain about all the back and forth between the Jeep and the booth. I'm sure she thought I'd lost my mind. She deserved an extra treat when we finally made it home.

I slid the final tote off the table and started toward the Jeep for the last time. Missy dutifully brought up the rear, her tongue hanging out the side of her mouth. As I walked across the park, I mentally planned the rest of my night. First, a hot shower. Second, a glass or two of Pinot.

"Hey, Cookie. Did you miss me?" Betty called out brightly.

Startled, I almost dropped the plastic storage bin on my foot. I set down the tote before whipping around. "Where the heck have you been? I've been worried about you." Immediately I was embarrassed I'd lost my temper.

Betty, on the other hand, didn't bat an eye at my outrage. "Talking to Officer Cupcake."

"For two hours?"

Betty squatted in front of Missy. With a thin hand, she patted Missy's head with great affection. Betty's white hair needed brushing, and her pajamas were rumpled. For the first time since I'd met her, she looked frail. That scared me more than not knowing where she'd been since she'd walked away with Officer Shughart.

"I had some things to take care of," she said.

"Like what?"

She straightened. "It's private."

"Privacy's never stopped you from poking your nose into my business."

"That's because someone has to keep an eye out for you, Cookie. You act before you think."

Look who's talking? The godmother of impulsiveness. I needed to calm down. What was I doing, interrogating a woman old enough to be my grandmother?

I inhaled deeply and counted to five, searching for a shred of patience.

"You look like you're about to pass out. Stop holding your breath." Betty said.

"Will you tell me where you've been?" I pushed one last time.

She shook her head.

I tried a different approach. "What did Shughart say?"

Betty sat on top of the storage container. I noticed her sneakers were no longer white, but grassy green. "You'd like her. She's a smart one. She's got two pugs, Charlie and Daisy. Cupcake promised to stop by the shop next week to check out our travel carriers. She's leaving on vacation next month."

"I meant what did she say about your involvement with Richard's death?"

She shrugged a delicate shoulder. "Don't leave town. Don't talk to the press. And if I see Stephanie to call her or that handsome Detective Malone."

"Holy cow, Betty. You're officially a murder suspect."

Betty clapped her hands and pressed them to her chest. Her gray eyes brightened with amusement. "I know. Exciting, isn't it?"

Chapter Nine

I DIDN'T CARE WHAT Betty thought; it was not exciting. More like terrifying.

By the time I got her loaded into her Mini Cooper and headed home, darkness had started to settle around us. I made her promise to call me once she'd arrived safely. Betty claimed I was overreacting. Maybe I was. But I couldn't shake the feeling that she was still keeping a secret. Something important.

I'd had a front-row seat the last time someone I cared about had kept a big secret—it had blown up in her face.

Malone had asked me to keep Betty out of his way. It looked like that wouldn't be as difficult as I'd originally believed. She was too busy disappearing.

I headed down the sidewalk for the last time and made a mental note to park closer to the entrance gate tomorrow. There were a handful of cars still parked along the canyon road. I'd luckily found a spot under a streetlamp. Once I reached the Jeep, I shoved the last plastic tote inside. I started to load Missy when I heard what sounded like a muffled howl.

"Stay."

Missy obediently waited for me to give the "load-up" command.

I concentrated on the evening sounds, picking out what belonged and dismissing it, instead waiting for what didn't fit in. Within a minute I heard the sound again. I glanced around but I didn't see an animal or a human. I closed the Jeep door.

"Let's take one last walk, girl."

Missy sighed, but dutifully followed.

We strolled along the sidewalk, perfectly lit by the overhead street-lamps that lined the walkway. I kept my eyes peeled for someone in distress. As I drew closer to a beat-up black Nissan, I heard the muffled howl of despair again. It came from inside the car. Had someone left a dog inside with the windows up? Granted, heat wasn't an issue this time of night, but why did people insist on taking their pets to run errands, only to leave the animals locked up in a vehicle?

I stomped up to the car intending to free the imprisoned dog, or at least check on his wellbeing and crack the window if possible. The second I got next to the Nissan, I knew I had it all wrong. Not about the dog in the car. I could see him clear as day, with his face pressed against the glass, leaving doggie kisses on the window. But the dog wasn't alone. And it wasn't just any dog.

It was Pickles. And Lenny.

Lenny didn't look happy that I'd found him hiding in his car. If he hadn't caught me peeking in the back window, I'd have walked away. I'm sure the nasty look engraved on his face was meant to frighten me off. Silly me, I took his stare as a challenge. I knocked on the passenger window.

He rolled it down a smidge. "Go away," he shouted through the crack.

"Are you okay?"

"We're fine."

The man obviously didn't know the definition of "fine." The smell of leftover fast food wafted from his car. His droopy eyes could barely focus on me. I'd either woken him up or he was drunk. At the moment, I believed he was drunk.

"You're not driving anywhere are you?"

"What's it to you?" he growled.

I pointed to the white bag on the seat. "If that's what I think it is, you shouldn't be driving."

He cursed, shoving the bag under the passenger seat. He fumbled with the handle before he finally managed to open the door. I jumped back, almost falling over Missy. The dome light blinked on. There were piles of dirty clothes; bags of food, gum, and candy wrappers; liquid cold medicine; and bottles of what looked like vitamins.

Lenny crawled out, yelling at me. "You're a nosy bitch. If I want to drown my misery, that's my business." He slammed the door shut. Pickles immediately started to howl.

I pointed at the dog. "Is he okay?"

Lenny crossed his beefy arms across his chest, effectively blocking me from getting closer. "Does he sound okay? He's depressed. If he's not racing, a little piece of him dies."

He wasn't the only one. From Lenny's rumpled state, he could have been referring to himself. He looked down at Missy and squinted. "My first dog was a bully. A faithful breed. Good choice."

"Ah, thanks." Instinctively, I gripped Missy's leash tighter. "What about you? Are you upset about the race or Richard's death?"

He stepped forward, eyes flashing. "Aren't you upset about it?"

He was too close. I could smell his breath, which surprisingly didn't smell like alcohol at all. His breath was actually quite refreshing. Like mouthwash. I stepped back. "Well sure, but I'm not going to get wasted because of it."

"I'm not wasted. This is all her fault," he ground out.

I was afraid to ask. "Whose?"

"Gia Eriksen."

I thought for sure he was going to say *Betty.* "Do you think she shot Richard?"

He looked up with red-rimmed eyes. "What?"

I tried a different tactic. "What's Gia's fault?"

"She convinced Hagan to postpone the race. We were ready today. We would have won." He smacked his humongous fist into the palm of his hand, flexing his bulging biceps in the process.

"Let's be reasonable. Her husband had been murdered. I don't think postponing the race was too much to ask."

"But we were going to win." His voice broke. "Finally."

Good heavens. Was he going to cry? He was way too sauced to make any sense. And if he wasn't making sense, he shouldn't be behind the wheel of a car.

"Lenny, what hotel are you staying at? I'd be happy to drop you off."

He puffed his chest, and for a second I thought his cotton shirt would rip in half and fall off his body. "I don't need your help. Scram."

"You shouldn't be driving."

"I told you. I'm not drunk." He motioned toward the backseat of the car. "Besides, do I look like I'm going someplace? Get out of here." I looked at the pillow and blankets shoved on the floorboards of the backseat. He was sleeping in his car?

As long as he wasn't driving in his current condition, I was good with leaving. With a quick wave, Missy and I skedaddled to the Jeep.

On the drive home I wondered if there was more to Lenny's outburst than he'd let on. I don't care what he said—the man was toasted. Maybe he was embarrassed that I'd found him sleeping in his car. Poor Lenny really was down on his luck. No wonder he wanted to win so desperately.

Yet I couldn't help but wonder if he wanted to win badly enough to kill Richard to ensure Pickles stood a fighting chance.

Love made people do crazy things.

Chapter Ten

ONCE HOME, I left the totes in the Jeep and set the alarm. The alarm was new. Not too long ago, my vehicle had been beaten within an inch of its precious Jeep life. I won't bore you with all the details. After two months of bodywork and a new paint job, she was as good as new. I'd decided a state-of-the-art car alarm system was appropriate.

I took Missy for one last walk so she could do her business, which she managed in record time. As soon as we walked inside the house, I yanked off my motorcycle boots and ditched them by the front door. Missy headed straight for her dog bed.

Circle. Circle. Knead. Knead. Circle. Circle.

Once she worked the pillow exactly the way she wanted, she dropped with a sigh. After tossing my handbag on the couch, I padded toward the kitchen and grabbed a wineglass from the cupboard. I popped the cork from a bottle of Pinot, filled the glass, and sipped my wine. The warmth of the alcohol spread through my body. I sighed in contentment. For the first time today, I felt like I could breathe. Relax.

My thoughts immediately turned toward Grey. Nope. I wasn't going there. Unwilling to wallow in self-pity about the possible demise of our engagement, and thus our relationship, I set my glass on the breakfast counter and attacked the dirty breakfast dishes I'd left in the sink.

I'd placed the last bowl in the dishwasher when it dawned on me that I hadn't heard from Betty yet. Had she made it home okay? Would she tell her daughter that the police considered her a murder suspect? What would Betty tell Duane about the missing gun? Would the girl with the dachshund tattoo come back? And if she did, would she have Betty's gun?

I heard my cell phone ring. It had to be Betty. I rushed to the couch where I'd left my bag. I managed to pull out my cell as the ringing stopped. Dang. Within seconds, a notification popped up that I'd missed a call from my mama.

I gripped the phone tighter. She never called to chat. I loved the woman, but she was a drama queen with an agenda. And usually the agenda was about what she wanted. The woman had a knack for finding a way to make any situation or circumstance, whether good or bad, about her. It was a true talent.

My cell chirped again. She wasn't giving up easily. I took a fortifying breath before I answered. "Hey, Mama. I was just thinking about you."

Her soft Texas sigh settled in my ear. "If that's true, Melinda Sue, tell me—why did I have to hear from your brother that you and Grey were talking about a wedding date? Why do you hate me?"

I rolled my eyes. "I don't hate you, Mama. By the way, I'm fine. Thanks for asking."

She paused, then inquired in a polite, but overly sweet voice, "How are you, darling? How's Grey?"

"I'm fine. Grey's fine. How are you and Daddy?" I continued the charade. If my tone were any sweeter, I'd give myself a cavity.

"I'm busy as ever. Your daddy keeps to himself. Locked away in his office, planning who knows what without me. If you're considering a fall wedding I need to know. The country club books years in advance. Although, if that's what you really want, I can call in a few favors. Lord knows I've bailed out that Lydia Marshall more than a handful of times. Her society contacts are rather lackluster. She owes me."

I returned to the kitchen for my wine. I'd need more than one glass for this chat. Membership at *the* Dallas Country Club was a long-standing tradition in the Montgomery family. One joined by invitation only, and to my knowledge, there hadn't been a Montgomery yet that hadn't been invited. It was the last place I'd choose to get married. I'd left that life behind and could honestly say I didn't miss it. Not one iota.

I drank deeply before replying. "I don't know what Mitch told you, but Grey and I have not set a date." Heck, at this point, we couldn't even be in the same room without arguing. Not that I'd admit that to her.

"Melinda, you listen to me, sugar. You must get a ring on his finger before you do something stupid. You know how you are. You're a lucky girl, Grey seems enamored by your impulsiveness."

I guzzled the last of the wine in my glass, then refilled—to the rim. "Thanks for the support, Mama."

"Support is what you get from your friends. Truth is what you get from me. Now, when are you two picking a date? And do not even think of robbing me of a wedding. My heart couldn't take another elopement. I can't believe your brother was so selfish."

I dropped to a bar stool and pretended to listen as she continued to prattle on about Mitch and his bride's, Nikki, disregard for tradition. I liked to call this, "Confessions of a Drama Queen."

I smiled wryly. Thank the good Lord, Mama didn't know how to Skype.

I FINALLY GOT THE hot shower I'd been daydreaming about. It was exactly what I needed to wash away depressing thoughts of Grey, my crazy mother, and worrying about Betty, who, for the record, I still hadn't heard from. I'd left her three messages to call me. Nothing. I had to believe that no news was good news.

I pulled on my favorite pair of yoga pants and an oversized T-shirt that read, "Don't judge the dogs." I grabbed a large glass of water, then sank onto the couch. Missy was still in her bed where I'd left her hours ago.

It was time for the news, and I was curious if MacAvoy had filed a report. I flipped on the TV in time to see his face pop up on the screen. Damn him. He looked refreshed and polished. He certainly hadn't downed a half bottle of wine and survived a round of Mama Take-Down. The noon reporter had managed to make it to prime time.

"A day of fun turned into a day of terror. Richard Eriksen was found shot to death during the Laguna Dachshund Dash." He paused. His beseeching eyes looked through the camera and landed into every viewer's home. "In the dog-eat-dog world of wiener racing, has Zippy's rivalry with his fellow competitors finally been pushed to a new level?"

"Oh, please," I muttered, disgusted.

"The police have yet to make an official statement, but witnesses claimed to have seen an elderly woman threaten Mr. Eriksen with a gun earlier in the day. No word on the woman's identity at this time. The final races are set to start Sunday at two o'clock," he finished.

I knew he couldn't be trusted. He'd just thrown Betty under the bus. Sure he didn't call her by name, but it was only a matter of time before her identity became public knowledge.

Callum "Mac" MacAvoy had better hope I didn't lay eyes on him tomorrow. I had a few choice words to give him. On the record.

Chapter Eleven

I'VE LEARNED THE best way to start the day is with an early morning jog on the beach. Today was no exception. The crisp air cleared the cobwebs from my head and gave me a jolt of energy. Energy I'd need for the day ahead.

After a quick shower, and a bowl of cereal, I pulled on a pair of skinny jeans, an event T-shirt, and my motorcycle boots. I'd remembered to slip on my engagement ring too. Considering all the action yesterday, I decided to leave Missy at home.

I backed out of the driveway and pointed the Jeep toward PCH, then headed to the boutique. Stray dark clouds had moved in. Morning fog wasn't unusual in Laguna, but these clouds were different—heavy and low—plus the air didn't smell salty, but like rain. Not a good sign for a race day.

Just blocks from the shop, I pulled over and parked in front of the Koffee Klatch. I was in desperate need of a chai latte.

The Koffee Klatch's funky décor, large comfy couches, and free Internet, made it a local favorite. It didn't hurt that the owner and employees loved dogs. The line was short for a Sunday morning. Sven, a lanky twenty-something who looked like he stepped off the pages of a Hans Christian Andersen fairy tale, towered over the customers from behind the glass counter. Three years ago, he'd left his family's Danish vineyard in Santa Ynez Valley for our laid-back beach town. From all appearances, he seemed to like it here.

Before I could utter a word, Sven asked if I wanted my usual Sunday order of a chai latte and a blueberry muffin. Okay, so maybe it wasn't *exactly* a last-minute decision to stop.

I nodded. "Please. To go."

"Sure thing," he said with wink and a nod. While he rang up my order, I stuffed a couple of ones into the tip jar.

"Is it true you were at the race yesterday? And you found the dead guy?" He didn't sound excited, but he was certainly curious. News traveled fast in Laguna. Especially gossipy bad news.

"I did." I paid for my food and stepped to the side, hoping that would be the end of the questions. I wasn't about to get off that easily.

"What happened?" He dropped a blueberry muffin inside a small white bag and handed it to me.

I eyed the other two people waiting to place their order. Neither one was shy about hiding interest in my answer. I groaned silently. Malone liked to keep his information out of the public eye if possible. In the past, I'd followed his lead. There was no reason to stop now.

"Honestly, I'm waiting to hear just like everyone else."

Sven wiped off the espresso machine's steam wand with a wet cloth. "Do the police have any leads?"

"I don't know. I haven't talked to anyone since I gave my initial statement."

Two quick bursts of steam shot from the wand. "I met the wife. You just missed her."

"Gia was here?"

He nodded. "She doesn't appear to be too upset about her husband's murder."

"Why's that?"

His lips moved, but I couldn't hear a word. The noise of the espresso machine heating the milk drowned out most of his answer. The second the machine stopped, his raised voice shot through the café. "She acted like she didn't have a care in the world. Other than her dog winning today's race."

I wished I could have heard the first part of what he'd said. Didn't anyone tell Gia that the spouse is the first suspect? The best course of action for her would be to fly under the radar and not draw attention to herself. Was she really that obtuse? Or could it be that she believed she'd get away with killing her husband?

Sven finished preparing my chai, snapped on the lid, then slid it across the counter. "Are you going out there today?"

"I have a few things to take care of at the shop first. What about you?"

"I'm here all day. Would you do me a favor?"

"Sure."

He pulled a twenty from his pants pocket. "Would you make a bet for me? Put this on Pickles." He shoved the money into my hand.

What the heck was he talking about? "You're putting money on Pickles?"

He motioned for me to follow him toward the back of the café. I grabbed my drink and followed.

"After meeting Gia, I'm rooting for the underdog," he said.

"Well, you obviously haven't met Lenny, have you?" I said wryly. "Seriously, I don't know anything about betting."

Sven shoved his hands in his apron pockets. "You don't have to pretend with me. I know all about the underground gambling. I heard from a friend that the bagman will be behind the chili tent."

"Bagman?"

"You know. Rodney. The money runner."

"Since I'm the one with your money, doesn't that make me the bagman?"

Sven laughed. "I guess it does. You're much better looking than Rodney, by the way."

I looked at the twenty in my hand. "I really don't know about the gambling."

His blue eyes widened as he ran his hands through his spiky, blond hair. "Look, I don't want to get into trouble. How about you forget we had this chat? Keep the cash." He moved to push past me, but I blocked his path.

"Whoa, there. I didn't say anything about trouble."

The front door opened. We both turned to see who'd walked inside. Well, surprise, surprise. If it wasn't Mr. TV himself. I had a lot to say to him, but not here. There was no sense stirring up more gossip than was already brewing around town.

MacAvoy wore the same grey blazer as he had yesterday, but today he had on black jeans and a black T-shirt. Interesting. He dressed like Malone now? They say imitation is the best form of flattery.

Mr. TV's gaze bounced between Sven and me. By the curious look on his face, I thought he'd join us, but instead, he strode straight to the counter and waited in line. But that didn't stop him from watching us like a neighborhood busybody.

I turned my back to the nosy reporter and spoke quietly. "Is there betting at every race?"

Sven shrugged. "Sure. Like I said, it's not a big deal." He inched away from me, eager to escape my questions and return to his customers.

He didn't strike me as a typical wiener race fan. As far as I knew, he didn't even have a dog. "How'd you learn about it?"

"Friends. Online."

Translation: his gambling buddies. "Who's Rodney? Is he a local?"

"He's from the valley. He's watched too many gangster movies, but he wouldn't harm a fly."

Against my better judgment, I said, "I'll find a way to get your bet placed." I was curious about the gambling, and there was no better way to nose around than by placing a bet.

"I've got customers." Without another word, he rushed back to his station, apologizing to everyone in line for the long wait.

I shifted my drink and bakery bag to the same hand so I could shove the twenty in my jeans pocket.

Don't you hate it when everyone knows more than you? Granted, Sven wasn't everyone, but he certainly knew about a covert activity I didn't know existed in my own community.

Did it have anything to do with Richard's death? At first blush I wouldn't think so, but there's only a handful of reasons people kill—love, hate, revenge . . . and greed. I was looking forward to meeting Rodney.

I sipped my chai as I walked past MacAvoy. I felt his determined stare fixated on my back. It was farfetched to believe he'd followed me to the Koffee Klatch. But I knew this wasn't the last time today our paths would cross.

In fact, I was counting on it.

I WAS IN THE MIDDLE of ordering paw-wear when the front door of Bow Wow Boutique opened. I looked up from my computer screen to see a woman in a black, belted, silk dress stroll inside. Valerie Andrews. Ugh. Betty's daughter stomped in my direction.

"Hey there, Valerie." I tried my best to be chipper.

"Hello, Melinda." She narrowed her stormy eyes on my face as she dropped her three-thousand-dollar purse on the counter with a thud. "I need your help. My mother has lost her mind."

There were many times when I felt as if my mother had lost her mind, but I knew better than to make that announcement to someone outside of our immediate family. "What seems to be the problem?" I hedged, unsure what Betty had shared with her daughter about the recent events.

"I'm sure you know about the dead body Mother found yesterday."

I cleared my throat. Actually, *I* had found the body. Not that it mattered. Although it was obvious, Valerie wasn't used to being corrected.

"This is a problem," she continued without waiting for a response.

"I can't have my mother traipsing around town talking about dead bodies and claiming that she's a murder suspect." She fiddled with the long delicate gold chain hanging around her neck. "I'm on numerous boards of prominent organizations. Her actions could have irreparable repercussions. Not to mention how her behavior is affecting *my* reputation within the community. I've tried to talk some sense into her, but she refuses to take my feelings into consideration."

I hadn't had much interaction with Valerie, but after each experience I've learned I liked her less and less. What kind of person puts their reputation above their mother's welfare? Not someone I'd choose to spend a large quantity of time with, that's for sure.

"Aren't you worried about Betty?" I asked.

She looked genuinely surprised for a moment. Shocking, because I'd always assumed she was a Botox disciple.

"It's true? Mother really is a suspect?"

Obviously Betty hadn't mentioned she'd threatened the dead guy with a handgun. "The police talk to everyone. It would help if Betty would tell them exactly where she was when Richard was killed. And even better if we could find her gun."

Her face paled. She pressed her blinged-out hand against her chest. Every finger sported a large colored gem. Valerie didn't follow the "less is more" rule.

"I thought she was exaggerating. You know how she is. Why wouldn't she tell the police where she—" Her eyes narrowed. "Did you say gun? What gun?"

"The one your husband gave her?" I meant to word that as a statement, but the confused look on her face caused me to end on a questioning note.

"Duane did not give her a gun."

I locked my computer. Ordering would wait. "Are you positive? He doesn't own a 9mm Berretta Nano?"

Her bejeweled hand gripped the leather strap of her purse until her knuckles turned white. "Yes, he owns that model. But it's locked away in his safe. In his study."

I had a strong suspicion Betty had been involved in a few things her daughter wasn't aware of. "Um, I don't believe it's there anymore. I've recently seen that gun. Betty was pointing it at Richard shortly before he was found dead. He'd been shot."

Valerie blinked rapidly, her face suddenly colorless. "My mother's a murderer," she wailed. "I'll never be asked to chair the children's charity committee for the women's club. Oh. My. God. She'll die in jail. What will I tell my sister?"

I scooted around the counter and guided her to my office at the back of the store where she could sit before she collapsed and knocked over a display of dog treats.

"Betty isn't going to jail," I stated. "Not if I can help it. She didn't kill anyone."

"But you just said she shot him."

Holy crap. This woman could not talk to the police. She was too easily confused. "No. I did not. Pointing and shooting are completely different. Where's Betty? She was supposed to come in to work an hour ago."

"She said she had some errands to run this morning. You don't suppose she's hiding evidence?"

She hopped up from the chair and started to pace. "Melinda, you have to help me. My mother doesn't listen to reason. She does what she pleases, regardless of my wishes. She's been very sneaky lately. Comes and goes at all hours of the day. She won't let me inside her cottage." Valerie skidded to a stop and grabbed my arms, squeezing them tightly. "Last night, I thought I'd heard her making some strange cat-like sounds. She insists I'm hearing things. She told me to make an appointment with an audiologist. She has to be hiding something. Help me find out what."

The only thing less appealing than helping Valerie was shopping with my mother. I shook off her hands. "Have you asked her what she's hiding?"

"Of course. She tells me to mind my own business."

That sounded like good advice. "I'm not sure what you want me to do about it."

"Talk to her. She likes you. Although, God knows why." She eyed me up and down, assessing my worth. Her scrutiny hardly stood up against my mother's disapproving eye.

I wasn't looking for a dog fight, but Valerie had to know she held some responsibility for the way Betty acted.

"I have talked to her. I adore your mother. The best thing you could do is to show her she still matters. Stop bossing her around. Stop undermining her worth. You'll find she may actually take your advice." So sue me, I lied. I didn't believe for one second Betty would do anything her daughter told her to.

Valerie turned glassy-eyed. "At least promise you'll look out for her.

She has always had a tendency to run into trouble, which has escalated since she's met you."

I was about to explain Betty didn't need my help to find trouble, when the bell for the front door chimed.

"Excuse me, I have a customer." Valerie stared at me, blank-faced. I turned her around and ushered her into the shop. "I'm not leaving you alone in my office. Let's go."

"But you didn't promise," she whined.

I was finished making promises.

"Hello," I called out. "Welcome to Bow Wow Boutique."

Much to my surprise, Gia and Zippy, each wearing designer jogging suits, stood inside in the shop. Gia didn't look happy. I'm sure her emotional state had nothing to do with the fact that she'd pulled her hair back into the severest bun I'd ever seen. I was certain her hair would rip right off her scalp at any moment.

"Hi, Gia. I'm surprised to see you here." I couldn't stop staring at the way the sides of her face were yanked back into a poor man's facelift. It looked painful, yet at the same time impressively effective.

"In all the chaos yesterday, Zippy's favorite blue ball has gone missing. He can't win today without it." She rattled off the brand name.

"I have a few left. It's very popular item. Let me grab you one. Feel free to look around," I called out over my shoulder.

"I'm in a hurry. Richard may be . . . gone, but that doesn't mean Zippy can't keep to his schedule."

What type of schedule could he have? Eat, sleep, do his business, play. Rinse and repeat. Wasn't that the universal dog schedule?

"I'll be right back." I made my way toward the front of the store and grabbed one of the many blue treat balls in a woven sea-grass basket. Valerie followed right on my heels.

"Melinda, I'm not leaving until you promise," she hissed.

I lowered my voice. "That is the recently widowed Mrs. Eriksen. At this moment, she has no idea who you are. If you leave right now, you won't have to kiss her butt apologizing for you-know-who's behavior yesterday. I'd think you've already done enough of that. Do you understand what I'm telling you?"

Valerie stiffened, then pasted on a smile I'd seen on a thousand other faces—a disingenuous airbrushed smile that only fooled the person giving it.

"I understand." She nodded briskly.

"Thanks for stopping by, Valerie." I opened the door, letting in the fresh air. "I'll let you know when your order comes in."

"I look forward to hearing from you . . . *soon*." She breezed through the doorway and outside.

I *may* have let go of the door just a tad too quickly, tapping Valerie's backside as she walked out. My bad.

I joined Gia and Zippy next to a display of dog breed charms. "Is this what you're looking for?" I handed her the ball.

She squeezed it a couple of times, then bent down and let Zippy sniff it. He snatched the toy from her hand and ran. She had him on a short leash—he didn't get past the rack of flying discs. Undaunted, he collapsed to his belly and gnawed on the ball. His soft floppy ears got in the way of his ability to grip the toy with his paws.

"Looks like he likes it. Is there anything else you need?" I asked.

She pointed toward the register. "I love those red sneakers you have in the showcase."

"Would you like to see them?"

She chewed her perfectly polished nail. "I really don't have a lot of time," she hesitated. "I guess if we're quick."

Not one to pass up a sale, I motioned for her to follow me. "Zippy's fine. Leave him there."

I pulled out the sneakers from behind the locked case. "Aren't they adorable? The canvas body is very soft, and the soles are nonslip."

"I love them." She didn't bat an eye at the fifty-dollar price tag. She placed them on the counter. "What about those?" She pointed to a pair of black boots with a zippered front.

I smiled, sensing a large sale within the next couple of minutes. "These are my favorite. Although confession time, I am partial to motorcycle boots." I hiked up my jeans and kicked my leg, showing off my own black boots.

Suddenly, Gia had plenty of time to waste. She weaved from one side of the store to the other, her face flush from stacking item after item on the counter for me to ring up. When she wasn't looking I tossed Zippy a couple of treats. He was a very well-behaved pooch.

While Gia shopped I asked, "You mentioned Zippy has a schedule. I'm curious what type of schedule a dog like him would have? Practice runs? Push-ups?"

"It's important that he practice the fifty-yard dash, keep hydrated, and stick to his feeding schedule, which is twice a day during the off season and three times a day during racing season." She fingered a sunflower-yellow bathrobe. Meeting her requirements, the robe was tossed on top of the growing pile of merchandise. "He has a very strict diet. Racing on a full stomach slows him down."

Oops. I glanced down at Zippy. He hadn't left a crumb of evidence. Good dog. I lifted my finger to my lips, swearing him to secrecy. He shook his head, his ears slapping the sides of his long nose. I guess I was on my own.

Gia's dilated eyes widened as she looked at the stack on the counter. "I think I got a little carried away." Her normally commanding voice sounded small and a little unsure.

"Everything is returnable. If you get home and decide you don't like an item or you've changed your mind for any reason, bring it back for a full refund."

She bit her bottom lip. "Do you have a shop in Laguna Hills?"

"No."

She slowly handed me a credit card. I caught a quick look inside her bag. She carried a purple water bottle that looked like the same one I'd seen Richard carrying yesterday. "Does Zippy only drink bottled water?"

She followed my gaze. Realizing I could see inside her purse, she closed it with a loud snap. "No, he does not only drink bottled water. It's my vitamin water."

Yeah, I didn't believe her for a second. She didn't have bloodshot eyes, and she wasn't slurring her words, but there was something about her body language that suggested she was lying. That and the fact that she had completely overreacted to my question.

"Why does Lenny Santucci hate you? You said that at one time he was your number-one fan? What really changed that?"

She stiffened. "I told you. He's a jealous loser."

I tapped her credit card on the Formica counter. "Nope. He hates you and he hated Richard. That's more than jealousy."

She eyed the card, biting her bottom lip. "Lenny tried to pass Pickles off as an offspring of Chip."

"Chip?"

Her eye-roll was so dramatic her lashes actually stuck together momentarily. For a second, I thought I might have to peel them apart for her. "Chip Ahoy. He's the ultimate champion. He retired from racing five years ago. Lenny claimed Pickle carried Chip's bloodline. Richard knew he was lying and threatened to discredit him."

Now that was a motive to hate someone. "Is Lenny from around here?"

"Up north. Redding or someplace boring like that."

"Did you see him around the time Richard was shot?"

She sighed. I was clearly wasting her time with all my questions. "I had more important things on my mind when I was looking for Richard than noticing if Lenny was following me around like a sick puppy. Are you going to ring me up?"

"Sure thing." I slid her credit card through the reader, expecting an approval.

Denied.

Holy moly. I looked up and plastered a fake smile on my face. "The machine's been acting funny lately. Let me try this again."

"Wait. Try this one." Gia handed me a different piece of plastic. She looked as uncomfortable as I felt.

I rubbed the magnetic strip on my jeans before sliding the card through the machine.

Not only was it denied, but I was also instructed to call the bank.

Hells bells.

Chapter Twelve

GIA AND I STARED at the silver plastic card in my hand. This could play out one of two ways. I call the bank and receive a verbal approval after Gia answers a couple of simple questions. Or I call the bank and the charge is denied. And possibly be asked to confiscate the card. Judging by the way Gia worriedly nibbled on her bottom lip, verbal approval was the unlikely outcome.

She caught my eyes dead-on. Her fake lashes were as thick as Grandma Tillie's fur coat and looked equally as heavy. I knew what she wanted me to do. The tension was broken by a ringing cell phone.

"That's me." I grabbed the phone and answered without looking to see who was calling.

"Hello." I didn't exactly turn my back on Gia, but I tried to give her some privacy. If she decided to put some, or all, of the merchandise back, I wasn't going to draw attention to it.

"Hi," Grey's deep voice filled my ear.

My pulse quickened. "Hi. I, um, didn't realize it was you." I tucked my hair behind my ear.

He chuckled. "Removed me from your contact list already?"

An easy smile spread across my mouth. He was back. "I thought about it. Are you at the gallery?"

"For a while. I thought you might want to grab lunch. Unless you're at the race."

I stole a glance at Gia. She was digging through her purse, apparently not ready to walk away from her mountain of dog paraphernalia.

"Not yet. I'm finishing up at the shop. Then I'd planned on heading over. Hagan asked me to come back and set up the boutique booth again. Are you coming to the dog park?"

Silence on the other end. Had he hung up? Or was he trying to come up with a decent excuse as to why he didn't want to come to the race? Most importantly, when had I started to sound so pathetic?

"Hagan asked you personally?" he finally asked.

"Yes, he was very sweet."

"What time does the race start?"

I could hear faint voices in the background. "Two. Is there someone there you need to take care of?"

"No. He's just looking. Did you find Betty's gun?"

I turned my back on Gia, fingers crossed she didn't grab her stash and run, but I didn't want her to overhear my conversation. "Not yet. I thought if I got there early, I could look for the filmmaker."

"How about dinner in Newport tonight?"

I nodded, eager to spend some time with Grey. "That sounds great." I studied my engagement ring. "And then we can talk. Right? That's what this is all leading up to?"

"Yes. We'll talk," he promised.

I closed my eyes and released a long pent-up breath. "Okay. I'll see you tonight. 401 Chop Oceanside?"

"That's where I proposed. The second time." I felt his smile as strongly as if he stood across from me. "Plus they have the best lamb chops."

We ended the call, agreeing he'd pick me up at eight. I shoved my cell inside my back pocket feeling very generous. Grey was ready to forgive and move on, and so was I.

"Gia. Here." I held out her credit card.

It took her a second to accept it, but when she did her claw-like fingers wrapped around the plastic card like a lifeline. She stuffed it in her purse before I could change my mind.

"Why?" she asked.

"Weird stuff happens all the time. Technology can be finicky. What works today may not work tomorrow." I pulled the toy she'd originally come to the store to find from the bottom of the pile. "This is a good-luck gift from me and my bulldog, Missy, to you and Zippy. It's been a rough twenty-four hours. We all want a fair race, right?"

She looked pained. I immediately felt bad that she'd taken my comment as a dig about the doping rumors. I dropped the ball on the counter.

She bent down, picked up Zippy's leash off the carpet, and snapped it back on his collar. "I heard you say you were looking for the filmmaker."

I nodded slowly, steeling myself for a possible tirade. "Have you seen her?"

"We were at the dog park earlier this morning, me and Zippy, working out. She was talking to that veterinarian."

"What did you think of Dr. Darling?"

"He was exactly as you described."

I'd accept that as an admission that I was right. "Did you talk to her? The gir—the filmmaker?"

Gia frowned, channeling her inner desperate housewife. "You could say that. She has a lot of nerve. She begged for an interview with Zippy and me, since he was the favorite. Of course, everyone knows he's the obvious winner. So, I agreed to meet. You know, doing my part to advertise the event. But that wasn't what she wanted to talk about."

I cringed, pretty sure where this was headed. To be honest, it would be difficult to brush over Richard's death. Talk about real-life drama.

"I'm sure if you explained—"

Gia's eyes sharpened under her tarantula lashes. "She accused me and Richard of doping Zippy. Can you believe it? My husband was just murdered and she wants to talk about why I won't willingly submit Zippy to a urine test. She shoved her camera right in my face and kept asking me over and over why it was so important to harm my dog in order to win a race. The nerve. I shoved her back and told her what she could do with her camera. I really hate that woman."

I cleared my throat. I was pretty darn certain Gia was about to regret her actions. "Was she recording when you attacked her?"

She stilled. "Oh, hell. I have to get that tape."

Gia frantically scooped up Zippy and cradled him in her arms. At the last minute, she grabbed the treat ball. Without a word, she scurried out the door and disappeared down the street.

It looked like the girl with the dachshund tattoo, aka Stephanie, had some things a couple of us wanted back. I wondered which of us would find her first.

Chapter Thirteen

BETTY NEVER SHOWED.

My calls continued to go directly to voicemail, while I continued to be concerned. Valerie's unexpected visit confirmed Betty had at least checked in with her daughter. I'd waited for as long as possible for my flighty assistant. I hung a sign on the front door informing customers they could find us at the Dachshund Dash, then closed up the boutique for the rest of the day.

Although the sun had burned off some of the morning fog, it remained slightly overcast with a chill gripping the air. I quickly swung by my place to let Missy out. She sniffed a few trees and a handful of bushes before she finally relieved herself.

"Do you want to go for a ride, girl?"

She peered up at me with squinty eyes, then trotted back toward the house, leaving me standing by the Jeep in the driveway. Apparently, she was passing. I couldn't blame her. Her stubby legs had carried her stocky body a long way yesterday.

We walked back inside the house, Missy headed to the kitchen. She sniffed her food dish; finding it rather lackluster, she lapped up some water instead.

"Alrighty, girlfriend. I'll be back later." I grabbed my Gap hoodie and black Moschino backpack from the couch.

At the last minute, I decided to print the photo of Fallon Keller that Darby had emailed me last night. I planted a quick kiss on Missy's head and reminded her to guard Grandma Tillie's brooch while I was out. Caro had to be aware by now that the heirloom was in my possession. She wanted the brooch as much as I did. In the past, we'd proven neither of us was above a little breaking-and-entering to get what we wanted.

I pointed the Jeep toward the dog park. Traffic was light for a Sunday afternoon, which was unusual. Maybe the possibility of rain had kept people home. I pulled into the parking lot and was lucky enough to find space to park near the entrance.

I noticed Lenny's car was no longer parked along the street. I wondered if he was off searching for a shower or a decent meal. Noting the size of his muscles, he didn't strike me as the kind of guy who'd happily eat fast food three meals a day and be content.

The park was quiet, basking in the calm before the energetic crowd trampled the lawn for the second day in a row. I carried the totes across the damp grass to my booth, greeting my fellow vendors along the way. I also kept an eye open for Betty.

I shoved the unpacked totes under the table, next to the cooler I'd left behind last night, with the intention of setting up later. My first priority was to find the girl with the dachshund tattoo and locate Betty's gun. I slid my backpack over my shoulder then slipped my hands in my jean pockets. My fingers brushed against the money Sven had given me earlier in the morning. I also needed to find where to place the bet for Sven.

I wandered toward the food area. Food trucks and canopy tents coexisted in an area not much larger than the parking lot. The aroma of BBQ, along with ethnic and typical fair food filled the air. My stomach growled in appreciation. The trucks came in all sizes and colors, some newer than others, while a handful looked like they had been pulled straight out of the junkyard and abandoned at the park.

Sven had made it sound as if the betting was a known fact. But I had a strong feeling that wasn't the case. The Red Hot Chili truck was easy to find. The words "Chill at the Chili House" were stenciled in green on the side. The huge serving window was locked down, so I knocked loudly on the side of the truck.

"Hello," I called out.

"Rodney isn't here," Lenny spoke from behind me.

I turned around. So he *was* here. I wondered where he'd parked his car today. He looked much better than the last time I'd seen him. His body-hugging T-shirt and khaki shorts, although stained and slightly wrinkled, didn't smell like he'd pulled them out of a dirty clothes hamper or, in his case, off the floorboard of his car.

"Do you know when he'll be back?" I asked.

Pickles lay at Lenny's feet looking rather subdued. Or bored. He was a dog so it was hard to tell what he might be feeling.

"You here for the chili?" Lenny slurped his coffee out of a to-go cup.

"Sure."

He watched me with bloodshot eyes over the rim of his cup. "Rodney's making change."

I wasn't sure if that was gambling slang for something nefarious or if he was literally making change. "Okay. Thanks, I'll check back later." I pivoted on my heel and started to walk back to the vendor booths.

"If you don't get back before the race, he can't help you."

"Good to know."

"You've never bet on a race before have you?" he called out.

I stopped mid-step. Clearly he had something to say. Curious by nature, I couldn't help but turn back around and close the distance between us. "Is it that obvious?"

An amused smile hung on his normally angry mouth. "Yeah. You working with the cops?"

Lordy, don't let Malone hear him say that. He'd think I was sticking my nose in places he'd specifically told me to stay out of. I admit, sometimes I didn't always follow directions well, but this wasn't one of those times. "Regarding Richard?"

"In any way." Beads of sweat dotted his forehead.

Was he sick? It certainly wasn't hot enough for him to be sweating. I'd wager he had a hangover. "Nope, I'm here as a favor for a friend."

"Where's your dog?"

"She was exhausted from all the back-and-forth yesterday. She chose her bed over another day being shown up by wiener dogs."

He finished the last of his drink then tossed his empty container in a yellow trash can. "Damn straight. Who you bettin' on?"

Ah. His interest in my wager was purely personal. I pointed at the long wire-haired guy resting in the grass. "I was told to bet on Pickles. To win."

Lenny rubbed the back of his head, his expression grave. "Good. Good. This is our time. It's now or never."

His comment struck me as odd. "Why do you say that?"

"Look at him. It kills him to race and never win. He can only take defeat for so long. Eventually he'll give up."

"That's tough. I'm sorry." Gia had taunted Lenny that his dog was a depressed loser. From Lenny's comments, it seemed she was right.

Pickles did look down in the dumps. Did dogs take antidepressants? Did they see dog therapists . . . like Caro? If we were talking, I'd ask her. But we're not, so I made a different type of suggestion.

"Maybe he just needs a treat." Missy always seems to perk up at the mention of the "T" word.

Right on cue, Pickles lifted his head. After a thump of his tail, he let out a small bark.

"He looks happier already," I said with an encouraging smile.

Lenny, on the other hand, looked like he was about to cry. He squatted next to the love of his life and stroked him adoringly. "I'll do everything in my power to keep him that way."

Everything? That was such a subjective word. I'm guessing "everything" probably didn't mean the same to me as it did to Lenny. And since we're now keeping score, did that mean Lenny would kill Richard Eriksen in order to keep Pickles happy? Where was Lenny when Richard was killed?

I kept my questions to myself because I was not sticking my nose into Malone's investigation. But I have to tell you—it was killing me to keep my curiosity to myself.

Lenny stood. "Hey, have you seen that filmmaker lady around?"

"No. I've been looking for her myself, but I haven't seen her yet."

He looked concerned. "She better be here. She's supposed to film our race. She promised."

Interesting. Why would she make that promise? "When was that?"

"Yesterday, when she interviewed us."

"Was that before or after Richard's body was found?" I know, I know. I just said I wasn't going to ask those types of questions.

"I thought you said you weren't working with the police?" He twisted his head side to side, popping his neck. He crossed his humongous arms across his chest, flexing every muscle I could see. And probably flexing those I couldn't. I noticed a brightly colored tattoo of the word "Marine."

It would take more than a military tattoo, some neck-cracking, and bulging muscles to intimidate me. "I'm curious. I haven't met the filmmaker yet. Do you know if she interviewed Richard?"

He snorted. "Of course."

"You really hated the guy."

"He was a cheat and a phony."

Interestingly enough, according to Gia, Richard had felt the same about him. "Did Richard tell you about the interview?"

"No. She followed him to the waiting area. It was disgusting the way she fell all over him. Zippy's not special. God, I hope she filmed Richard's stupid rituals. He was such a fool."

"Rituals?"

"About six months ago, in San Diego, I overheard him and Gia arguing about Richard's superstitions. Get this—he carried a lucky rabbit's foot like a freakin' kid. He brought a special water dish to every event. The fool even made Zippy walk in six large circles, backwards, two hours before each race. He was a nut job."

That could have been what Betty had witnessed, except she'd thought he'd hurt Zippy. "Was that all they argued about?"

"Heck no. What do all married couples argue about?" He rubbed his thumb against his sausage fingers. "Money. His therapy sucked up all their funds. Can you believe it?" An evil laugh rumbled up from deep inside him, causing Pickles to bark.

I could. I also believed Lenny knew an awful lot about a person he hated. What was that saying, "Keep your friends close, but keep your enemies closer?"

I added Lenny to my suspect list.

Chapter Fourteen

AFTER I LEFT LENNY and Pickles, I dashed toward the veterinarian tent to talk to Daniel who, according to Gia, might know where I could find the girl with the dachshund tattoo, aka Stephanie, the mysterious filmmaker. I found it rather suspect so many others, except for me, had talked to her. Plus, I suddenly had a number of questions to ask my favorite vet about depressed dogs.

The tent, which was really a portable clinic, was nestled in between the Doxie Lovers of OC and The Pet Palace—the finest five-star dog-houses money could buy. The clinic's doors were propped open, which I took as an invitation to enter.

Amazing. It was a fully functioning clinic stocked with general supplies and all the necessary equipment—including an x-ray machine—to care for a sick or injured animal.

I found Daniel crouched in front of a rolling cabinet at the back of the tent.

"Knock, knock," I called out lightly, not wanting to startle him.

He stood and brushed off his khakis. His welcoming smile spread to his warm brown eyes when he realized it was me. "Hi, Mel. Come on in."

Daniel was ripe with boyish charm and sharp intellect. Somehow he'd dodged the broken-down-hockey-player look after he'd busted his nose three years ago in a freak surfing accident.

"Hey, Daniel. How are you?"

"I'm good. How about yourself? How's Missy's new toothbrush working out?"

I grimaced. "She hates it. To be honest, so do I. The triple headed brush is difficult to get into her mouth. I'm going back to the regular toothbrush I had."

"Whatever works. Dental care is equally important for canines as for us humans. Although, I'm sure you didn't stop by for a lecture about dental care. What can I do for you?"

"Do you have time for a couple of questions?"

"Sure. Have a seat." He pointed at three plastic chairs that looked uncomfortable and not conducive to long-term sitting.

I glanced around for another option, but unless I was willing to sit on an exam table, an unforgiving chair was it. "Trying to keep the line short, huh?"

He chuckled. "Definitely not the most comfortable, are they?"

We dragged a couple of chairs to face each other, the metal legs chewing up the grass then spitting up dirt. I dropped my backpack on the ground and sat.

He rolled the sleeves of his gingham-checked blue sport shirt to mid-forearm. "So, what's going on?"

I leaned forward, resting my elbows on my knees. "I was curious; how would you treat a depressed dog?"

His eyebrows knitted in concern. "Are you worried about Missy?"

"No. I was talking to Lenny Santucci a few minutes ago. His dog Pickles is racing today. He was telling me how depressed Pickles has been lately."

He nodded. "Pickles could be picking up on Lenny's anxiety."

That was a definite possibility. From what I had seen, Lenny was not only high-strung but he also had a lot to be anxious about. "Do you medicate for that? Or, you know, do dogs go to therapy?"

Daniel smiled knowingly. "Caro could talk to you about therapy."

I leaned back in my chair and rolled my eyes. He knew my cousin and I weren't on speaking terms. He'd heard both sides of our whole muddled history. As a true friend to both of us, he refused to pick a side. "I see you haven't lost your sense of humor."

Daniel popped up. "I have something for you." He walked across the tent to the rolling cabinet and dug through the top drawer. He pulled out a pamphlet and brought it over to me. *Behavioral Medications for Your Dog*. The front page was a photo of an adorable Corgi barking at his owner.

"Treatment depends on the animal. It doesn't have to be one or the other. They can be medicated and attend therapy. Either one can be costly. Without insurance, the medication can cost as much as seventy dollars a month."

I flipped through the brochure. "If Pickles was on antidepressants, would he have an unfair advantage?"

He shot me a half smile. "Pickles might experience an increased heart rate, but an antidepressant could actually slow him down."

Could Pickles be on medication, and that's why he continued to lose? I tapped the pamphlet, debating what I should do next. Lenny didn't seem like the kind of guy who'd appreciate unsolicited help. I shoved the information in my backpack.

Daniel checked his watch. "The race starts in about ninety minutes. Did I answer all your questions?"

I grabbed my backpack and stood. I needed to make this fast; I still had to set up the booth. "I ran into Judd Malone yesterday and he mentioned you examined Zippy. How was he?"

He raised an eyebrow in amused skepticism. "You just *happened* to run into a homicide detective?"

I grinned. "Well, you know."

He leaned against the exam table. "No, I don't know. I'm not sure I want to. But to answer your question, yes, I examined Zippy Eriksen. Other than acting a little skittish after being handled by a couple of strangers, he seemed fine."

I wasn't a specialist, but in my humble opinion, I also thought he seemed fine when he was at the boutique this morning. "So you cleared him to race today?"

He shrugged. "Why wouldn't I?"

"Even after all the doping rumors?"

He blinked in surprise. "What have you heard?"

"Mostly Lenny spouting off about the Eriksens juicing their dog. But it was Gia's reaction that got me curious. If she has nothing to hide, why not volunteer Zippy for a urine test?"

"Actually, Gia agreed to let me run a few tests. Everything came back negative."

Why keep that a secret? She was proving to be an accomplished liar. "She's not doping him?"

The boyish grin transformed into his serious doctor scowl. "It's not that simple. I have to test for specific drugs. I tested for five drugs; he tested negative for those five."

"Did you suggest which drugs to test for?"

He nodded. "I did. After I'd talked to the filmmaker—"

"I wanted to talk to you about her," I said.

Daniel looked confused by my sudden interjection. I was about to ask him about Stephanie, when Mr. TV strolled inside, hijacking my tête-à-tête.

"Well, hello there. We meet again." He flashed a roguish smile at me.

"I thought I left you at the coffee shop. I'd think a *serious* journalist wouldn't choose to hang out at a wiener race."

"Ah, but as you pointed out yesterday, not everything is what it seems."

There was no way to tell if he was talking about himself, me, or the race. Either way, I didn't want to know. I'm sure there were those who found his twinkling eyes and witty conversation adorable, but I wasn't one of them.

"I find that we're both here to question the good doctor intriguing." He held out his hand in Daniel's direction. "Callum MacAvoy, *Channel 5 News.*"

"Noon reporter," I clarified, with a cheeky smile.

They clasped hands. "Daniel Darling." Daniel's curious gaze darted between the reporter and me.

"Daniel and I are friends. I wasn't questioning him," I said, clearing up Mr. TV's assumption.

"My apologies. It only *sounded* like an interrogation."

Daniel's brown eyes narrowed. "How can I help you, Mr. MacAvoy?"

"I was hoping you could shed light on the doping allegation. I've heard from a couple of sources who are concerned about Zippy taking a supplement. Can you confirm if that's true?"

I was surprised to hear he was investigating the doping angle. Had he overheard my conversation with Daniel?

"To my knowledge, the dog is clean."

Mr. TV pulled out a pen and notebook from inside his blazer pocket. "Then you *have* tested the dog?"

"I thought murder was your story?" I asked.

"A good reporter follows every thread."

A good reporter follows every thread, I mimicked silently. I didn't want to listen to him pontificate on how to be a great reporter. Could he possibly be anymore condescending?

"Doctor, did you test Zippy at the urging of the racing organization?"

Daniel shoved his hands in his pockets. "I'm not at liberty to answer your questions. Perhaps you should talk to Hagan Stone. Mel, is there anything else you needed?"

I wanted to ask him about Stephanie. I bit my lip as I quickly searched for a way to get rid of Mr. TV.

MacAvoy tapped his notebook with his pen. "I can tell you're itching to ask him something, Melinda. Don't let my presence stop you."

"Don't flatter yourself." I faced Daniel wide-eyed, hoping he'd get the message I was sending. "About your early morning visitor," I prompted.

Daniel looked like a confused charade player who had no idea how to interpret his partner's clues.

"She's talking about the girl with the dachshund tattoo," MacAvoy butted in.

I jerked my head around and slung an irritated glare at him. "You are annoying."

"Who?" Daniel asked.

"The filmmaker," I explained. "Did she say where she'd be today?"

"Not specifically."

I smiled insincerely at MacAvoy. "Excuse us." There was no need to play coy any longer.

I grabbed Daniel's arm and dragged him away from MacAvoy. As quietly as I could, I recounted Betty's story about how Stephanie, aka the girl with the dachshund tattoo, had taken Betty's gun.

"I wish I'd known about this sooner. I could have helped," he said softly. "I wonder why Betty didn't mentioned this when I saw her yesterday," he mused.

"You saw Betty yesterday too?" My voice squeaked. I looked over my shoulder at MacAvoy. He waved. Ugh.

"Yes," Daniel said.

I knew him well enough to know when he was keeping something confidential. "When exactly? Give me a time."

He walked toward the door. "I'm not sure. I wasn't watching the clock."

I grabbed his arm, forgetting all about MacAvoy. "If you can give her alibi, please do."

He shook his head. "I can't. I saw her after Richard's shooting."

"Did she come here or did you see her around the park?"

With a heavy sigh, he crossed his arms and asked, "What's with all the questions, Mel?"

"Besides the fact that she's a murder suspect, and Mr. TV over there stopped short of reporting her as a person of interest on the news last night?"

He whistled softly. "There's more?"

"Yes. Betty's disappearing without a word to anyone, dodging her daughter, and missing work. I'm concerned."

Daniel turned more tightlipped than usual. "If she is hiding something, I'm sure she has a very good reason."

I wanted to shake the information out of him. "She confided in you?" I had no idea they were so close.

Daniel shrugged. "I'm sorry. That's all I can say."

"I might be able to help." MacAvoy's rich voice shot through the tent like an arrow.

For a price. He didn't say the words, but they hung in the air nonetheless.

Accepting assistance from Callum MacAvoy would be like dancing with the devil.

"I'll take my chances elsewhere. Daniel, thanks for the help. I have to set up the booth." I spun around and marched out of the tent.

Chapter Fifteen

I BARGED OUT OF Dr. Daniel's tent and smacked into a frazzled petite brunette, knocking her off her feet. The contents of my backpack spilled onto the grass like candy from a busted piñata.

"I'm so sorry. Are you okay?" I offered her a hand.

The woman looked up. Dark eyes peeked through limp locks of hair. It was Fallon Keller, the protester who'd been arguing with Richard before he died. The day was turning around.

"I'm fine," she replied through gritted teeth, refusing my offer.

I dropped to my hands and knees and gathered my personal items. I scooped up my keys, the dog antidepressant brochure, lip balm, and wallet. Fallon handed me my cell phone.

"Thanks. I think I've seen you before. Weren't you protesting yesterday?" I kept my head down and aimed for a nonchalant tone of voice.

She scrambled to her feet. "Maybe."

I gathered the last few items out of the thick grass, cramming everything inside my bag as quickly as possible before jumping to my feet. We each took a moment to brush ourselves off. I wasn't very meticulous since I was wearing yesterday's jeans and T-shirt. Fallon, on the other hand, had worn a trendy, long maxi-dress with a white jean jacket. A little dirt and grass stains would be noticeable.

As she continued to inspect herself, I pressed for a little chat. "I have to admit, I was surprised to see picketers. I had no idea there was any type of controversy around wiener racing."

Her small face tightened with passionate disapproval. "These races promote animal exploitation, cheating, and gambling. Our organization would rather encourage competitions which demonstrate doxies' natural agility and field-tracking skills. Did you know there are Dachshund Dashes held on ice rinks? That's extremely dangerous. The lack of traction has led to horrible spinal injuries."

I didn't know. As fanatical as she sounded, she made valid points. About ice races anyway. "But we're racing in the grass. At a dog park."

"You have no idea what these owners are willing to do behind the scenes. It's appalling." She pointed at a sheet of paper lying in the grass behind me. "You missed something."

It was the photo of Fallon and Richard. My breath caught. This could be bad.

"Thanks," I said, as we reached for it at the same time.

She snatched it from my grip. "Where'd you get this?" Her voice rose in what sounded like panic.

I grabbed it back. "The event photographer took it yesterday." No use beating around the bush now. "How do you know Richard?"

She hesitated. "Everyone knows Zippy and the Eriksens."

"But not everyone wants to beat Mr. Eriksen with a picket sign. What were you two fighting about?"

"We weren't fighting. We hardly knew each other."

I looked at the photo. I wasn't buying it. People who didn't know each other, didn't glare at one another with that much emotion. I held up the paper. "Really? Looks like you were about to whack him with your sign."

"That's not what happened," she denied, stepping back.

"What was it then?"

"I was surprised. I lost my grip on the wooden handle. That's all."

My eyes narrowed in skepticism. "Surprised about what?"

She pressed her lips together. "That's not really any of your business."

"You're absolutely right. But the police have a copy of this photo." I shook the paper. "It's only a matter of time before they talk to you. Whatever you're hiding will come out. Think of this as an opportunity to hone your answer."

"Was he upset that you'd tipped off the filmmaker about Zippy's retirement?" MacAvoy asked from behind me.

I spun around to face Mr. TV. Damn him. Why didn't I hear him creep up on us? How much had he overheard?

"How did you know about that?" Fallon's eyes darted around like a runaway bride looking for an escape route.

It was true? Well that could be a real game-changer.

"Yeah, how *did* you know about that?" I didn't want to be impressed, but I felt a temporary crack in my disdain for Mr. TV. Maybe he was better at research than I had given him credit for. Or more likely, he had real sources.

"Isn't that what you told the filmmaker yesterday? That Richard

Eriksen had confided in you about retiring Zippy after this weekend's race?" he asked Fallon.

"I-I don't know what you're talking about."

He pulled out the same small notebook he'd held just minutes earlier and flipped through it. "I saw her interviewing the protesters for her dogumentary. You were there."

"That doesn't prove anything," she snapped.

She was right. But I was finally starting to push past my distrust of Callum MacAvoy and decode his insistence that he had something I wanted—the girl with the dachshund tattoo. "It does if the filmmaker told MacAvoy."

He smiled. "You're starting to pay attention."

"Well, you did try and tell me you had something I wanted. I just didn't realize 'something' meant 'someone'," I conceded reluctantly. "This doesn't mean we're friends. I'm angry that you talked about Betty on the air."

He grinned. "You saw that?"

"Don't sound so impressed. I'm not signing up for your fan club." I switched my focus back to Fallon who trembled like a frightened Chihuahua. In the words of Grandma Tillie, she was "as antsy as a Baptist at a poker table."

"Why would Richard confide in you? He didn't seem like someone who spilled secrets to random strangers or acquaintances," I said.

Her amber eyes darkened with emotion. "We weren't random strangers."

"So you have some type of history? I heard there was an altercation last year between a protester and a racer. Was that you and Richard?"

"You heard wrong. Lenny Santucci argued with a judge. He thought she was playing favorites. There were no problems between anyone in our organization and a racer.

"So you and Richard were what? *Friends?*" As in friends with benefits?

Fallon started to answer, but Hagan Stone suddenly called out my name, stopping her cold. The three of us turned in his direction as he bounded our way. MacAvoy cursed under his breath. I had to agree, Hagan had horrible timing.

"Hello, Ms. Langston. I wasn't sure you were here." Hagan sounded out of breath. What was so important that he felt the need to run?

"I'm definitely here." Oh, dang. The booth. I still needed to unpack the merchandise.

Hagan sucked in one last deep breath, then let it out in a rush. "I won't need you as a judge after all. Thank you for your willingness to help. I do so appreciate it."

While I was distracted with Hagan, Fallon seized the opportunity to slink off without a word. Darn. I had more questions for her.

"I'm glad it all worked out." Because my promise to judge had completely slipped my mind. I was about to excuse myself so I could chase after Fallon until I noticed Hagan's gaze collide with MacAvoy.

The intensity was palpable. Hagan's expression morphed from gratitude into a mixture of surprise and then worry. I would have thought he'd be happy to know the event was being covered by the media. Even if it was by the noon reporter. Everyone knows, beggars can't be choosers.

"It's nice to see you again, Mr. MacAvoy," Hagan said. His normally charming tone lacked sincerity.

"Stone. I hear congratulations are in order." MacAvoy's smile was anything but happy for Hagan. "I heard you bought a bar in the Florida Keys."

Hagan's face became unreadable. "My, it's a small world. That's not public knowledge." His words came out stilted, forced, as if suppressing the urge to lose his temper. "Who told you?"

MacAvoy held out his hands, palms up. "As a reporter, I can't reveal my sources."

The words were innocuous. An excuse you'd expect from reporter. But there was underlying meaning floating over my head that only they understood. By the glares they shared, I got the feeling they didn't just dislike each other, but they didn't trust one another either.

I was clearly at a disadvantage in this conversation. But that didn't stop me from jumping in with both feet.

"Hagan, I was curious. There's a filmmaker at the event. She's shooting a dogumentary about wiener racing. Have you talked to her?"

He shifted a fixed gaze in my direction, body stiff. "I met with her yesterday. I believe I was one of the first people she interviewed. Fascinating young woman." His tone suggested she wasn't a good kind of fascinating.

"Have you seen her today?"

"I can't say that I have. Did you need to speak with her?"

I'd wanted Betty's gun back, but I kept that to myself. "I'd like to talk to her about the alleged doping and gambling operation."

"Pardon?" His eyebrows lifted in surprise. "You must be confused."

"No, not at all. In fact, I've talked to enough people that I know it's all true."

"As the Chairman of the Board, the doping allegations shouldn't be a shock to you," MacAvoy piped up.

For a second I thought Hagan's strained smile was because of what I'd said, until I realized he was looking at MacAvoy. I shot Mr. TV a "back off" look. Why did he have such a difficult time staying out of my Q&A session?

"She might have mentioned the possibility of some contestants using supplements of some kind," Hagan conceded.

"I'm not trying to get anyone in trouble." I held up my hands in an effort to ease the building tension. "There are a lot of rumors floating around about doping. Today I heard about an underground gambling group. And another thing I've been wondering. Does anyone know why her company, Bright Eyes, decided to film our race? Was it luck of the draw or does she have information the rest of us don't? Is this supposed dogumentary really an exposé and we're going to get caught up in it?"

MacAvoy jerked his head around. Had I actually thought of a scenario he hadn't?

"I know nothing about gambling. Perhaps you've been hanging around the wrong crowd." Hagan quickly shot a hostile look at MacAvoy before managing to look at me with concern. I wasn't convinced of his sincerity. About being concerned, that is. I believed his hostility. I was prone to feel it myself when it came to the handsome reporter.

"I have numerous tasks to attend to before race time. And I do believe your booth has yet to be unpacked, Ms. Langston." Hagan turned on his heel and charged off, effectively dismissing us.

I'd just been served.

Hagan was hiding something. Just like Fallon. I'd get to the bottom of it, sooner or later.

MacAvoy continued to watch Hagan walk away. "You gave me some advice yesterday. Let me return the favor. Don't get too comfortable around him."

"Hagan Stone?"

He nodded.

I shrugged, unconcerned. "He's harmless."

"He's dangerous."

His flat tone made me turn and look at him.

"O-kay. Dangerous as in he'll turn a blind eye to potentially harmful conditions for the dogs? Or dangerous as in he'll kill me?"

MacAvoy aimed his intense green eyes on me. "If you keep him from getting what he wants most, he'll remove you."

Hells bells. Getting in the way was my forte.

Chapter Sixteen

I RUSHED TO THE booth, ignoring my growling stomach as I passed the food trucks. The delicious aroma of fish tacos, chicken alfredo pizza, and gourmet hot dogs begged me to take a minute for lunch. But I was strong. Okay, let's be honest. I was in complete panic mode. Any other day, I'd have stopped for a fish taco. Maybe even a hot dog with grilled onions, cheddar cheese, and bacon. My mouth watered thinking about all the delicious food options at my fingertips.

All the other vendors in my row had their merchandise arranged and ready to sell. Fans started to trickle in. The second I reached Bow Wow Boutique's booth, I tossed aside my backpack and went to work.

Dog bowls and boxes of treats. Collars and leads. Paw-wear and outerwear. Key chains and dog toys. I was a stacking, folding, and hanging maniac. Out of the corner of my eye, I caught a glimpse of Darby heading my way.

Without a word, she stashed her camera and messenger bag under the table. She grabbed the last plastic tote and immediately started to unload.

"You are a godsend. How much time do we have?" I asked.

"First race starts in an hour."

I scooped up an armful of grooming supplies. I hung the soft bristled brushes as quickly as possible. "I got sidetracked with Doctor Daniel. Then I literally ran into Fallon Keller." Once the brushes were displayed, I started on the combs.

"I still haven't heard from, nor seen, Betty since yesterday. Who knows what she's up to?" I continued to rattle off the morning activities at warp speed. "Get this, Valerie showed up at the boutique today, begging me to talk to Betty and get her to confess all of her dirty little secrets. And to top it all off, Callum MacAvoy knows Stephanie."

Darby pushed back the hair from her eyes. "I'm not even sure where to start. The only person you didn't mention was Grey."

"That's because his was the only name you were listening for." I stacked the last metal grooming comb next to the other four on the table. "We're having dinner tonight. To talk." Anticipation and anxiety knotted in my stomach.

After I hung the last pup sweater, we stepped back to survey our handiwork. It wasn't Betty-Beautiful, but we were ready for business.

I hugged Darby. "I couldn't have done it without you. You're the best."

She tilted her head. "I've always got your back. Mel, I know it's none of my business, but if you need to talk about whatever is going on between you and Grey, I'm here."

I nodded. I desperately wanted to confide in her. I needed a sounding board and levelheaded advice. But in order to do that, I'd have to divulge the truth about Grey's FBI job, and that option was off the table.

"I know. I appreciate it. There's not a lot to tell. I crossed a line and he has every right to be mad. We're working it out. I promise."

A sliver of sunshine broke through the dark clouds, as Darby said, "I can't imagine you've done anything he can't forgive."

Guilt kept me from looking at her for too long. I stashed the empty totes under the table. "Did you find Malone and give him your photos yesterday?"

She nodded. "He was actually very receptive. He even thanked me."

I laughed, picturing how difficult that must have been for him. "How very un-Malone-like. You know, he's done a couple of un-Malone-like things lately. I wonder why."

Darby shrugged. "I try not to think about him."

Talking about the ever-so-serious detective made me remember the bet Sven had asked me to place. I reached for the crinkled twenty shoved in my pocket. "Have you heard anything about a gambling ring?" I asked Darby.

"No, but I've heard talk between some of the other vendors and fans about friendly wagers being placed."

I pulled my hair back into a quick ponytail and sighed. "I think there's more to it than that."

"Like organized crime?" Darby asked in a hushed voice.

I shook my head. "Sven, from the Koffee Klatch, made it sound like he was placing a low-key wager. At the time I believed him. But when I ran into Lenny at Rodney's chili truck, I got the feeling it was more serious than a simple friendly wager. Speaking of chili, I'm starving. I haven't eaten lunch."

Darby opened her messenger bag and pulled out a snack-sized energy bar. "Here."

"Are you sure?" I practically had it unwrapped before she could answer.

"I've got two more."

"Thank you," I managed to say around a mouthful of rolled oats and chocolate chips.

The mini-bar was gone in two bites. I was about to suggest a quick trip to the food trucks before we were swamped with customers when I saw Grey pop out from behind a young family of four who were all dressed like Underdog—capes included.

"Grey's here." I sounded like a teen girl who was about to be caught with a boy in her room.

Darby leaned against me, peeking over my shoulder. "I thought he wasn't coming."

I turned toward my best friend, quickly wiping the crumbs from the corner of my mouth. "Do I have chocolate smeared across my face?"

Darby held me at arm's length and gave me a quick best-friend-once-over. "You look fine."

"Yeah, well, if my Mama was here she'd tell me to slap on some lipstick." My mother thought everything was better, or at least easier to ignore, if she was in full makeup. And jewelry. Mama could easily be confused with a model at a Tiffany's photo shoot.

I looked back in Grey's direction and waved. He nodded in acknowledgment. He'd dressed down today. Dark jeans with an untucked cobalt blue, button-up shirt. It felt like my stomach was performing an Irish clog dance. The closer Grey got, the stronger the clog-stomping.

"Do you want me to leave?" Darby asked.

"Absolutely not." I may have sounded slightly panicked, which, given the fact that I felt like I was about to go on my first blind date, was perfectly normal.

"Does he have a Gina's Pizza to-go bag?" Darby asked.

I sighed in food lust at the brown paper bag clutched in his left hand. Gina's Pizza was my favorite restaurant. "Yes, he does."

"Good afternoon, ladies." Grey's deep voice shook me to my toes.

"Hey," I said, dividing my attention between his handsome face and the food.

"Hi," Darby said through an amused smile. "She missed lunch."

My mouth watered as the smell of marinara tickled my nose. "Please tell me that's a meatball sandwich." If this was his version of a peace offering, I accepted.

Grey peeked inside the bag and acted like he wasn't sure I'd want it. "Well, it's only a half and no longer warm. Oh, and I have a bottle of water."

I held out my hand. "Perfect."

He chuckled as he handed me the food. "I took a chance you missed lunch."

If I wasn't already in love with him, I'd fall in love all over again. Obviously, I could be bribed with food.

"Any sign of Betty and her gun?" he asked.

"Not yet. We're no longer the only ones looking for the filmmaker either. Apparently, she recorded Gia threatening her. Now Gia wants the video."

"I hate to say it, but that would make great footage," Darby said.

"What about you? Did you have any luck?" I asked Grey as I pulled out the sandwich and unwrapped one end. I inhaled the sweet smell of marinara as I lifted the sandwich to my mouth. My teeth bit into the toasted bread with a loud crunch. I closed my eyes and sighed. Heaven.

He shook his head. "Unfortunately, no. Have you heard from Malone?"

I shook my head while I finished chewing. "Nothing. Although Darby did give him a copy of all her photos yesterday. He was very appreciative."

Darby scoffed. "I don't know about that. But he did mutter the words, 'thank you'."

"Does anyone want a bite?" I held up what was left of my sandwich. They both declined, and I was thankful. Darby and Grey made small talk as I finished my lunch.

"Have you seen Hagan Stone today?" he asked Darby.

"Oh, yes. I met with him early this morning. He's around here somewhere. Did you need to talk to him?"

He shook his head. "No."

"I noticed the two of you talking yesterday. I didn't realize you knew each other." She wiped her palms on her jeans as if she were nervous.

I watched Grey with a sideways glance, curious to hear his answer.

"We don't. I met him while looking for Betty's gun."

Darby's blue eyes blinked repeatedly. "Oh, it seemed like you were awfully friendly."

Grey's shoulders tensed. If you didn't know him, you probably wouldn't have noticed. But I did know him, and he was being very cautious with his answer. "He's a friendly guy. He was telling me about the dogumentary and how excited he was to have the promotion."

I frowned. That wasn't the story he'd given me. Grey was lying to one of us.

Darby grabbed her camera and messenger bag. "I've got to go. The race will start soon, and I want to shoot some pictures of the crowd beforehand."

"Is everything okay?" I asked her.

She nodded, a tentative smile pasted on her face. "I realized how late it's getting. Can't document the race without the photographer."

"True. Good luck. I hope today runs smoother than yesterday."

"Don't we all. See ya later, Grey."

"Good-bye." He waved as she walked away.

I cracked open the water bottle and drank deeply, washing down the last of my sandwich. "I'm surprised to see you."

He leaned against the table. "I had some unexpected free time so I thought I'd swing by. Where's Missy?"

"At the house. Yesterday was too much excitement for her. She'll be disappointed she missed you." I gathered my trash and looked around for a garbage can. Not seeing one, I said, "I'll be right back."

"Can't stand being alone with me?" Did he actually look worried or was that wishful thinking on my part?

I gestured to the budding crowd and excited dogs. "This is not alone. I'm looking forward to being alone with you later tonight." Feeling confident in our relationship for the first time in weeks, I kissed him lightly on the mouth without an ounce of hesitation. "Hold down the fort. I'm going to find a place to toss this before a dog sniffs it out. If someone stops, entertain them until I get back."

My stomach was full, and my heart was optimistic. I felt a huge goofy smile slowly spread across my mouth. I picked my way through the crowd toward the bright yellow barrel, thinking about the different possible endings of my dinner with Grey later tonight.

A blur of blue velour sped ahead of me, knocking a dog walker aside. It looked like Gia and Zippy. I bobbed to the right but lost sight of them after they slipped behind the Feline and Me tent.

I reached the trash can and pitched my garbage inside. Before returning to Grey, I decided to make a quick side trip in the direction where I thought I'd seen Gia and her dog dash off. Sure enough, they were there. With her back to the crowd, Gia bent over and poured the contents from her purple reusable water bottle into Zippy's special bowl. The dog lapped up the liquid almost as quickly as she poured it.

I wish I'd paid more attention to her when she'd rattled off his schedule earlier. Normally, I wouldn't be suspicious of an owner pouring her pooch a drink. But Gia had been adamant that whatever was in the bottle was hers. "Vitamin water," she had said. I wasn't so sure.

She'd purposely hidden behind a tent, away from public viewing, before giving Zippy his drink. What was Gia Eriksen hiding? My long stride ate up the distance between Grey and me at a quick pace.

It was possible I'd just caught Gia red-handed breaking the rules. I had to find a way to get that water bottle to Doctor Daniel.

Chapter Seventeen

I HAULED MY BEHIND back to the booth, skidding to a stop in front of Grey who was leaning against the table reading email from his phone. I grabbed his shoulders and practically shouted, "I think I just saw Gia doping Zippy."

Grey looked up, surprised. "What?"

I tamped down my excitement. After stepping to the side, I pointed toward the Feline and Me booth. "Over there, behind the tent. Lenny might have been telling the truth. We've got to get Gia's water bottle."

"You're leveling a pretty serious allegation. Are you sure she was drugging him?"

What a joy-killer. I dragged my gaze away from where Gia and Zippy were tucked away like a couple of paparazzi-ducking celebrities. "Nooo," I dragged out the one syllable word. "That's why I said we have to get the water bottle from her. We need proof."

He didn't say a word. At least not verbally. I ignored his nonverbal cues and took his silence as an invitation to sway him to my way of thinking.

"Don't you find it odd that she hid behind the tents to give her dog a drink? Why be so secretive?"

"Maybe she wanted privacy."

"She could have gone to the veterinarian clinic or her car. What if Lenny was right? What if she's been cheating this whole time?"

He pocketed his phone with a sigh. "You're scheming."

"No," I lied, my eye twitching.

A wry smile settled on his mouth. "The eye spasm gives you away."

I pressed my fingers against my eyelid.

"You need to stay out of it," he said.

I sighed, frustrated. "Why? Why do I need to stay out of it? If Gia is cheating, aren't I just as guilty for turning a blind eye?"

He attempted to hide a pained look, but I saw it and recognized the furrowed brow for what it was—resignation.

"What did you have in mind?" he asked.

I wasn't one to gloat over a win. Believe it or not, I am willing to so-licit suggestions if warranted. To be honest, my motives weren't one hundred percent pure. If I could find a way to get him emotionally in-vested in helping me, it might rebuild the trust I'd broken.

I stepped closer until we were an arm's length apart. I lowered my voice. "You're the FBI. What do you normally do?"

He crossed his arms across his chest. "First of all, I have facts, not assumptions. I get a warrant. And I don't go off half-cocked. I have backup."

The air around us dropped twenty degrees. What was I thinking, consulting a process-driven rule-follower?

I stepped back. "We don't have three months to execute your standard operating procedure. We have an hour before the first heat. No pressure, but if you don't come up with a suggestion, I'll go with my idea. And we both know you won't like my grab-and-dash plan."

Grey and I stared at each other as he silently strategized. My plan was simple: confront Gia and make her hand over the bottle and con-tents for Daniel to analyze. I even had a backup plan if she refused: grab the container and run. It was plan B that I knew Grey wouldn't like.

"Unless she admits to cheating, Zippy will run in the race. If she is cheating, any possible fallout will come after today's event."

There were times when Grey's logic was rather deflating. This was one of those times. "I realize that's a possibility. But we still have to at least try."

I was so wrapped up in snatching the water bottle away from Gia, I didn't notice Betty approach.

"Hey Cookie, Stephanie's here sniffing around the food. I called Officer Cupcake, like I promised."

Betty shuffled toward us as if nothing was amiss. But after one look at her, I knew that wasn't the case. She looked like she'd wrestled the last brownie away from a starved serial-dieter and had paid for it dearly. She wore elastic polyester pants (since when did Betty wear polyester? She's a cotton-and-silk type of gal), a wrinkled graphic tee with multiple stains, and grassy sneakers. Her straw handbag hung on her arm. Where were her silk printed pajamas? Her pearls?

Most importantly, where were her lipstick eyebrows?

All thoughts of Gia and the water bottle were pushed aside by my concern for Betty.

"Where have you been?" I wrapped my assistant in a hug. "Are you okay?"

Her small frame felt delicate in my embrace. Her coarse white hair, which needed a good brushing, tickled my nose. I stifled a sneeze. As we hugged, I detected an unusual scent surrounding her. I quietly sniffed her shirt. Unless she'd bought a new perfume, she smelled like hamburger. Maybe she'd brought her lunch with her.

She patted my back then stepped away. "You're holding up traffic. How are we supposed to make money if you block the only entrance to our booth? Where is everyone?"

I gently held onto her arm. "Sweetie, I've been worried about you."

She brushed off my hand as if I were being overprotective. I suppressed my surprise at the large bruise developing under her paper-thin skin on the back of her hand.

"You don't need to worry about me. I can take care of myself," she assured me.

It sure didn't look like it.

She gave Grey an appreciative onceover. "Nice to see you again, handsome."

He smiled warmly as he made his way to her. "I'm glad you're here."

As she lifted her cheek for him to kiss, the neckline of her shirt dipped, exposing two long red scratches at the base of her neck. I couldn't let that pass.

"What's going on? You're dressed like a bum. There are scratch marks on your neck. You never called me last night to let me know you made it home. And you were supposed to be at the shop hours ago."

She raised her hand to cover the scrapes. "It's really none of your business."

You know what? I was tired of people telling me what was my business and what wasn't.

"Wrong. It became my business when your daughter showed up at the boutique, begging me to keep *you* out of trouble."

Betty snorted her disgust. "That child only thinks about herself. It's none of her business either. I'm a grown woman. I don't have to answer to anyone."

"No, you don't. Have you looked in the mirror today? You're a disaster. For goodness' sakes, did you really think I wouldn't notice you're wearing polyester pants?"

She cast a sideways glance toward Grey who was being unusually quiet.

"I-I fell. This morning," she admitted, never looking me in the eye.

"You're okay?" he asked.

"I'm fine."

I wasn't convinced that's all there was to it. But Betty had her own ideas, and she didn't like to be told what to do. I understood that about her. There wasn't much more I could do, except dispense some tough love.

"Alright. Then as your boss, I expect you to be at work when you're scheduled and dressed in your Betty clothes. Do you get what I'm telling you?"

She nodded. "I hear ya, Cookie. No more playing hooky. Ha. I made a rhyme." Once she was finished laughing at her pun, she shoved her hands on her hips and tsked. "You may be the boss, but you stink at displaying our products. No wonder we don't have any customers."

She hooked her straw handbag on the crook of her arm and stomped toward the haphazardly-hung dog leashes.

"I was a little pressed for time." Great. Suddenly, I was on the defensive.

"Humph."

As she passed Grey, a dollar bill fell from her purse.

"Hey, you're dropping money." I picked it up.

She snatched the bill then shoved into her purse, once again avoiding eye contact. I couldn't help but notice there was more cash inside her handbag. A lot more.

My eyes narrowed. "Betty, is your purse stuffed with dollar bills?"

She hugged her handbag to her chest. "I don't loan money to friends or family."

I lifted my eyebrows. "Please tell me you haven't been hanging out at the drag queen bar again."

"Oh, that's a great idea. I have plenty of tip money." She swiveled her hips. "I may have to leave early today. I love that Cher gal." She danced as she hummed a Cher tune.

Wait. Were those chili stains on her t-shirt? That would explain why she smelled like hamburger. Then it hit me. Oh. My. Gosh. I shook my head in denial, but I knew it was true. "Betty, have you been betting on the wiener races?"

She froze. Blinked a couple of times, then lowered her handbag to her side. "How do you know about that?"

I couldn't look at Grey, especially after I heard his groan of dismay.

"You have been gambling," he stated flatly.

She shrugged. "There's no need to fuss. Just a half dollar here or there. I had to get in on the action." She patted her purse. "I'm on a roll too. Today's race is going to be big. *Big.* Guaranteed a huge payout. Odds are in favor of Pickles."

A half dollar? What did that even mean? Was that more gambling slang, or had she really only bet fifty cents? Maybe Sven should have asked Betty to place his bet. She obviously was more informed than I was on terminology.

"No more, Betty." Grey's tone brooked no argument. Neither did the stern look on his face.

She winked at him, undaunted by his commanding authority. "No problem. I've already placed my wagers for the day. Pickles to win." Betty traipsed to the display of leashes and collars. "Make yourself useful handsome. Hold out your arms."

Grey frowned. "Only if you promise, no more gambling."

"You have my word." Betty crossed her heart.

I don't know about Grey, but I didn't believe her for a second. His frowned deepened, but he did as she asked. Betty draped the merchandise over his arms, quickly sorting by size first, then color.

"I thought you didn't like Lenny?" I asked, as Betty made quick work of reorganizing my rush display job.

"Just because he's a loser, doesn't mean his dog can't win."

Confession time. If Sven wanted to place a bet, legal or not, that was his choice. But Betty was a different story. I felt protective of her, both physically and financially.

"Grey, do you think we can get her money back?"

She looked up from hanging the last handful of leashes. "Why would I want to get my money back? Do you have an aversion to money? Maybe you should talk to someone about that."

"I have plenty of money. Don't you worry about me."

No longer Betty's personal hanger, Grey rubbed the back of his neck. "The best thing you could do is forget about it. Don't go back."

"If I win, I'm getting my money," Betty promised, full of attitude.

"Leave it alone. Underground gambling is an illegal business."

"I bet on the ponies every summer. That's not illegal," she argued.

He sighed, frustrated. "That's different."

Betty sniffed. "I don't see how."

"Well, it is."

Betty stared at his unbending face. "Now you tell me. Is that why Rodney, the bagman, keeps hiding from the judges?"

Grey rubbed his face. "Stay away from the chili truck."

"Listen handsome, if I win, I'm collecting my money."

"No. You are to stay away." His eyes lit on Betty's face, imploring her to do as he said.

Grey was agitated. I had a nagging feeling he was holding back vital information. "What aren't you telling us?"

"I'm telling you, these are serious criminals. Stay away from them." His voice was tight, irritation written all over his face.

I could feel myself getting cranky. I'd already told Betty to stop betting. He'd already told her to stop betting. Why was he picking this hill to die on? Surely there were more important arguments to win.

I met his eyes and held them. I wanted his complete attention. "Look around. This is a wiener race. Rodney isn't going to break Betty's knee caps because she won twenty bucks. How would you know they're dangerous criminals?"

"You don't want me to answer." He glanced at Betty who was taking in our discussion wide-eyed.

"No, I do." I motioned for us to move aside so we could talk in private. He shook his head no. I felt like he was purposely pushing my buttons. Picking a fight.

"How do you know the people behind the gambling ring are hardened criminals?" I repeated my question, refusing to back down, all the while knowing I was being just as unreasonable as Grey. But I couldn't seem to stop myself.

He shrugged. "I'm speculating."

No, he wasn't. That answer was for Betty's benefit. His shrug was stiff and unnatural. He knew something, and he was keeping it to himself. I thought we'd moved past this a year ago when he promised to share more. I wasn't expecting specifics. But how hard was it for him to pull me aside to tell me he was working a case? That's all I wanted.

I suddenly wondered if he was here to keep an eye on me, and not because he actually wanted to spend time with me.

"Why are you here?"

We stared at each other. My chest rose and fell with each breath as I waited for an answer. Hoping he'd tell me the truth, and at the same time worried he'd evade or deflect my very direct question.

"To bring you lunch." His flat eyes caught me off guard.

He'd closed himself off. I wanted to believe him. But I didn't. I caught my breath on the huge lump in my throat.

Grey broke eye contact and turned toward Betty who watched us intently. "Did you talk to the filmmaker?" he asked.

She shook her head. "Nope. She was sniffing around the food

trucks this morning. I lost my phone, so I found that charming Hagan Stone. He promised to call the police for me."

His cheek muscle twitched. "Hagan called the police for you?"

She nodded. "He said he'd take care of it."

Grey's cell rang. He frowned at the name of the caller. "I'll be back." He looked at Betty. "Behave."

To me he said nothing. Which was good. I'm not sure I could have held my tongue. We watched him walk toward the same group of trees where I'd gone to take his call yesterday.

Once he was out of earshot, Betty asked, "Why is he mad? Did you do something?"

I gave her a half shrug, unwilling to put my suspicion into spoken words. Besides, this was between me and Grey. "I thought I knew. But now . . . I'm not sure. Let's stop talking about Grey. How much did you really put on Pickles?"

She rubbed her hands together. "One hundred."

I opened my mouth, then shut it. There was nothing I could say. She was a grown woman. Who was making poor decisions. "Seriously, no more gambling."

"I said I got it. Hey, where's Missy?"

"I left her home. She's worn out from yesterday."

"Do you kennel her when she's home alone?"

"Not anymore. She's too lazy to rummage around in stuff she shouldn't."

"But you used to kennel her?"

"Sure," I replied, puzzled at why Betty was asking so many questions. "Some dogs actually like their kennel. It's comforting. But you have to do it right. You have to train them. You can't make the kennel a place of punishment. Why all the sudden interest in dog care?"

"Can't a body be curious?"

Nah, this was more than curiosity, but for the life of me, I had no idea what it could be. She was probably plotting her next crazy marketing idea.

"So what were you two doing before I arrived?" Betty puckered her lips and made kissing sounds.

She couldn't have been further from the truth. "We were talking about Gia. She and Zippy were hiding behind the cat tent. She was acting very secretive as she poured something from her purple water bottle into Zippy's special bowl."

"What?"

I shook my head. My earlier excitement returned at the possibility of catching Gia cheating. "I'm not sure. It's possible she's doping Zippy like Lenny said. Grey and I were brainstorming a way to get the water bottle so we could take it to Daniel."

"I never liked her. What's the plan?"

"But what about our merchandise?" Now I sounded like my sales-crazed assistant. Seriously, why did I even bother setting up the booth if we weren't going to be there?

Betty looked torn. "How 'bout we give ourselves fifteen minutes? If we don't find her, we come back and make some money."

I looked over at the grove of trees. Grey was gone. My heart hurt knowing he didn't seem to find it necessary to include me on his comings and goings.

My biggest reason to stay put had simply vanished.

I grabbed Betty's arm, not willing to let her disappear too. "Fifteen minutes. Let's go."

Chapter Eighteen

GIA WAS GONE.

It wasn't surprising. She couldn't hide behind the tent forever. I was self-aware enough to admit I was jumping to conclusions about her juicing Zippy. For all I knew, it really was her vitamin water like she'd claimed. But my gut told me Gia had a secret, just like everyone else.

"Thirty minutes until the first heat in the heavyweight race. All competitors report to the waiting area." Hagan's distorted voice thundered over the PA system.

"Do you want to keep looking for Gia?" Betty stopped under a eucalyptus tree off the pathway to pull up her socks.

"What's with the rainbow-colored socks?"

She looked up. "I don't judge your boots."

"Point taken. Yes, I want to keep looking for Gia."

She stood and rested a hand on her narrow hip. With a mischievous smile she said, "Let's look for Stephanie too."

I know what you're thinking. We'd promised to let the police handle it. But the police were a no-show at this point, and Betty's gun was still missing. "If we find her, we call Malone directly."

"Let's grab a corn dog, first. I haven't eaten lunch." Betty patted her stomach.

What could I say? I had been in that exact position thirty minutes earlier. We circled back toward the food area.

"No chili truck," I insisted. "And I'll pay. The last thing we need is for you to start a riot showing off a purse full of money."

Betty grinned. "I won't turn down free food."

Just one more thing we had in common. The more time I spent with Betty, the more convinced I was that she was what I'd be like in fifty years.

I'd hoped we'd stumble upon either Grey or Darby at some point, but we hadn't laid eyes on either of them. I kept watch for the enigmatic filmmaker since this was where Betty had last seen her.

The gray clouds had disappeared, and the sun warmed my back as we followed the well-worn pathway toward the food area. I recognized a number of clients, which wasn't unusual at an event like this. I enjoyed seeing their smiling faces. Betty and I were a few yards from the food area when loud shrieks and excited barking resonated throughout the park.

We looked at each other. With a nod, we agreed to check out what was going on. We followed the wave of people rushing toward the arguing voices.

"Hey, there's Luis." Betty waved in his direction.

He held his doxie, Barney, in his arms, their attention locked on whatever was occurring inside the human circle. Suddenly, a recognizable female screech rose above the whispers of the crowd.

"Gia," Betty and I exclaimed in unison.

We elbowed our way in between Luis and a ginger-haired man who hid his wind-battered face behind a pair of thick, black-rimmed glasses.

"I love a good fight," the man said. The sides of his mouth curved upward, deepening his tanned wrinkles.

If crowd size was an indication, he wasn't the only one eager to witness a good scuffle.

"Luis, what's going on?" I asked.

He smiled sheepishly, finally noticing Betty and me. "Some lady picked a fight with Mrs. Eriksen."

The "lady" was Fallon Keller. They faced off, surrounded by a ring of drama-thirsty onlookers waiting for one of the women to throw the first punch. I had a flashback to middle school playground fights. This would not end well.

"I said, leave. You're in violation of the restraining order," Gia demanded. Her face screamed she was willing to wage a battle between good and evil. Terrifyingly enough, I couldn't tell which side she was defending.

"That's ridiculous. There's no such thing." Fallon thrust her picket sign between herself and Gia.

Zippy barked as he lurched for Fallon. He wasn't threatening. He acted like Missy when she rushes toward me after she hasn't seen me for a while. I found his reaction to her curious.

"Stay," Gia commanded. She slung her large handbag on her shoulder. In an attempt to keep her energetic pooch close, she wrapped the leather leash around her free hand. "Yes, there is. Our attorney filed it the same day we sued you for harassment. You've followed us from race to race for two *years*. You're obsessed with us."

Fallon's face remained eerily calm. "I don't know what to tell you except Richard lied."

"No, he didn't." Gia stomped her foot, plunging her heel into the grass.

Someone behind her laughed as Gia's arms shot out to catch her balance. Zippy barked again, triggering the canines in the crowd to join him.

Mr. TV appeared out of nowhere. He managed to wedge himself next to me. "I've checked. There is no restraining order," he said under his breath.

I begrudgingly made room for him. "When did you do that?"

"Yesterday. I searched the public records database for any info on the Eriksens."

I was about to ask if he'd dug up anything of interest when Gia continued her verbal attack on Fallon.

"You have an irrational attachment to Zippy. And—and you've sent us death threats."

Whoa. Death threats? That was out of left field. Why in the world would she send them death threats? I looked at MacAvoy for possible answers since he seemed to know more than the rest of us. He shrugged.

I studied Fallon's face. She wasn't just calm, she was confident. As if she knew something Gia didn't. I pulled out the photo of Fallon and Richard from my bag. In the picture she looked angry.

"You don't know what you're talking about." Fallon turned to walk away. Zippy lunged after her again sending all the dogs into another bark-fest.

"I saw you in your car outside of our house," Gia shouted.

Fallon stopped.

"That's right. I saw you. I know about all the pathetic voicemails you left for Richard on his cell phone."

Fallon slowly faced Gia again. Her smiled slipped, revealing a tiny crack in her confidence that wasn't there six seconds ago.

Gia didn't hold back from spewing her venom. "But you crossed the line when you broke into our house and ransacked it. Destroying our family photos. Shredding Zippy's bed. You're a horrible person. You belong in jail."

Fallon shook her head. "I didn't break into your house. I would never hurt Zippy." She glanced at the "Save our Doxies" sign she clutched. Was she about to whack Gia with it?

For those of us paying attention, she didn't deny calling Richard repeatedly. I studied the photo again. Had Darby captured a lover's quarrel? Maybe Richard always looked angry. I didn't know him well enough to know his true temperament.

MacAvoy looked over my shoulder. "Where'd you get that?"

I shoved the photo back inside my bag. "I don't reveal my sources."

He smiled. "What were they arguing about?"

"I don't know."

"You're in violation of the 'no contact' order," Gia told Fallon. "You need to leave."

I elbowed MacAvoy. "Tell her that's not true."

He cleared his throat. "I'm afraid she's correct," he spoke loudly, attracting Gia's attention. "There isn't a restraining order."

She whipped around and glared at MacAvoy. "Yes, there is. My husband filed it two months ago. He promised me he'd take care of it. Right after she"—Gia pointed a finger at Fallon—"broke into our house."

"Unfortunately, your husband lied to you," MacAvoy said.

"I knew he was no good," Betty muttered under her breath.

"Shh," I whispered back. I didn't believe either woman would admit to killing Richard, but there was a chance they might say something incriminating, and I didn't want to miss it. You know, so I could fill in Malone later.

Gia scowled. "You're wrong. He wouldn't lie to me. She stalked us. I have proof."

Fallon shook her head. "I wasn't stalking anyone. Richard could have told me to leave him alone at any time. He didn't. Not once."

Okay, it didn't take a genius to see where this was going. Gia was also putting two and two together and coming up with the same conclusion I had. I felt badly for her. It was one thing to learn your dead husband might have cheated on you. It was a whole other story to find out about it from his mistress in front of fifty strangers.

Gia rallied quickly. "Your pitiful attempt to take what didn't belong to you failed."

"You're wrong," Fallon bit out.

"You're a jealous vindictive witch. He didn't want you so you shot my husband."

There was a collective gasp at Gia's accusation. Oh, it was on like Donkey Kong.

"I didn't kill Richard." Fallon's dark eyes glared at her enemy.

"Someone call 911. There's a murderer among us," Gia wailed, pointing at Fallon.

"It's you. You're the killer." Fallon's condemning words fell into an expectant silence. "He was going to leave you, but you murdered him first."

I felt like we were watching two B-list actors act out a scene from Clue. I half expected her to finish her declaration with, "In the dog park with the revolver."

All at once, Gia dropped Zippy's leash and jumped Fallon. The picket sign landed with a solid thwack on the grass.

"You tramp," Gia screamed.

"Murderer." Fallon managed to wrangle free, and push Gia away. "You're crazy."

Zippy jumped around, dragging his leash behind him as he barked his head off.

"That dog's jacked up," Betty said.

I called Zippy, but he refused to come. He was too worked up to obey, and Gia was too upset to notice her pooch needed her.

"You killed my husband you selfish harlot." Gia's face grew redder with each word. "You couldn't have him, so you shot him."

"I loved him." Fallon pounded her chest. "I was the best thing that ever happened to him. We were going to start our lives together. You killed him. He hated you."

"Liar!"

"You're the liar. You refused to give him a divorce. You didn't love him. You just wanted his money. He was going to leave you and retire Zippy after this race."

I met MacAvoy's gaze. We knew that was the truth. He'd confirmed it with the filmmaker.

Gia lurched for Fallon again, who quickly backed away, keeping out of Gia's threatening clutches.

"You told him the only way he'd get rid of you was over your dead body. Well, look who's dead. Richard." This time Fallon lunged for Gia, shoving her in the chest.

Gia stumbled back, dropping her purse at her feet. Zippy frantically pawed at the bag, managing to unearth the purple water bottle I'd been wanting to nab earlier.

The women circled each other like the *Mob Wives* cast at a Hollywood premiere. It was about to get ugly. Where were the police? Hadn't Hagan called the police like he'd promised Betty?

"That's it. You're dead." Gia shoved Fallon so hard she tripped over Zippy, barely managing to stay upright. Zippy yelped, jumping to the side.

The mass of onlookers stumbled back, granting wide berth. I scanned the faces in the crowd. We all had the same stunned look of fascination and horror. Although judging by the number of people who'd whipped out their cell phones to snap pictures of the fight, the allure of drama had outweighed their alarm.

Zippy ran in circles around his owner and Fallon, wrapping his leash around their legs. The fighting women toppled to the ground with a loud thud. Gia wrangled Fallon onto her back and sat on the poor gal. Within seconds, the screaming match escalated into an all-out brawl, which included hair-pulling, scratching, and rather impressive foul language. Gia never relinquished her advantage.

"I've got twenty on the crazy one," Betty shouted.

"Which one's that?" the ginger-haired man asked.

"Damn, I don't have a camera." MacAvoy looked over his shoulder, presumably for his cameraman, Ryan.

I jerked my head in Mr. TV's direction. "That's what you're thinking about?"

"It's my job," he said unapologetically.

I was worried about Zippy being injured. I watched for an opportunity to grab the dog without being kicked when his leash somehow managed to untangle itself from the women's thrashing legs. Zippy raced off toward the track with his ears flapping in the breeze—all four paws taking flight as his long body stretched out to full length. Barking dogs tugged on their leashes, yearning to give chase to the current wiener champion.

"Sweet baby Jesus," Betty cried out. "Look at him go."

Luis set Barney on the grass. "We'll get him." They took off after the runaway pooch.

It was a complete and utter madhouse. I pulled out my cell to call the police when I felt a heavy presence loom behind me.

"Break it up." Malone's voice roared over my shoulder.

Startled, I fumbled with my phone almost dropping it. *Holy crapola.* Where'd he come from?

The crowd parted, inviting Malone to wade into the lion's den. Gia and Fallon continued to pull hair and scream vicious names at each other, oblivious to the police's arrival.

"Enough!" Without a second of hesitation, the detective effortlessly lifted Gia off Fallon and set her aside.

Well, I don't know about everyone else, but I was certainly thanking the good Lord for Malone's timely appearance. At the rate those two were going at it, someone was going to end up dead.

And we all know, I'm the last person who should be reporting a dead body to the cops.

Chapter Nineteen

THE POLICE USHERED the bystanders to the side, keeping Gia and Fallon separated. Officer Salinas stood next to Fallon, his crossed arms resting on his large muscular chest as if daring her to leave. At the moment, she continued to stay put, but the girl looked like she was ready to bolt at the slightest provocation.

Detective Malone's forceful voice hovered above the curious buzz as he questioned Gia. I couldn't make out the words, but the low-pitched tone and wide-legged stance communicated clearly that he meant business.

The women looked like two rolled drunks with blades of grass and leaves stuck in their hair like barrettes. Angry red scratch marks trailing down their necks. Fallon's white jean jacket was covered in grass stains, and the bottom of her maxi-dress was torn. Gia's bedraggled blue jogging suit hung awkwardly on her frame.

"Who called the cops?" Betty whined.

We hung back with the remaining handful of gawkers. For once, Malone hadn't ordered us to wait around so he could talk to us later. Betty and I were simply being nosey. Plus I also had some information I thought Malone might find helpful.

"In a manner of speaking, you. You asked Hagan to call when you spotted Stephanie."

"Oh, yeah. That was a long time ago. I forgot with all the excitement. They sure took their sweet time getting here. Stephanie's long gone."

Something wasn't adding up when it came to the filmmaker we'd dubbed Stephanie. Between the murder of Richard Eriksen and the physical altercation between Gia and Fallon, that was prime drama for any film. Let alone a dogumentary about the underside of wiener racing.

Yet, she wasn't anywhere to be found. Why not? Where was she? What could be more important than filming unscripted drama? Even MacAvoy's first response was to look for his cameraman. Nope, something was off. I was beginning to wonder if she was a filmmaker or if that was just a front for something more sinister. But if she wasn't making a dogumentary, what was she up to?

"Hey, do you think Rodney was taking bets on the fight?" Betty asked excited by the possibility.

"No." He was a bookmaker. Of course he was. Just one more reason Stephanie should have been around.

"Too bad. I'd have put money on Gia. She's a scrappy gal."

"No, you wouldn't. You're not betting anymore."

"What's one more wager?"

Malone suddenly looked in our direction. He wasn't that far away from where we stood. It was possible he'd overheard our gossip about the illegal gambling. He watched us long enough that I got a little nervous. Betty, on the other hand, waved at him.

She sighed like a lovelorn school girl. "I think he missed me."

Doubtful. "Let's stay back and let him do his job."

"Isn't it his job to solve murders? Those two were just fighting. And not doing a very good job at it until the end."

"He's here because of Stephanie. The fight is coincidental. Although, it is possible one of them killed Richard."

When you think about it, each had motive. Fallon could be a suspect because it was possible Richard wasn't leaving his wife for her as he'd promised, and that ticked off Fallon. Gia could be a suspect because she knew her husband was having an affair and was planning to leave her for a new life with Fallon.

That's when I noticed the purple water bottle. Zippy had managed to paw it out of Gia's purse, and it had rolled under a wooden picnic table adjacent to where Mr. TV stood attempting to snag an interview with the police. Malone and the other police officers dealt with the fighters, leaving the water bottle fair game.

"Don't go anywhere. I'll be right back," I said to Betty.

"Where are you going?"

"Hopefully to grab evidence that will prove Gia's cheating. I'll be right back."

No one paid any attention to me as I made my way toward the potential evidence; their focus was on Malone, Gia, and Fallon. I hustled toward the container before anyone could beat me to it. MacAvoy glanced over his shoulder. I gave him a half wave, keeping my eyes on him as I bent down and reached for the bottle under the table. Only my fingers didn't grasp the bottle, but another hand.

I gasped. I turned my head only to find myself face to face with Grey.

"What are you doing?" I asked in a harsh whisper.

"Apparently the same as you."

"Where have you been?"

He looked around. "This isn't a good time."

"Melinda, what do you have?" MacAvoy called out.

I pulled the bottle from Grey's grasp. "We'll finish this discussion later. Let's go before he comes over here."

I left Grey and rushed back to where I'd left Betty on the grassy pathway. I heard Grey and MacAvoy tailing me.

"Good job, Cookie." Betty rubbed her hands to together. "I like how you got those boys to follow you over here. You get Grey; I get the reporter."

I shook my head in exasperation. "He's all yours."

MacAvoy stopped next to me. Grey was only a couple of steps behind him. Mr. TV nodded at Betty and Grey as he smoothed his Ken-doll hair.

"Hello," he said, in his on-screen persona.

I rolled my eyes in Grey's direction.

"You're even more handsome in person." Betty smiled broadly. "Are you available?"

"Sheesh. At least tell him your name first." I chuckled.

"I'm Betty." She batted her eyes at him. "You got a girlfriend?"

Grey coughed back a laugh.

MacAvoy was clearly caught off guard, "We broke up." He turned to me. "What are you up to Melinda?"

"Nothing that concerns you. Go back to eavesdropping on an official police-questioning."

MacAvoy looked at me, amused. "I wasn't eavesdropping."

"Only because you weren't close enough then."

MacAvoy laughed. "Be careful. You're warming up to me."

"Hardly."

Grey looked at me with surprise in his eyes. "A new friend?"

I found it hard to believe Grey didn't know who'd joined our cozy little group.

"I don't believe we've met. I'm Callum MacAvoy. Reporter for *Channel 5 News*."

"Grey Donovan. Melinda's fiancé."

They shook hands, taking each other's measure. Sheesh. This

wasn't the first time Grey had introduced himself as my fiancé, but this was more than an introduction. He was marking his territory. Which was completely out of character.

"Grey owns the ACT Gallery. If you're serious about publicizing locally-owned businesses, his would be the perfect opener. He has a great eye for promising artists."

"I'll keep that in mind." Translation: not happening.

I unscrewed the lid of the water bottle and looked inside. The bottle was still half full of a dark liquid. I inhaled, smelling the contents. My eyes widened. I knew that smell—an energy drink. Was that safe?

"Don't drink that," Grey ordered.

I wrinkled my nose. "I hadn't planned on it. But even if I did, it wouldn't hurt me."

I'd downed my share of highly caffeinated drinks throughout my college days. Other than shaky hands, a racing heart, and an extended focus period, I'd never needed to seek medical attention.

"What's the importance of the bottle?" MacAvoy asked.

"Gia's a cheater and Cookie's got the proof," Betty explained. "If you'd like an exclusive on how we broke the case, I'd be happy to give you one over dinner."

I sighed. "For once, can you at least try to keep a subject under wrap? Betty is my assistant. I'd like to tell you she's harmless, but that's a lie."

She stroked her white hair. "I'm free tonight." She cocked a boney hip toward MacAvoy.

The poor reporter looked like he wasn't sure if she was serious or pulling his leg.

"I have to take this to Daniel. I think I know what he needs to test for," I said.

"You should tell Malone. I'll get him." Betty bounced on the toes of her sneakers eager to get her man. And just that quickly, MacAvoy was forgotten, and she was back to the handsome detective.

I was about to burst her bubble. "Leave him be. Feeding your dog caffeine isn't against the law. But it is against the race rules. We should give it to Daniel and let Hagan know."

"Don't tell Hagan yet. Let Daniel run his test. If it's positive, then you can tell Hagan." Grey had been awfully quiet until now.

"Why wouldn't you want to inform Hagan?" MacAvoy challenged. "As the chairman, he should know that there's a possibility of duplicity. It's his obligation to remove any contestant if there's a suspicion of cheating, race-rigging, or animal exploitation."

I looked at Grey. "He has a point." I grimaced as I realized I'd sided with Mr. TV over my fiancé.

"If there is a possibility of cheating, the accusation holds greater weight if it comes from the event's veterinarian than us. Gia doesn't strike me as the type of person who will walk away quietly."

An equally valid point.

All four of us looked in her direction. Somehow, she managed to look self-righteous and pouty at the same time. She caught us staring at her. She must have told Malone because he turned in our direction.

"Great. He's coming over here," I complained.

"Yippee." Betty cheered.

"How can you tell?" MacAvoy asked.

I sighed. "Experience."

Sure enough, the minute Malone finished his interview he made his way toward our group. As we watched him draw closer, I wondered if I was the only one who felt anxious about what he may have overheard. Not that we had anything to hide, but Betty was in enough trouble as it was; she didn't need to add illegal gambling to her list of offenses.

If the looks on the others' faces were any indication, Grey and I were the only ones wishing Malone would stay on the other side of the grassy area. The other two looked like they were about to be granted their greatest wish.

"Mel, Betty." Malone acknowledged the men with a nod.

"Detective Hottie," Betty cooed.

He avoided Betty, instead turning his attention toward me. His crossed his arms and wide-legged stance indicated he wasn't in the mood to play games. "Gia claims you have an item that belongs to her."

Of course she did. Darn her.

I scowled. "First, let me tell you that I have not shoved my nose into your murder investigation."

He stared at me, unimpressed. "Yet, you're still here."

"I did discover some information you might find helpful. Or maybe not. But before we get to that, may I ask you a question?"

"If I say no, will that stop you?"

I smiled. He finally understood me. "Not at all."

"Get it over with."

"Have you or your crew talked to the filmmaker? I find it odd that she's not here, recording all the crazy drama. Look at MacAvoy, he can't stay away, and he's the noon reporter."

"I'm a serious investigative reporter."

I tossed him an apologetic smile. "No offense. Just stating the facts."

Malone watched Gia and Fallon shoot daggers into each other for a second. "We were sidetracked. But no, to my knowledge, we have not talked to the filmmaker yet."

"You should put a lookout for her," Betty suggested. "What's that called? A BOGO?"

"A BOLO," Grey corrected automatically. "Be On the Look Out."

I couldn't decipher the expression on MacAvoy's face, but Betty was impressed. Malone and I had to be thinking the same thing—was Grey trying to blow his cover?

Grey shrugged unapologetically. "I like cop dramas."

"Oh, me too," Betty agreed, excited to have someone who shared a mutual interest. "I like the dark gritty shows with the handsome cops."

Her taste in cop shows was no surprise to any of us.

Malone changed the topic back to his original question. "Is Gia correct? Do you have an item that belongs to her?"

My grip on the bottle tightened for an instant before I reluctantly extended the potential evidence in his direction. "This."

"We're taking it to Dr. Darling." Betty glared in Gia's direction.

Malone tried to take it from my hand, but I couldn't let go. He raised an eyebrow. "Thank you," he deadpanned.

I release my hold. Dang, dang, dang. I wanted to take it to Daniel. I had questions that only he could answer. Like would caffeine actually make the dog run faster? If so, how much caffeine would a dog need to ingest? How much was too much caffeine for a dog?

As I had done minutes earlier, he unscrewed the cap and smelled the contents. He cast a sideways glance in my direction.

"I'm pretty sure it's an energy drink. I saw Gia behind a tent, pouring the contents into Zippy's special bowl. If that's an energy drink, Lenny's accusation, as obnoxious as he is, was accurate—the Eriksens were most likely juicing their dog. We were on our way to see Daniel."

"In other words, they're cheaters," Betty spit out.

Malone recapped the bottle. "Wait here."

He stalked away toward Gia, his boots crushed the grass, leaving behind determined footprints. He asked her a few questions. She nodded vigorously and reached for the bottle. Malone pulled it out of her reach. He called one of his uniform officers over, spouted orders as he pointed at Gia, then returned to where we waited.

"I'll have someone deliver this to Dr. Darling," he said as he approached.

"We'd be happy to do that for you," I offered.

"I'd rather you find Zippy and take him to the onsite clinic so he can be tested. If this is what we think, the dog should have a complete examination."

"The last time we saw him, he was racing toward the track. Luis and his dog, Barney, went after him. I'm not sure if they caught him or not."

"Zippy ran like he had wings," Betty interjected. "A true champion."

"Or hopped up on caffeine." Mr. TV jotted down a couple of thoughts on his notepad. "How much caffeine does it takes to affect a canine?"

Malone's voice was tight. "This is not a formal interview. Understand?"

MacAvoy nodded and put away his notepad.

"I will make sure this reaches Dr. Darling. Anything else you want to tell me?" Malone asked me.

I tilted my head toward MacAvoy and Grey. Malone understood my unspoken request and motioned for me to follow him to an open grassy area a short distance away. I kept my back to MacAvoy, not sure if he could read lips.

I could feel three sets of curious eyes on us. I was sure they were talking about us too. Except for Grey. He'd keep his comments to himself. Hopefully he'd manage to keep Betty from jumping MacAvoy. She did like men.

"Thanks. I don't trust the reporter," I said.

"Keeping your enemies close?"

"Something like that."

"That doesn't explain why you don't want to talk in front of your fiancé."

I shrugged. "He'll tell me to stay out of it."

He actually smiled. "Sounds like good advice."

"Do you want to know what I learned or not?"

He shrugged. "I don't seem to have a choice. Go ahead."

"Sven, at the Koffee Klatch, told me about a gambling ring here, behind the chili truck. When Gia was at my shop earlier today, she tried to buy out the store, which I thought was great. Until I ran her credit cards. Both were denied. She's obviously having some type of financial issues. And by now you know all about the affair between Fallon and Richard."

"Tell me about this rumored gambling ring."

I ignored his request. I was on a roll. "Here's my working theory. If the Eriksens were doping Zippy, which we now know is likely, it's possible they could have been betting on him in order to make money. I admit, it's a stretch, but possible. What if what Fallon said was true, Richard planned to leave his wife for Fallon? MacAvoy said Fallon told the filmmaker Richard intended to retire Zippy after this event. If he took the dog, Gia would run out of money in a hurry."

"That's a lot of what-ifs." His eyes narrowed. "Let's go back to the gambling ring. Did Sven tell you that the Eriksens were placing bets?"

My mouth disengaged long enough for me to realize that I may have gotten poor Sven into trouble. "No."

"Did you see either of them by the chili truck?"

I shook my head, nervous the conversation wasn't proceeding the way I'd imagined.

"Have you seen anyone placing a bet?"

I inhaled deeply, unsure how to answer his question. "Not exactly," I hedged.

"What does that mean?"

I pushed my lips together and chose my words carefully as to not mention Betty's new pastime. "Sven asked me to put twenty dollars on Pickles. I went to the chili truck, but Rodney, the bookie, wasn't there."

"You're admitting to placing an illegal bet?"

I stumbled over my words, "No—I didn't think—I mean." I took a breath and started over. "I did not place a bet. But I did go to the truck to verify Sven's story."

"When was that?"

"Around one o'clock. Maybe a little before that."

He was silent for a full minute as he mulled over what I'd told him. "Did Gia tell you she had money problems?"

"No, but in my retail experience, the only other time I've had to retain a customer's credit card, he was bankrupt and later arrested for fraud. We both know people have killed for a lot less than that."

We stared at Gia for a minute. She glared back at us.

"What are the odds that she or Richard owns a gun?" I asked.

"Pretty damn good. Richard bought a 9mm Beretta two years ago. He reported the firearm stolen last month."

Hells bells.

Chapter Twenty

I WAS STILL REELING from the knowledge that Richard had owned a gun and had reported it missing. After my talk with Malone, I felt confident Gia would be uncovered as the killer, clearing Betty of all suspicion.

I returned to Grey, Betty, and Mr. TV with a spring in my step and a reassured smile on my face. They had waited exactly where I'd left them. I take that back. Not exactly as I'd left them.

Grey had drifted a few feet back from the others. His blue eyes sparked with amusement as he watched Betty hit on MacAvoy. She'd managed to link her arm with her favorite noon reporter, showing him the stains on her T-shirt and, I suspected, inadvertently her cleavage.

I felt a twinge of guilt at the pained expression on Mr. TV's face. Leaving Betty alone with two good-looking men had been a lack of forethought on my part. I rejoined the group with an apologetic glance at MacAvoy and shrugged. Betty was Betty.

He tilted his head toward the older woman glued to his side and mouthed, "Help me."

"Cookie, you're back. Me and Stud Muffin were about to grab a corn dog." She batted her eyes at her captive.

Who would have thought I'd feel sorry for Mr. TV?

"Cut him loose. We'll grab some food for you in a minute."

"Thank you." MacAvoy flashed me a grateful smile. "Does this mean I owe you one?" He tugged at his blazer sleeves, which had bunched around his elbows.

"I'd rather you not owe me anything."

Grey rejoined the group as well, and within seconds, I was peppered with questions from all of them.

What did I need to talk to Malone about in private? (Grey)
Did the police have any new suspects? (Mr. TV.)
Were they close to an arrest? (Also Mr. TV)
Did he have dinner plans? (Goes without saying—Betty)

"Malone and I didn't talk about his dinner plans. Nor did he name suspects or suggest there would be a pending arrest." I studied Mr. TV with narrowed eyes. He grinned in return, enjoying my scrutiny.

He knew there had never been a restraining order. Did he know about Richard's gun? If he was as good of a reporter as he claimed, I had to believe he knew. The urge to ask him about the gun was powerful, but on the off chance he didn't know about it, I wasn't willing to violate Malone's confidence.

So instead of asking him about the gun, I asked, "Who do you think killed Richard Eriksen?"

"Gee, now you want my opinion?"

I really wanted to erase that nettlesome smirk off his face. "A moment of weakness. It won't happen again."

"You want suspects other than Gia and Fallon?"

I sighed, already tired of his buildup. I vowed I would never ask for his opinion again. "Obviously."

He lobbed an accusatory looked in Betty's direction.

"Me?" She placed a bruised hand over her heart. "I'm offended you consider me a suspect."

"You threatened the victim with a gun."

"I was protecting myself," she corrected him.

"Had you actually talked to her before you broadcasted that salacious tidbit, you'd know Betty felt threatened by Richard," I argued, inching closer to him. "She didn't kill anyone."

"It was a fact. Just because it doesn't fit neatly into your explanation of events doesn't mean I shouldn't report on it," he countered, his voice tinged with righteous conviction.

"It was sensational and meant to drive ratings." Pangs of indignation bubbled inside of me.

"That's my job," he said. "I'm sorry if that offends your misguided sensibilities."

I could feel my blood pressure rise at his criticism. He didn't know anything about me. I felt Grey's hand on my shoulder. I breathed through my nose and counted to five.

"So your prime suspect is a senior citizen?" Grey asked dryly.

"Melinda didn't let me finish," Mr. TV said.

"Cookie is easily excited. I've changed my mind. I'm flattered you think I'm dangerous. I accept your dinner invitation." She leered.

His brows furrowed. "Um, I don't believe I asked you to dinner."

I enjoyed watching him squirm for once.

"You will." Betty shimmied side to side. "You haven't seen me decked out in my sexy outfit."

I pulled her next to me giving MacAvoy breathing room. "I want to know what he thinks. You can scare him off later."

Mr. TV eyed Grey. "Are you sure you want to talk about this now?"

Confused as to why he'd be suspicious of Grey, I edged closer to my fiancé. Certainly he didn't think Grey was a killer? "Why wouldn't I?"

He shrugged as if to say it was my funeral. He pulled out his notebook and flipped the pages. "As you wish. Hagan Stone—"

"Whoa." I waved my hands to stop him. "Are you serious? Why him?" I didn't see that coming. I mean, Lenny I would have understood, but Hagan?

Grey crossed his arms, his posture rigid as he studied MacAvoy. "I'm curious to hear that myself."

"I'm sure you are." His flat tone surprised me. After a tight smile aimed at Grey, he continued. "Gia and Richard argued with Hagan yesterday about not paying the entrance fee. Their check had bounced. That was a revelation to Richard, which started an argument about money between him and Gia. In the middle of their argument, Richard announced their marriage was over."

"How do you know this?" Grey asked.

MacAvoy thumped his notebook. "I overheard them."

I could easily imagine, lurking in the shadows with his voice recorder, capturing the whole sordid affair. Apparently, his job was to overstate facts and to eavesdrop on conversations that didn't involve him. Not that I was in any position to point fingers on the latter. I'd been known to listen to a conversation or two that didn't include me. How else did you find out what people were thinking?

"Did you film the fight?" Betty asked excitedly.

"Unfortunately, no."

His news scoop corroborated what Lenny had told me. It also supported my theory about probable financial trouble with the Eriksens. Unfortunately for Gia, the information made Fallon's claim that Richard was about to leave his wife credible.

"A husband and wife arguing about money doesn't make Hagan look like a murder suspect. It makes the wife a prime candidate." Grey uncrossed his arms and glared dismissively at MacAvoy.

I was surprised at Grey's strong reaction. He clearly didn't value the reporter's opinion. That wasn't like Grey. He'd always been the fair and balanced half of our relationship.

MacAvoy faced off with Grey, accepting the silent challenge Grey had issued. "Richard threatened Hagan. He told him he knew his secret, and if he didn't let Zippy run, he'd go to the local authorities and tell them everything he knows."

"What did he know?" Betty pushed closer to MacAvoy, stepping on my foot. "What's Hagan's secret?"

I shot her a look and took a large step away from her.

"He didn't say. But Hagan grew very quiet and told him he would accept a new check. That's why Richard had gone back to his car."

"Did you tell this to Malone?" Grey asked.

"Of course. *I* don't withhold information." MacAvoy gave me a pointed look.

Excuse me? For once, I was keeping my nose clean. Well, mostly clean. My gaze bounced between the two men, the heavy duty posturing unmistakable. Was he insinuating that Grey was the one withholding information?

I sandwiched myself between the men and directed MacAvoy's attention toward me. "I'm sure you've searched Hagan's background. Did you find anything suspicious?"

"Sure. Nothing the police don't already have access to. I do know Hagan doesn't have an alibi. A reliable source told me Hagan was alone, running a sound check."

"Certainly someone saw him?" I asked.

MacAvoy shook his head. "No one has confirmed his claim yet."

"I wonder what he's hiding." I mused.

"Melinda," Grey said under his breath. He'd dragged out my name until I almost didn't recognize it.

I tilted my head to the side and lifted one eyebrow. "I'm curious. There were hundreds of people here yesterday. Someone had to have seen Hagan. Unless he lied."

As Grandma Tillie used to say, "The hamster was on the wheel." What could be so detrimental to Hagan's reputation that he had basically let Richard blackmail him into allowing Zippy to race? Did his secret have to do with the Dachshund Dash? Or was it a personal matter? Did any of this have to do with the bar Hagan had recently bought?

If all of this was true, and I didn't have any reason to believe MacAvoy was lying, Hagan had fibbed when he'd said he didn't know the Eriksens very well. They had to be close enough for Richard to know Hagan's secret.

I looked at Grey and asked softly, "Do you think Hagan knows about the illegal gaming? Could that be the secret Richard was talking about?"

"I don't know. You need to stay out of if." He checked his watch. "I have an appointment at the gallery with a potential new artist. I have to go. I'll pick you up at eight." After a quick kiss, and a steely glare at MacAvoy, he walked away.

My head spun at the speed of which he rushed off. If I didn't know better, I'd think he had been looking for an excuse to leave.

"Humph. He's in a hurry." Betty stated the obvious.

Mr. TV watched Grey walk away. "Do you plan to marry him?"

I was shocked at the amazingly personal question.

"Of course she does," Betty answered. "Cookie, I've got to use the little girls' room. You two still gonna be here when I get back?"

"I'm not the one who keeps vanishing."

"And you're not the one I want waiting for me. I'll be right back, sugar buns." Betty blew her newest crush a kiss. She floated toward the port-a-potties, giggling.

MacAvoy blanched. "Are you two related?"

"No," I said with a laugh. "Let's just say she adopted me. So, why do you want to know if I'm marrying Grey?"

"It's none of my business."

I raised my brow. "Agreed. But that didn't stop you from asking. Look, I can read people pretty well. You think you know something, so get it off your chest. If you haven't put two and two together yet, I'm rather direct. I may not like what you have to say, but I'd rather hear the truth than a lie."

He tucked his notebook inside his jacket. "Do you trust him?"

"With my life," I replied with conviction.

He nodded a couple of times. "Remember what I said about Hagan, that if you get in his way he'll do whatever it takes to get rid of you?"

"Yes."

He pushed back his blazer and shoved his hands in his pockets. On a heavy sigh he said, "I've seen your fiancé and Hagan confiding in each other on more than one occasion. Whatever it is they're talking about is very secretive. Don't let Hagan's suave persona suck you in. He's a skilled gamesman. Whatever house of cards Hagan has conned him into, your fiancé is undoubtedly in over his head."

His concern took me aback. I blew my bangs out of my eyes and searched for a way to explain Grey without explaining Grey. "Um, I appreciate your concern. But you don't need to worry about Grey. He's been known to outfox a schemer or two."

He gave me a half shrug, obviously unconvinced. "Suit yourself. But when you're bailing that guy out of jail, just remember I tried to warn you."

A half smile tugged on corner of my mouth. Most likely it would be the other way around—Grey would have to bail me out of jail.

MacAvoy strutted off to secure his own one-on-one with Malone. My smile slipped, and I sighed heavyhearted. Grey wasn't at the race because of me. He was on a case. Possibly one that involved Hagan Stone and an illegal gambling ring. My heart sank.

When had he started to keep secrets again?

Chapter Twenty-One

"YOU RAN OFF ALL the men, Cookie." Betty sauntered up next to me. She'd reapplied her lip gloss and had drawn on cherry red eyebrows. Maybe one day she'd divulge why she preferred lipstick to an eyebrow pencil.

I pushed away the feelings of betrayal and anger toward Grey, and focused on what Malone had asked me to do.

I smoothed my hair back from my face and forced myself to grin at Betty. "We have an errand to run for Malone. He wants us to find Zippy."

She rubbed her hands together. "Well, we can't let Detective Hottie down. Let's go."

I wrapped my arm around her and gave her a quick hug. "First, let's get you a corn dog. You can eat it while we walk."

We followed the smell of fried calories toward the corn dog truck, aptly named The Dog House. The side of the truck was designed to resemble a popular comic strip's dog house. We'd lucked out; the wait was short. As we stood in line, my stomach growled. I know, I'd just eaten a meatball sandwich. In my defense, Grey had only brought me half a hoagie.

Since we were already there, I bought a corn dog for myself too. I slathered mine with mustard. Betty dribbled two lines of ketchup on her fried masterpiece.

We polished off our dogs as we headed to the racetrack by way of cutting through the vendor area. Betty insisted we check on our booth, which we'd left unattended for far too long. I couldn't deny she had a good idea.

No surprise, there wasn't a single customer at our booth. Quinn, the owner of the Wag and Treats bakery, had pitched a vendor tent across from ours. She said she'd been watching our merchandise in our absence. I thanked her profusely with a promise to make it up to her.

Betty found a note Darby had taped to the display of dog treats, an invitation to watch the races with her at the starting gate. Betty jumped on the offer, ready to leave immediately. I quickly reminded her we needed to find Zippy first and take him to Daniel.

Truth be told, I'd been relying on Luis to catch Zippy, and once he had, that he'd maintain possession of the dog until someone came for him. A rather brazen assumption on my part, but if you knew Luis, my supposition wasn't that inconceivable.

We found Luis within minutes. He and Barney anxiously paced in the waiting area with other racers and owners. The racetrack and waiting pen were the only areas where dogs were allowed off their leashes, and the dogs were taking full advantage of the situation.

I didn't see Zippy. Darn. I might have overestimated Luis and his ability to catch a champion wiener racer. Besides Barney, there were two smooth-haired doxies, one black and white, the other one red. Then there was my personal favorite, a long-haired chocolate-and-tan dappled beauty. She was adorable and very friendly. She raced up to Betty and me as we squeezed through the gate.

"Hi, Luis." I bent down to greet the congenial pup. "And who are you, cutie pie?"

"Hi, Mel. Betty," Luis greeted from the far side of the fenced-in area.

"That's Chloe," her owner, a tall, warrior-princess looking woman answered. She smoothed her sleek ponytail. "Careful, she likes to nip."

Hearing her name, Chloe eagerly nosed my hand demanding my attention. I rubbed the pooch's deep chest. "She's a sweetie."

Betty stepped to the side and called Barney over. She loved him up. Nose to nose, she whispered doggie-sweet-nothings. In return, he licked her cheek repeatedly. Had her purse not been full of money, I'm sure she'd have pulled out a handful of Bowser treats for all the dogs.

I straightened and carefully backed away from the dogs that ran circles around my feet. "Did you catch Zippy, Luis?"

"Sure did." I caught a flicker of pride in his dark eyes. "Took him to the veterinarian tent. I thought he should be checked out. You know, in case he was injured in the fight."

I smiled. "You're a good man."

He looked down, but not before I glimpsed the pink tint spreading across his cheeks. He cleared his throat. "Who won the fight?"

Betty snorted. "Detective Hottie broke up the brawl. Before he showed up, I'd call Gia the winner, hands down."

Luis nodded thoughtfully. "I could see that."

"What time is the race supposed to start?" Betty stood and patted her handbag.

I narrowed my eyes and nodded at her purse, silently communicating she needed to cease the betting references. She shrugged as if she had no idea what I meant.

"The first heat has been postponed. Again. At this rate, we'll never run that last race," Luis muttered.

Affable Luis was actually a little pessimistic. I wasn't sure why that realization tickled me, but it did.

"Trust me, the show will go on." I patted him on the back.

"Yeah, what else could go wrong?" Betty said.

That lame comment was just an invitation for catastrophe.

While Betty and Luis chatted and shared strategy tips, I observed the other competitors as they ran through their paces. I recognized the side-glances, the silent sizing-up of the other racers, and the occasional condescending backhanded compliments meant to chip away at someone's confidence. The similarity wasn't lost on me—whether a beauty pageant or a wiener race, the need to win pulsed through every true competitor.

I didn't miss the mind games and subterfuge.

Out of the corner of my eye, I saw Darby taking candid photos near the track. I waved until she saw me. She waved back and pointed toward the starting gates. I guess we were supposed to meet her there.

"Great. Look who's coming," grumbled one of the female doxie owners. She pointed behind us.

We all turned and watched Lenny and Pickles chase Hagan toward us. I wasn't sure if she was unhappy about the arrival of Lenny or Hagan. I looked forward to chatting with each of them. I had a few questions pertaining to their respective relationship with the Eriksens.

"Don't ignore me," Lenny shouted at Hagan's back.

Lenny no longer looked as refreshed as he had this morning. He looked rumpled and dirty. The bottom of his shirt was torn, and there was a black smudge of what I suspected could be grease on the leg of his shorts.

Hagan, who was definitely ignoring Lenny, tromped toward us with long strides. He stopped at the gate and announced, "I'm here to inform all of you the race will start in fifteen minutes."

Betty and Luis high-fived; the other owners cheered.

"You got Barney's chicken?" Betty elbowed Luis. He grinned, patting the fanny pack.

"Game on, Chloe." Xena The Princess Warrior picked up her pooch and kissed her soft head.

Lenny marched up behind Hagan. He grabbed him with a brawny hand and yanked him around. "You have to disqualify the witch." He poked him in the chest with his beefy finger. "I told ya she was cheatin'. You should have listened to me."

Hagan straightened his narrow shoulders, then stared down his beakish nose into Lenny's angry face. "I beg your pardon." His Cary Grant accent was extra thick, magnifying his indignation.

"Beg all you want, but you can't have it. I was right. You have to kick Gia Eriksen and her dog out of the race." Lenny cracked his knuckles.

Hagan held his hands out, palms up. "I don't have proof of any misdeed."

He didn't seem particularly upset about that either. I had to admit, with my newfound information I looked at Hagan in a new way. What I once found as awkwardly endearing facial features now looked somewhat creepy and sinister.

Lenny's face turned brick red. "Yes, you do. You don't want to admit it." He jabbed a finger in my direction. "Tell him, Melinda."

Great, why was I being dragged into his fight?

I walked over to where Lenny stood, keeping the fence between us for good measure. "How do you know about that? We didn't tell anyone." And I highly doubted Daniel or Malone had informed him.

His red-rimmed eyes stared at me unapologetically. "I saw the police bring Gia's water bottle to the veterinarian tent. Pickles and I stood by the door and listened."

I leaned forward catching a whiff of his minty fresh breath. Was the guy drinking mouthwash? Maybe he was attempting to mask an alcohol smell with mouthwash.

"You eavesdropped?" Betty asked, appalled.

I kept my mouth shut. You already know where I stand on that topic.

He snarled. "Damn straight I did. I wasn't about to let evidence get swept under the rug this time."

This time? As in, there had been evidence of cheating in the past? Fallon had mentioned Lenny had argued with a judge last year. Could it have been about cheating? A year was a long time to carry a grudge.

I looked at Hagan. His face was emotionless, but his fixed eyes assessed the situation. Probably calculating a way out.

"I heard the cop tell the doc that Melinda had seen Gia give whatever was inside the water bottle to Zippy." Lenny's face contorted into a hardened mask of scorn. "You have to act Hagan. You have to disqualify Zippy from the race."

The sun disappeared behind a dark billowy cloud. I rubbed my arm, feeling suddenly chilled. An eerie quiet settled around us as we all waited to hear what Hagan Stone would decide.

One way or the other, someone was bound to end up very unhappy.

Chapter Twenty-Two

HAGAN RECOVERED quickly. His face softened, and his eyebrows drew together in concern. "Is it true, Melinda? Do you have proof Gia Eriksen was cheating?"

I couldn't figure this guy out. Was he mad or concerned? "I did. I gave the water bottle to Detective Malone. I believe Dr. Darling has it now."

He formed a steeple with his fingers and rested them against his lips. With all eyes on Hagan and Lenny, no one noticed Gia waltz up to the gate, Zippy in tow, until she opened her mouth and whined. "Are you talking about me, Lenny?"

I blinked a few times. This was the first time I'd seen her up close since the fight. Gia's face was battered and bruised. She'd managed to pull her black hair into a messy ponytail. Her designer clothes were grimy; her torn collar hung on by a handful of stitches. Gia's swollen lips pouted her displeasure at our horrified stares.

"What the hell happened to you?" Lenny bellowed.

"She got into a girl fight with her dead husband's mistress. But don't you worry. Gia kicked her butt. That is, until the cops arrived and broke it up." Betty beamed with admiration.

Good grief, next she'd ask for her autograph. I was concerned that Gia might need medical treatment. "Did you have someone at the first aid station look you over? Make sure you're okay?"

"I'm perfectly fine," she snapped.

She obviously hadn't looked in a mirror recently.

Lenny narrowed his eyes and glared at her. "You were caught fighting by the cops, cheating by the doc, and Hagan refuses to disqualify you. Are you two sleeping together?" His accusatory tone reverberated throughout the park. "What other explanation could there be?"

All eyes were glued on Gia and Hagan. Heck, I've learned over the past few years, anything was possible. I felt a little remiss that I hadn't thought of that possibility myself.

"That's enough." Hagan sounded very un-Cary-Grant-like.

Gia waved her hand in front of her as if to dismiss all of the overwhelming evidence of her misdeeds and any possibility of her fornicating with the Chairman of the Board.

"This is all the filmmaker's fault. She obviously wasn't a professional. She believed Lenny and has managed to somehow turn everyone against me."

I shook my head. This was suddenly Stephanie's fault? I wasn't following her logic. Maybe she had a head injury.

She turned her battered eyes toward Hagan and attempted to look sympathetic. It wasn't that difficult, what with all the bruises around her eyes. "You know how much we need to run this race." Her face may look broken, but her voice was steely and threatening.

Did he? Was she referring to her possible financial problems?

"That's not the whole story," Lenny growled.

"Gia, I saw you sneak behind the tents," I chimed in. Good grief, if Hagan didn't make a decision soon, there would be another brawl. Only this time Gia would not come out the victor. Lenny would pummel her into dust with one swing.

"You were spying on me?" she screeched. If she'd had something to throw at me, she would have.

"Not at all. I was minding my own business when I saw you and Zippy slink behind the Feline and Me tent. After your brawl with Fallon Keller, I noticed the same water bottle Zippy had dug out of your bag. I grabbed it. I unscrewed the cap and recognized the smell—an energy drink."

"You busy body," she hissed. "Why can't you stay out of my business?"

"Is this true?" Hagan finally spoke. "Did you give Zippy an energy drink?"

She threw her shoulder back in defiance. "I don't have to answer that."

He nodded, his face tight. "You're right. You don't. Mrs. Eriksen, I regret to inform you that Zippy has been disqualified for suspicion of unsportsmanlike conduct."

"Yes!" Lenny punched the air. "Let's get this race started."

"You can't do that. I—Zippy has to race. You agreed," Gia yelled. She charged after Hagan and grabbed the back of his shirt. "If you exclude us, you'll regret it."

"No, Mrs. Eriksen. Don't threaten me. Or you'll regret it." His face hardened like granite, but his smile was pure satisfaction. "Do I need to call security?"

Gia let go of his shirt as if it had suddenly caught fire. She stepped back, but she didn't stop glaring at him. "You'll be sorry," she promised.

"I don't think so."

MacAvoy's warning about Hagan Stone roared through my head.

"Can we run this race before another fight ensues or someone else drops dead?" Betty asked.

"I'm not particularly fond of your phrasing, madam, but yes, we can start the first heat. Racers to the gate." Hagan waved his hand in the air commanding that we all follow.

My heart was already racing. It had been years since I'd been in a bar fight, but if I needed to, I could hold my own. Unlike my cousin and Betty, I'd learned to defend myself through real-life situations and not in a classroom. For a couple of minutes I'd thought that's where the confrontation between Gia, Hagan, and Lenny had been headed.

Who'd have thought an innocent wiener race would incite such hot-headed competition?

THE DARK CLOUD drifted onward, allowing a sliver of sunlight to shine dimly on us. Hagan called security and had Gia and her dog escorted off the field. Lenny watched with a pleased smile plastered across his face. I was surprised he hadn't broken out in applause or his version of a happy dance.

Hagan grabbed the microphone and called for all the racers to report to the starting line. The race would begin in five minutes.

Betty and I joined Darby on the sideline.

"What was going on over there?" she asked. "I stayed back and took a lot of pictures. The whole scene looked intense."

"Gia and Zippy got kicked out for cheating," Betty explained.

"Technically for unsportsmanlike conduct," I added.

Darby whistled. "She didn't take that well."

Betty stretched up on her toes to peer at Darby's viewfinder camera. "You got some good shots there." Betty nodded, impressed. "I bet you could sell those to a celebrity tabloid and make some fast cash."

"I'll keep that in mind," she said, in all seriousness. Once Betty turned her attention to the track, Darby and I exchanged an amused look over Betty's head.

The three of us watched Lenny hand Pickles to the gate attendee in lane two. Luis and Barney were assigned gate five. The other contestants quickly took their places. After a murder, a fistfight, and the smack-down Hagan had just handed Gia, a wiener race felt, well, a little anticlimactic. *Does that make me a bad person?*

"I still have a chance to win big. Especially now that Zippy's been disqualified for doping." Betty patted her purse. "If I win big I'm buying an outfit off that shopping channel."

"Grey said to leave the money," I muttered.

She hugged her purse up against her tiny body. "No way."

This wasn't the time to convince her otherwise. Darby paced along the sideline snapping pictures.

"Darby, have you seen Stephanie? Shouldn't she be here?" I had a hunch there was more to the girl with the dachshund tattoo than her dogumentary.

"I haven't seen her." She lowered her camera, tucking a lock of blond hair behind ear. She surveyed the area quickly. "It's odd that she hasn't been around. Especially if she really is a filmmaker."

"Stop jabbering over there," Betty jeered good-naturedly. "The race is about to start. Darby, we can watch at the finish line, right?" Betty rubbed her hands together greedily. Okay, it was possible that was a show of excitement. But I was sticking with greed.

"Sure. Stay back and don't interfere. Remember, no matter what happens, you can't touch the dogs."

"You got it, sweet cheeks." Betty swung her handbag up on her shoulder and led the way.

Luis, Lenny, and the rest of the owners moved to the finish line. Each pulled their racer's favorite item out of a pocket or bag. Luis dug the chicken strips wrapped in tinfoil out of his fanny pack. Lenny unearthed a squeaky toy monkey from somewhere. A couple other owners had balls. The owner in lane three had a box of Bowser treats.

"Last call," Hagan's voice carried over the loud speakers.

The excitement for the race filled the air as the crowd cheered for their favorite doxie. Cries of well-wishes and encouragement blasted toward the field. I couldn't help but feel excited too.

The starting gate looked like a row of cubbyholes, open on the back side to place the racer inside. The front side was covered with a clear plastic door so the racer could see the owner at the finish line but not leave the block until given the signal. Once the starting gun fired, the designated volunteer at each end of the gate would pull the handle and the plastic door would lift up, releasing all the dogs at once.

"Racers are present," Hagan announced into the microphone, his energetic voice pumping up the crowd.

The cheers grew louder. Betty jumped up and down, alternating between squeals of excitement and ear-piercing whistles. Darby and I looked at each other and smiled.

"Ladies and gentlemen, I'd like to introduce our racers for the first heat in the heavyweight event. In lane one, we have Chloe from Long Beach. In lane two, is Pickles from Yreka. Lane three, is Dutch from Irvine. Lane four, is Maverick from Newport. And in lane five, our very own Barney from Laguna Beach."

We whooped and hollered as Barney's name was announced.

"Wouldn't it be awesome if Barney won?" Darby lifted her camera and snapped pictures, prepared to watch the race through her camera lens.

"That'd be great," Betty agreed halfheartedly. She wasn't as genuinely supportive as Darby. I knew she was thinking about her wager and possible windfall.

"On your marks," Hagan yelled into the mic.

"Get set." He raised the starting gun, and pointed it in the air.

My heart raced as I waited for him to pull the trigger.

BANG!

The clear plastic door lifted. Pickles, Maverick, and Barney shot out immediately. Their long wiggly bodies ate up the grass as they raced toward the finish line. Pickles was in the lead, his mouth open as he charged forward. He was focused on the toy monkey Lenny held in front of him. With Zippy out of the way, Pickles could experience his first win.

Poor Dutch stood at the starting gate, sniffing the grass where the other dogs had been seconds earlier. I giggled when he lifted his leg and marked his spot. Chloe got a late start, but she came on fast, gaining on the three leaders.

"Chloe is making a comeback," I shouted, bouncing on my toes, energized. "She's gonna catch up to the others."

"Run, Pickles. I got a hundred bucks on you," Betty shouted at the top of her lungs.

Darby swung around with a shocked look on her sweet face. "What?"

"Pictures, Darb," I said. "I'll explain later."

Suddenly, Chloe was within a nose of Pickles. Maverick and Barney started to run out of gas. It was down to Chloe and Pickles.

I cupped my hands around my mouth and shouted, "Go, Chloe. Come on girl, you can do it."

All of a sudden, Chloe bit Pickles on the behind. My breath caught. The crowd gasped.

Pickles whipped around and ran in the opposite direction. Chloe chased him, nipping his rear as they ran.

"No, no, no," Lenny screamed. The veins in his face pulsed with each "no" he uttered. "Come back, Pickles. Come!"

"Get the chicken, Barney. Get the chicken," Darby yelled. She lowered her camera for a second, then raised it again. I could hear the quick burst of the shutter as she snapped picture after picture.

Barney and Maverick raced in unison to the finish line nose to nose. I clenched my hands into tight fists. I caught myself holding my breath. I forced myself to breathe.

Luis yelled encouraging words, waving the chicken strip so hard it broke in half, sending a chunk flying across the finish line. Barney raced to the chicken then skidded to a stop. He dropped his head and ate the snack. Maverick raced past him, crossing the finish line first. The crowd roared in celebration.

"Oh, no!" Darby and I cried in unison.

I was heartbroken for Luis. They'd almost won. He'd been so close.

"The winner of the first heat is Maverick. Second place, Laguna's own Barney," Hagan announced once Barney crossed the line.

We continued to wait on the other three. Lenny swore at Pickles and Chloe, who were both out of bounds chasing each other in some kind of doggie dating ritual. And remember poor Dutch? Well, he slowly made his way toward his owner.

Luis lifted Barney and held him high. "Great job," he shouted. "Great job!"

He carried him toward us. We continued to hoot and holler our excitement like a bunch of Texans at a three-legged race during a family reunion.

"That was awesome." I rubbed Barney's head. "I bet you'll get to run in the finals."

Luis beamed. "I think so too."

"Come by the boutique tomorrow. I'll have something extra special for Barney."

"Yeah, well don't shake your chicken so hard next time. You still have the big race to run. And if you drop a piece, do it on the other side of the finish line," Betty grumbled.

"Don't be rude," I chastised. It wasn't Luis's fault she bet on the wrong dog.

"No, she's right. I was so happy, I forgot what we were doing." Luis smiled broadly, unperturbed by the unsolicited advice. "I'll pay more attention next time."

"You were fine." Darby gave him a quick hug. "I'm so proud of both of you. I got some great photos too. I'll show them to you later. I'll print copies for you."

"Thanks, Darby. Hey, here comes that TV reporter. Do you think he wants to interview me?"

"Absolutely," I said. If not, I'd make sure he did.

We expected to see MacAvoy and his cameraman, Ryan, ready to interview the winners. But he was alone. And running. His perfectly coiffed hair windblown, his face pasty white.

"Where's Detective Malone?" he asked out of breath.

"I haven't seen him since Gia and Fallon's fight. Why? What's wrong?" A shaken MacAvoy wasn't normal. His blazer was off, and there was blood on his hand. My heart jolted, not from excitement—from dread.

He caught his breath, then shoved his bloody hand through his hair. "I found the filmmaker. She's dead."

Chapter Twenty-Three

I KNOW THIS SOUNDS awful, but I was relieved I wasn't the one to find the dead body. Let's get real here. How many dead bodies can a girl stumble over before she becomes a suspect? That's a rhetorical question. No answer needed.

Darby rummaged around the bottom of her messenger bag and found a clean tissue for MacAvoy to clean the blood off his hand. I slipped my cell from my pocket and pulled up Malone's number, then handed the phone to MacAvoy. He quickly explained why he was using my phone before he updated Malone. He returned my cell with a shaky hand.

"Thank you for your help." His voice wavered. He cleared his throat. "He wants me to meet him at the chili truck."

The same chili truck I'd visited earlier this afternoon. The same chili truck where Betty had placed a bet. The same chili truck Grey had insisted Betty and I stay away from.

Coincidence? I didn't think so either.

MacAvoy split without another word. He never did explain why there was blood on his hand.

"He's really upset," Darby noted, her voice heavy with concern.

I agreed. I hadn't pegged him for the emotional type. MacAvoy had barely held eye contact with us. Even after he'd talked to Malone, the reporter's tanned faced had looked an unhealthy white.

I felt badly leaving Luis to celebrate his almost-win alone, but the dead girl had Betty's gun. That took precedence over any party. Darby, Betty, and I hustled to the to the crime scene. I formed a suspect list in my head for the new murder as we power-walked toward the food area.

Gia was obviously the prime suspect. She'd threatened Stephanie for questioning her about the doping, and the filmmaker had recorded Gia's tirade.

Fallon had spilled the secret about Zippy retiring. Maybe she'd asked for that portion of her interview to not air and Stephanie had refused. They argued, and Fallon killed her. Flimsy, but possible.

My newest suspect, courtesy of MacAvoy, was Hagan Stone. If Stephanie had proof of illegal gambling, he might want to stop her any way he could. That theory had legs.

I wanted to add Lenny to my list. He certainly had the type of temper to off someone. But other than me, Stephanie was the only person who'd taken his claims of cheating seriously. I put him at the bottom of my list.

Of course, this was all before we knew how she'd died. Since MacAvoy had blood on his hand, I guessed she wasn't poisoned.

By the time we reached the crime scene, Malone and his people were already there and had taped off the area. For the second time in as many days, the dog park looked like a scene straight out of a cable police drama. Sans the foul language and naked butts.

"She'd better have your gun." I looked over my shoulder for Betty, but she'd disappeared again. Damn.

"Good grief. Where'd Betty go now?" I asked Darby.

She shook her head equally confused. "I-I don't know. She was behind us a minute ago."

How was it possible someone as colorful as Betty could slip away unnoticed as often as she had recently?

A small crowd had gathered. A couple of uniformed officers ushered everyone aside to allow the technicians to work uninterrupted.

Malone stepped out of the food truck. He pinned us with his steely blue eyes. I raised my hand in acknowledgment. He'd lost his leather jacket at some point in the day. He wore an average short-sleeved black T-shirt. Somehow, it looked intimidating on him. He moved in our direction with a deliberation that made poor Darby freeze in place.

Her eyes widened. "Why is he coming here?"

I wondered for a moment if he'd developed his deliberate walk to intimidate people like us or if that was just who he was. Either way, it worked. "Whatever the reason, answer the questions honestly," I instructed, never taking my eyes off Malone.

Darby had a history of keeping important information from the police. I hoped she'd learned her lesson. If he wanted to talk to Betty, lying about where she was or wasn't wouldn't help anyone.

He planted a hand on each of our shoulders and led us away from his crime scene and toward the park entrance gate. "Ladies. What brings you to this end of the dog park?"

I didn't bother beating around the snapdragon bush. "Is it true? Is it the filmmaker?"

He nodded, his impassive look gave nothing away.

"Does she have Betty's gun?" I pressed.

"Where is Betty?" He deflected, looking past us.

I felt Darby tense beside me. I shifted, uncomfortable. "I don't know. She was right behind us, but she slipped away unnoticed. Did the filmmaker have Betty's gun?"

"Yes."

"Thank goodness," Darby said with a sigh, her pent-up worry faded with Malone's one word.

"Don't thank anyone yet." His lips thinned.

My stomach sank. Somehow, I knew what he was about to say. I shook my head. "Please do not say she was shot."

He stuffed his hands inside his jean pockets. "I'm afraid so, Mel."

That explained the blood on MacAvoy's hand and why he had been as emotional as the mother of the bride on her son's wedding day. He must have touched her.

"With Betty's gun?" Darby asked in a small voice.

"I won't know that for a few days. We have to run some tests. But it's possible."

"Any sign of Richard's gun?" I grasped for anything that would shift the investigation away from Betty.

"No." His voice wasn't clipped, but it wasn't reassuring either.

I rubbed my temples trying to gather my thoughts and push back the throbbing pain threatening to explode from behind my eyes. "Don't get me wrong, but normally you keep this type of information to yourself. Why tell me now?"

"Since the reporter found her, he'll likely broadcast his findings on the evening news. I've asked him to keep this quiet while we investigate, but . . ." He shrugged.

Just because he asked, didn't mean the reporter would comply, especially a reporter whose top priority was to make a name for himself at a new job. "Does he know that's Betty's gun?"

Malone shook his head. "There was no need to tell him about the gun. We found blood under the victim's nails. It's possible she fought with someone."

I closed my eyes. I felt sick to my stomach. Malone had seen Betty's scratch marks. "Betty's probably a hundred pounds dripping wet. She'd never win a fight."

"Which is a motive to shoot the victim." His calm demeanor did not pacify my anxiety.

"Self-defense?" My voice broke. If I were any sicker, I'd throw up on Malone's black boots. Betty had told anyone who'd listen about her self-defense class. Heck, she'd been showing off her moves just yesterday, acting like a martial arts, superhero action figure. For all we knew Stephanie had filmed Betty's exhibition.

Darby reached for my hand and squeezed reassuringly. "You need to talk to Betty, don't you?" she addressed Malone. I was momentarily impressed with the strength in her voice. Feisty Darby had come out to play.

He ran his palm over his chin. "Officer Shughart is looking for her. Should you find her first, bring her here. To me. I still have a crime scene to process and other witnesses to talk to."

He was giving us the opportunity to find my unpredictable assistant. "Betty really was with me this time. She didn't do this," I pressed.

He cocked his head to the side and offered me a stony face. "I don't have an exact time of death yet."

"But?" I heard it in his voice. He had a timeframe. And I wasn't going to like it one iota.

"The victim was seen alive around nine o'clock this morning. The murder could have occurred anytime between then and two this afternoon. Was Betty with you that entire time?"

I swallowed hard and shook my head.

His jaw tightened. "Find her. Now."

I believed in Betty, and, deep down, I knew Judd Malone did too. I wouldn't be me if I didn't remind him there were other suspects. "We will. Don't forget Gia Eriksen and Fallon Keller also had motive to kill her. And Gia's husband had a gun. After talking with MacAvoy, Hagan Stone had a motive too."

"I'll keep that in mind." His dry tone clearly indicated he was more than aware of the particulars and didn't appreciate my two cents. "Don't make me regret telling you about the case." He turned and walked away.

"I wouldn't dream of it," I called out.

He stopped mid-step, faced us, and asked. "Where is Mrs. Eriksen?"

"Hagan disqualified her and Zippy for suspicion of cheating and had security physically remove her," I explained, more than eager to share what I knew. "Oh. If Gia *did* kill her husband, and now the filmmaker, someone might want to keep an eye on Hagan Stone. Gia was none too pleased that he disqualified Zippy. She vowed to get even with him."

Malone sighed. "You just can't help yourself, can you?"

I smiled. "Not really."

"Find Betty. I'll have my team look for Gia." He stalked off.

I elbowed Darby. "You heard the man. Let's find Betty."

Chapter Twenty-Four

"WHAT DO YOU make of all this?" Darby asked as we hustled through the park searching for Betty.

It wasn't lost on me that recently I'd spent an inordinate amount of time looking for Betty. Seriously, what could possibly require her to disappear at the most inconvenient time? I realized there was a lot about Betty that I assumed I knew.

I readjusted my backpack. "I'll admit, I thought there was something fishy going on. I mean, she should have been everywhere filming. I didn't think it was because someone had killed her. This whole thing doesn't make sense."

"Do you think the two murders are related?"

I slid Darby a sly look. "Are you poking your nose in Malone's investigation?"

My buddy's face blossomed into an attractive shade of pink. "I was just curious. I know you're thinking about it."

I laughed in delight that I was slowly pulling kindhearted Darby to the dark side. "Gia could be the killer. She had every reason to shoot her unfaithful husband. And we know Stephanie recorded Gia's threats." I grimaced. "I even told Gia that the video could be used against her."

"Her bad choices are not your fault." Darby adjusted her messenger bag. "At least we know where Betty's gun is."

The whole situation with Betty's gun was like a nightmare come to life. Why did Betty have to bring it to the race in the first place? Talk about bad choices. Sheesh. By now we'd covered the entire food area. We made our way back toward the racetrack.

"Like Malone said, that's not necessarily good. With Stephanie dead, all Malone has is Betty's word that Stephanie took her gun. And what if that gun was used to kill Richard and Stephanie? I'm not convinced this is good news for Betty. You've seen her. You can't tell me you didn't notice the red marks on the lower part of her neck."

Darby shuddered. "I'm trying not to think about it. I'm scared for her."

I was sure this whole situation stirred up unwanted memories for her. I stopped. Darby stopped next to me with a questioning gaze. I rested my hand gently on her arm. "Look, I totally understand if you need to sit this one out. I can look for Betty on my own."

She shook her head with a great deal of determination. "No way. You helped me when I was in trouble. The least I can do is help Betty."

I was all about paying it forward. But there was a big difference between settling the bill for the people behind you in the drive-up and purposely poking around in an active murder investigation.

We started walking again. I wondered where Gia was hiding and if she'd heard about Stephanie. Apparently, Darby was also thinking about Zippy's owner.

"Do you think Gia left for home once she was kicked out of the competition?" she asked.

"Not a chance. She's already proven she doesn't handle public humiliation well," I said, referring to her brawl with Fallon.

"Hey," Darby gasped in surprise. "Is that Betty?"

I turned in the direction Darby had pointed. Sure enough, there was Betty in her ugly polyester slacks and oversized T-shirt sneaking off toward the street where she'd parked her Mini Cooper.

This was it. I was about to catch her in the middle of her disappearing act. "I'll be back."

"Wait. What are you going to do?"

"Malone said to find her. Well, we did. Now it's time to follow her. She's not as sneaky as the thinks she is. Besides, it's better if I find out what she's hiding than Judd Malone. He has no misgivings about tossing people in jail. Not even the grandmotherly type." I sprinted toward the parking lot where I'd left the Jeep.

Darby chased after me. "Hold on. I'm coming."

We had to run past the crime scene to reach the parking lot. I caught Malone off to the side talking to one of his officers. His head jerked in our direction as we darted past. I refused to make eye contact, worried he might order us to stop.

As soon as we reached the Jeep, I asked Darby, "Are you sure? You're the official photographer. The big race will start soon."

Darby opened the door and gently set her bag behind the passenger seat. "You're wasting time with all that talking."

A big Texas grin spread across my mouth. "I love it when you talk dirty."

I opened my door and shoved my backpack behind my seat. We

scrambled inside and slammed the doors. I yanked my cell from my pocket and tossed it into the cup holder, then shoved my key into the ignition. The engine made a sad "wrrrr" sound, refusing to start.

"Seriously? Now?" I tried again. It still wouldn't start. I pounded the steering wheel. "Argh. What's the deal?"

"Come on. We'll take my car. I'm parked a couple of rows behind you."

We jumped out of my Jeep and grabbed our bags. I followed Darby to her blue Fiesta. We piled in and fastened our seatbelts.

"Betty's not the best driver," I warned.

"That doesn't surprise me," she muttered.

Thankfully, Darby's car started on the first try. She shifted into reverse, but the car didn't move.

"What are you waiting for? She's getting away." My voice rose in frustration. I motioned toward the direction where Betty had somehow managed to hop the curb as she sped off. Lordy, she was a horrible driver.

"Over there." Darby pointed toward a row of port-a-potties. "Is that Gia and Zippy next to the black SUV?"

Gia had changed into a pair of jeans and red halter top. Her hair was still in a ponytail, but at least she'd brushed it at some point. I wondered where she'd changed her clothes. She didn't strike me as the type to change clothes in her vehicle.

She had her back to us. It was hard to tell for sure from where we were parked, but it looked like she was loading Zippy into his car seat. "There's no way she's talked to Malone yet."

"Do you think she knows about Stephanie?"

"Honestly, I think she killed her husband. I wouldn't put it past her to kill the one person who recorded her lashing out in anger."

Darby's thumbs beat out an anxious rhythm on the steering wheel. "We need to choose. Do we follow Betty or Gia?"

"Gia," we said simultaneously.

As soon as our suspect pulled out of the parking lot, we followed. Darby's economical sporty compact car followed Gia's eighty-thousand-dollar Lexus SUV up Laguna Canyon Road.

"Don't get too close," I said in a harsh whisper.

Darby shot me a funny look. "Don't be a backseat driver. Besides, her truck is so big, she probably can't even see us."

"Sorry. I'm a little caught up in the moment. Where do you think she's headed?"

Darby chewed her bottom lip contemplating the question. "To dispose of the murder weapon."

I blinked. "That's entirely possible. I should call Malone." I reached for my cell, but my pocket was empty. "Shoot. I left my phone in the Jeep. Do you have Malone's number?"

"Why would I have his number?" Her voice rose a couple of octaves.

"Well, you've found almost as many dead bodies as I have. Plus you were a prime suspect in a murder investigation."

Darby fixed me with a look that said I was two sandwiches short of picnic. "All the more reason to not have his number on speed dial. If I need to report an emergency, I'll call 911 like everyone else."

She had a point. I guess I had an unresolved need to solve crime.

We continued to follow Gia out of town. She hung a right on El Toro Road heading toward Laguna Hills. The brown rustic canyon slowly transformed into green trees and modern neighborhoods. Traffic was typical stop and go, but Darby never let Gia out of sight. The big SUV turned left at a mall, then sped up and cut a sharp right at a gas station and headed down a side street. Darby stayed on her tail.

"Hang back." I reached out for Darby's arm. "We need to keep some distance. There's not enough traffic here."

Darby eased up on the gas, allowing more space between us. Palm trees and security bushes lined the streets. Color-coordinated retail businesses were replaced with boring dreary warehouses.

"This is an industrial area," Darby said.

We continued a few more blocks when she made a left. All of a sudden, we had our answer. Gia turned her giant SUV into a rental storage business. Darby drifted to the side of the road, out of sight. We watched Gia pull up to the black wrought-iron security gate. She rolled down her window, then punched a code into a keypad. The gate pulled back, granting her entrance.

"Now what?" Darby asked.

"Park. We have to climb over and go on foot." Bless her heart, she didn't balk at the idea of climbing the gate.

She shut off the ignition and pocketed the key. "I haven't climbed a fence since I was a teenager."

We got out of the car. Darby pressed the button on her key fob. The car beeped, confirming it had locked remotely.

"We've broken onto a boat at the Dana Point Marina, how difficult can it be to climb the fence?"

"Well, the last time, I ripped my jeans." She flashed a self-conscious smile as we ran across the street.

I laughed. "I can't guarantee that won't happen again. Look, if we catch her red-handed with anything incriminating, we call Malone."

We'd reached the fence just as a large moving truck pulled into the drive. Darby and I exchanged a "it's-our-lucky-day" look. I waved them past us, and we quickly followed them inside the storage area.

We raced in the direction where we'd last seen Gia's vehicle. We jogged side by side down the middle alleyway; Darby watched the left, and I watched the right. We found Gia five rows down. Darby and I were both out of breath and a sweaty mess. We hid behind a tan concrete wall.

Darby peeked around the corner.

"Do you see her?" I asked.

"Shh." Darby slapped my leg.

Since I was taller, I peered over her head. We were looking at one of the largest units on the lot.

"How big do you think that is?" I whispered.

"Bigger than the shed my dad built in our backyard in Nebraska. And that was huge. Dad stored a riding lawn mower, snow blower, a couple of bikes, gardening supplies, and camping equipment and still had plenty of space to walk around without touching a single item."

I frowned. "I was thinking more like actual dimensions. I'd say ten feet by twenty-five feet."

Darby looked up at me and frowned. "I have no idea how big that is."

Gia and Zippy were out of the SUV. Zippy was off his leash, distracted by unfamiliar smells.

"Don't you worry, boy," she cooed. "They won't get away with disqualifying you. You're a champion."

I wished I could see her face as she repeatedly worked the combination lock.

"Why isn't this working?" Gia shouted, yanking on the lock. "Aaarg." She stomped her foot like a preschooler.

"Careful, princess, you'll break a nail." I chuckled softly. Darby shushed me again.

Gia wiped her palms on her jeans. "Damn it!" She tried again. "Six. Twenty-eight. Three." She tugged on the lock, and it released. "Finally."

This was it. My heart raced as the orange door rolled up. We sucked in our breath in anticipation.

"Hells bells. There's no way you're walking around in there." I wasn't sure if I was horrified or impressed.

From floor to ceiling, the unit was packed with furniture, cardboard boxes, trunks, and plastic totes. Some items were still in their store bags. If I had to make a guess, the tags were probably still attached. I was shocked. Was this why the Eriksens were broke? Not because of Richard's therapy, but because of Gia's shopping addictions? By the amount of possessions in the unit, she was a shopaholic hoarder. It didn't look like she'd thrown anything away. Ever.

"Now, where did I put that?" Head down, she tossed aside one mangled box for a sturdy one. She clumsily maneuvered though the storage room, tottering over boxes and plastic bags, almost landing on an outdoor metal butterfly chair. Sadly, she had good taste. I'd happily take the huge butterfly chair off her hands.

"What do you think she's looking for?" Darby asked in a hushed voice.

"Who knows? You'd need a treasure map to find anything in there," I whispered.

Zippy charged deeper inside. He rooted around while Gia frantically searched. The dog ran toward the front, nose to the ground, sniffing whatever his nose could touch. Something had caught his attention. He whined as he pawed at a water-stained cardboard box toward the door, only a few feet from where Gia stood.

"What did you find, Zippy?" Gia inspected the worn box.

"Give me your cell." I patted Darby's shoulder.

Darby coughed up her phone without question. Unless you counted her arched eyebrows as a question. I did not.

"I think I can remember Malone's number by the pattern." I concentrated on the key pad, practicing what I thought the configuration could be. "I didn't always have him programmed, you know."

Darby wisely kept her own counsel. She returned to our surveillance project. "She's opening the box," she warned.

I poked my head around the corner. Gia was bent at the waist, pushing her ample rear end toward us. "There you are. I've been looking for you." She straightened, then spun around, an animated smile on her bruised face.

Darby and I gasped. Gia gripped a very large handgun, which was pointed in our direction.

I ducked behind the wall, dragging my best friend with me.

"She has a gun. We're going to die," Darby cried.

Chapter Twenty-Five

WE SANK TO THE ground. The heat of the pavement seeped through my jeans. "I don't think she saw us." I said between the beats of my pounding heart.

I whipped out Darby's phone from under my butt, and punched in the pattern I remembered. *Please be right.*

"Malone." He picked up on the first ring.

"It's Melinda." I didn't bother to hide the panic from my voice. Times like this called for the man with the badge. Even if it meant the threat of a night in the pokey. "Darby and I followed Gia to a storage unit. She has a gun," I whispered.

"Why would you do something so stupid?" I didn't have to see him to know his stock-and-trade unreadable expression had been replaced with a set jaw and furious eyes.

"How were we supposed to know she was retrieving a weapon?" I asked in a harsh whisper. Following Gia seemed like a good idea at the time. I peeked around the corner to make sure she was still there.

"You don't. You're not the police," he barked into my ear. "Where are you?"

I rattled off the address and storage unit number. "You'll need a code to get past the security gate."

"What is it?"

I closed my eyes knowing my answer would probably push him over the edge. "I have no idea. We parked Darby's car and followed someone else inside. I don't know how much longer she'll be here. I'm not even sure if the gun is loaded. What do you want us to do?"

"Get back to Darby's car and get somewhere safe." His curt tone cut off any argument he thought I might give.

Joke was on him. For once, I wasn't about to quibble over being ordered around.

I turned to Darby who no longer looked terrified. In fact her light blue eyes snapped with worry. Luckily for us, I had good news.

I gave her the cell phone back. "Calvary is on the way. Let's get out of here."

"We should have followed Betty. At least we already know where her gun is." Darby's dry tone shook a laugh out of me.

Point taken.

DARBY AND I SAT in her small Fiesta with the back windows halfway down for what seemed like an eternity. It was probably more like ten minutes. Two Laguna Hills police cars and Malone's silver Camaro barreled down the street. No sirens. They whipped into the driveway, stopping at the security gate only long enough to punch a code into the keypad. The gate opened, slick as a whistle. They rolled through like they belonged. Unlike us.

"How did he know the number?" Darby asked, impressed.

"He's Judd Malone. He probably called the company and demanded the code."

Five minutes dragged along. I shifted in my seat. "Turn the key so I can roll my window down."

She rolled her eyes. I wasn't fooling her. She was well aware I wanted to hear what was happening. Being the amazing best friend that she was, she honored my request.

We continued to wait. Darby softly hummed the Jeopardy theme.

I looked at her amused. "What is 'bored out of my mind,' Alex?"

"I'd never make it as an undercover cop," she said.

After another five minutes went by without the sounds of guns firing, I opened the door.

"Mel, Malone said to stay here."

I didn't need Darby's reminder. "I won't get too close." I slid out and quietly closed the door. I moved to the front of the car, listening for an indication of what was happening on the other side of the gate.

Darby joined me. She nervously scanned the street. "This is a bad idea."

"Probably. But it won't be the last bad idea I act on."

"Aren't you supposed to have dinner with Grey tonight?"

I shoved my hands in my pockets. I hadn't forgotten about our dinner, but it hadn't been top of mind either. "Yes. What does that have to do with this?"

Her eyes widened. "You won't make it if Malone throws you in jail."

I laughed. "Okay. Okay. You win."

We leaned against the hood of the car. "What's wrong with the Jeep?" she asked.

I sighed. "I don't know. It worked fine this morning. Maybe I left the lights on and drained the battery. Hopefully, I just need a jump start." Sort of like my relationship with Grey.

One of the Laguna Hills police cars appeared at the exit, saving me from morose thoughts.

"Here they come." Darby announced.

We slid off the hood and watched. The gate opened; a police car rolled through the exit. Gia sat in the back seat. As they drove past, she noticed us and shot a death glare in our direction. She wasn't happy to see us. It didn't take a genius to guess we were the ones who called the cops.

"He arrested Gia," Darby exclaimed. "Where's Zippy? Do you think he's with her?"

I cringed as I imagined what Malone had to endure if he'd tried to take Zippy. "I can't imagine Gia going anywhere without her dog."

The second police car pulled around the corner with Malone's Camaro right behind. The police car headed out of town, Malone pulled up next to us and parked.

"Aren't you glad we stayed put?" Darby said.

Not really. I didn't like to be left out of the party. I wasn't exactly a wallflower type.

Malone unfolded from his car and made his way toward us. I liked to describe his walk as legal danger.

"Did you arrest her?" I asked as soon as he was close enough to hear me. I thought it was better to take control before the lecture started.

He stopped in front of us. His wide-legged stance kept us from escaping before he was finished with us. We were about to be royally scolded. "She's being taken in for questioning."

"What the heck was all that stuff?" Darby asked.

Malone shook his head. With his expertise at the neutral expression, I was hard pressed to guess if he was confused or appalled by Gia's hidden treasures. "Those are the items that won't fit in her house. She also rents two more units here."

"She's a shopaholic. That would explain the Eriksens' financial issues. You should have seen her at the boutique. She acted like a junkie getting her fix by binge-shopping."

He gave me a pointed look.

Yeah, yeah. I was theorizing. "What about the gun? Is it Richard's?"

He didn't answer right away. "She says it's not, but we'll run the serial number for verification."

"Of course she's lying," I said. Malone didn't respond. Not a blink of an eye, muscle twitch, or clenched jaw. A silent Malone meant a ticked-off detective.

"Is it the murder weapon?" Darby asked.

"We won't know that for a couple of days," he explained.

The midday sun peeked out from behind a gray cloud. Darby shielded her eyes from the sudden burst of bright light. "Can you at least tell if it's been fired?"

I shook my head. "You can't tell if a gun has been fired recently by looking at it," I explained.

Malone raised an eyebrow. "Care to enlighten me on how you know that?"

I shrugged. "I grew up in Texas. My daddy taught me how to shoot and care for my gun. I know you can tell if a gun is dirty, but you can't tell if it's been shot recently."

He studied me closely. I made myself hold steady under his scrutiny. Maybe he'd take me a little more seriously with his newfound knowledge.

I smoothed my hair back from my face. "Did she tell you what she was going to do with it? Was she going after Hagan?"

He shook his head. "She said she planned to sell it."

It was possible she was telling the truth. Depending on the type of gun, she could get a large chunk of money quickly. It was also possible she intended to shoot Hagan first. A girl has to have priorities.

Malone shifted his weight. "Since you're here, does that mean you didn't find Betty?"

Darby and I exchanged a look. Man, I hated that I felt like I was tattling on my grandmother. "She drove off the same time as Gia. We had to make a choice." I shrugged. "Is Zippy okay?" I inserted, to stave off the reprimand I felt coming, and to make sure an innocent dog hadn't been forgotten.

"He's fine. Don't do this again," Malone ordered.

I bit the inside of my check to keep from smiling. I wasn't sure which "this" he was talking about. There were a few choices. Although, I didn't think Malone was asking me a multiple choice question. "Do what?"

"Follow a murder suspect. You're not the police. You could have been hurt. Or could have gotten someone else hurt."

Darby nodded solemnly. Her blond hair caught the sunlight, casting a glow around her head. "We know. We're very sorry. I also have more photos from today's event if you'd like them."

I kept my trap shut and let Darby handle the apology. Her Midwestern sincerity was hard to resist. Plus, she had potential evidence. Evidence was a surefire way to get on Malone's good side.

He walked to Darby's side of the car and opened the door. "Get out of here and go home. Get me those photos first thing tomorrow."

Darby scrambled inside. Malone didn't bother opening my door. Instead he glowered at me, silently communicating to keep my nose clean, then strode back to his shiny Camaro.

Chapter Twenty-Six

IT DIDN'T TAKE long for Darby and me to return to Laguna Beach. Funny story, Detective Malone followed us the majority of the way, much to Darby's chagrin. I was proud of her. Other than repeatedly checking her rearview mirror, and sitting perfectly erect in her seat, she didn't let the fact the Malone was tailing us freak her out. I had to wonder if that was his way of ensuring we followed orders.

While Darby concentrated on not committing a traffic violation, I worked at piecing together the day's events. I couldn't pinpoint what it was, but I felt like we were missing something.

"Mel, I need to stop by the studio really quick. I'll only be a couple of minutes. I want to download my photos for today. Once I do that, I can drop off the memory card to Detective Malone. Now that there are two murders, I'm sure he'd like them as soon as possible."

I smiled at her. "No problem."

Darby's photography studio was conveniently located right next door to Bow Wow Boutique. We pulled up to the shop, and, lo and behold, there was Betty's Mini Cooper—parked haphazardly in front of the boutique.

"I can't believe it." I yanked my bag from the backseat. Betty had some explaining to do.

"Be gentle with her." Softhearted Darby grabbed her messenger bag and got out of the car.

She walked to her studio. I, on the other hand, headed for the boutique with brisk steps. I opened the door and entered. Betty was preoccupied, digging through a stack of chew toys.

I carefully set my bag on the floor. "Hello."

Startled, Betty jumped a mile high, dropping a handful of toys. "Don't sneak up on an old woman like that. You want to give me a heart attack?"

I waved away her dramatics. "If anyone around here has a heart attack, it'll be me. What are you up to?"

She jutted out her chin. "I had an errand to run." She sounded like a petulant child.

"I noticed that when you hot-rodded away from the dog park. Had you stuck around, you would have learned Malone found your gun."

A triumphant smile danced along her mouth. "I told you that filmmaker had it. I guess that wraps up that." She resumed her search, dumping the toys onto the floor.

"Not by a long shot. Malone wants to talk to you. You left without a word to anyone. Don't you realize that makes you look guilty?"

Betty scooped up the toys and dropped them back into the bin. Apparently, she hadn't found what she was looking for.

"Look, Cookie. No offense, but I got stuff to do. You head back to the park without me. I'll meet you there."

I sighed. "Not happening. There's no way I'm letting you out of my sight. Besides, my Jeep won't start. You'll have to take me back."

"Then how'd you get here?" Skepticism dripped from her question.

"I hitched a ride. Why won't you tell me what you're up to?"

Betty remained stubbornly silent.

I tugged my hair frustrated. "Of all people, you should know that I won't judge you. Trust me enough to tell me what's going on. Where have you been running off to? Are you in some type of trouble?"

She brushed past me, heading for the counter. "It's not what you think."

I grabbed my backpack and followed her. "That's the point. I don't know what to think. Is it money problems? Do you need some cash? Besides the wad of dollar bills you have stashed inside your purse? You should put your money in the safe until you can make a bank deposit on Monday."

"You keep your money, Cookie. Stop worrying about my cash and start worrying about yourself." She pulled her purse off the shelf from under the counter.

I sighed. The time had come to fill Betty in on my financial stability. I leaned against the counter blocking her only escape route. "I need to make a confession."

"What are you gonna tell me? That you're hiding a kid?" She cackled at her lame joke.

I grabbed her delicate hands and held them firmly in mine. "Look, there's no need for you to worry about money. I have enough for both of us. If you're in some type of dire financial situation, I'd be happy to help. Consider it a loan if it makes you feel better."

"I don't know what you're babbling about, but I have plenty of money."

"So do I," I reassured her.

"Sure thing, Cookie. Whatever you say."

She tried to pull her hands away, but I held tightly, careful not to apply pressure to her bruise. "I'm part of the Texas Montgomerys."

She narrowed her eyes and thought about what I was saying. "You mean oil?"

I shrugged, unwilling to go into details. "Among other things."

She whistled. "You're loaded."

I released her hands and straightened. "My family is wealthy. I'm blessed to be a Montgomery. The point is, I care a lot about you. If you need anything, please know you can count on me to help you out."

"Really? Anything?" She peered into my face.

"Absolutely." I nodded.

"Okay. Come to my place." She whizzed past me.

I blinked. "Right now?" I should be happy she was taking me up on my offer. I hadn't expected her to bite so quickly. I thought I would have had to work a little harder to convince her.

"You got something better to do?"

"I still need to pick up the Jeep. We left all the merchandise at the park. Malone wants to talk to you, and Grey and I have a date tonight."

"Then we better get crackin'."

I texted Darby informing her she was free of me. I slung my backpack over my shoulder and followed Betty to the door wondering where we were going and if we were about to do something illegal. We locked up the shop and headed toward her car.

"What were you rummaging around for in there?" I motioned to the boutique.

"You'll find out," she assured me. I wasn't reassured by the secretive look she wore.

Confession time. I'm a grown woman, but I was afraid to get in the car with Betty. I didn't have a phobia about tiny cars, but I didn't exactly feel safe riding in them. The majority of my fear came from Betty's horrible driving. The last time I'd ridden with her, I hadn't been sure we'd survive the experience.

I hesitated, my hand on the passenger door handle. "Do you think I could drive?"

She looked at me over the top of her Mini Cooper. "Do you know where we're going?"

"Not yet. But I can follow directions."

She opened her door. After a throaty laugh, she said, "No one drives my car but me. Get in."

I'm not Catholic, but I crossed myself. Insurance. At least I had my seatbelt fastened before she backed out of the parking space at record speed. She slammed the car into drive and stepped on the gas. I grabbed the Oh-Crap handle above my head, flashing back to our last memorable drive together.

"Do you think you could stay off the sidewalk this time?" I squeezed one eye shut and cringed as she narrowly avoided clipping a parked Land Rover.

She gripped the steering wheel like she was a NASCAR driver. She turned her head and looked me. "You're too wound up. You gotta learn to relax."

"How? You drive like a manic." I gasped in terror. "Watch the road."

My life flashed before my eyes. I was going to die and miss my dinner with Grey. It was suddenly clear what I needed to do to make it up to Grey.

Betty ran a yellow light, turned onto Pacific Coast Highway, and headed north. She gunned it coming out of the turn, slamming me against the door.

"Did you get your license out of a box of Cracker Jacks?"

I could practically feel my teeth grinding to dust, my jaw was clenched so tightly. I was afraid I'd cry out like a school girl every time the passenger tires blipped onto the shoulder, but I held it inside, lest she mock me for the remainder of our time together.

"I'm a fantastic driver."

"No. You're not. You switch lanes as often as a mother changes her newborn's diapers."

"I like to make time."

"I like to arrive at my destination alive."

Betty slammed on the brakes and hung a left into a gated community. She rolled up to the security gate and punched in the security code. I flashed a sideways glance. She was definitely full of her own secrets. This wasn't just any gated community. The cheapest mansion behind the gilded gate was a measly twenty-five million. In order to live here someone had to vouch that you weren't a fraud or criminal, and have a substantial amount of cash in the bank.

We wove our way through the meticulously kept neighborhood where even the soaring palm trees that lined the quiet streets were prestigious. The residential speed bumps were the only thing slowing down Racecar Betty.

She finally found the long driveway she was looking for. She pulled through and parked next to the bungalow hidden behind the huge mansion in the front.

"Who lives here?" I had to pry my fingers from the handle.

"Me."

I did a double take. Someone else was secretly loaded. "Okay then. I see you don't need my money."

"Nope. My daughter's husband has plenty of dough, and they pity me, so they're always paying me off. Enough about those losers. I need your help." Betty opened her door and jumped out. "Now I don't let just anyone in here. Swear on your Grandma Tillie's brooch you won't tell Valerie I let you inside. She'll take it personally, and I'll have to deal with her sniveling for weeks."

I climbed out of the car. I stretched my leg, working out the muscle cramp from being sandwiched inside her tiny clown car. "I won't say a word."

I followed her up the stone walkway to an adorable stucco guesthouse with flower boxes in the windows. Charming and inviting. I was a little nervous as to what waited on the other side of the door. Betty paused with her palm on the handle. A pathetic whining came from inside.

I gave her a long assessing look. What had she gotten herself into? "Is that coming from inside your house?"

"Yes. Now, don't dawdle. Come straight inside and shut the door. You have to move quickly. Got it?"

No, I didn't get it. "Whatever you say."

She unlocked the door and practically shoved me inside. My mouth dropped open.

Holy cow. Betty's cute little dream house looked like she'd hosted a frat party. Garbage, clothes and shoes littered the tile entryway and front sitting room. An overstuffed recliner had been knocked on its side, and two of her potted plants had been demolished.

"What the hell happened to your house?"

"Raider."

I tore my eyes off the mess and looked at Betty, more concerned than I'd been five minutes ago. "What or who is a Raider?"

A large Saint Bernard with used tissues and food wrappers stuck to his face bound down the hallway and into the sunlit room. He jumped onto Betty, knocking her to the floor. He licked her face over and over, slobber dribbling down her shirt. Raider's slobber. Not Betty's.

"Him." She wrapped her arms around his thick neck and buried her face in his fur, giggling.

Chapter Twenty-Seven

"YOU HAVE A DOG? Since when?"

I straddled the massive beast and pulled him off Betty. Good grief he was strong. He thought I was playing and knocked me on my butt.

"Sit," I ordered. He walked over me and pranced his way back to Betty.

"I found him last week." She pushed him back as she gathered her feet under her.

I scrambled to my feet and helped her stand. "He's a stray?"

"No. He's my dog. And before you get all crazy, I've already had Dr. Darling look him over and give him all his vaccinations."

That explained Betty's secret visit to Daniel.

"I read up on Saint Bernards on the Internet. They're supposed to be slow and lazy. But he runs around like a furry freight train destroying everything in his path."

"I can see that. Betty, he can't be more than eighteen months old. He's still in the puppy stage. I'm sure as he gets older, he'll calm down, but for now he's going to have a lot of energy. Is this why you've been disappearing?"

Raider ran down the hallway and brought back a Kong chew toy and dropped it at Betty's feet. She patted his head lovingly. "Look around, Cookie. He's destroyed my place. If Valerie sees this she'll insist I get rid of Raider."

I looked around. "She may have a point this time. He's chewed your furniture, dragged your garbage throughout the house." I picked up an empty box of dog treats. "Did you take this yesterday?"

She grabbed the box from my hand. "I'll pay for it. He eats a lot, and he's never satisfied with one treat."

At the word "treat," Raider left his toy and trotted into the kitchen. He barked. I held back my laughter. Betty shuffled to the kitchen and pulled a handful of treats out of a plastic container on the dining table. Was this the same woman who ordered Luis to put Barney on a diet?

"Last night he ate my favorite animal-print lounge suit. He doesn't like to be alone so I come home every couple of hours to check on him. I'm exhausted." She tossed him the treats. He dropped to the tile and immediately chomped on his snack.

"Separation anxiety," I said.

"No. I think he doesn't like to be left alone."

"That's what I said." I looked around the room. "You need help."

"That's why you're here. I thought we could take shifts—"

"Oh, no. This is not my area." I held up my hand. "I can't help you in the way you need. You need to train him. Now. Teach him who's the alpha dog. If you keep him, and he continues to jump on you, he could injure you."

"What do you mean, 'if I keep him'? Why wouldn't I?"

"Think about it for a second. When he's full grown, he'll weigh two hundred pounds. More, if you keep overfeeding him treats. He could knock you over with his tail. Besides, full grown, he won't fit in your car."

"I'll buy a new car," she said stubbornly.

I rubbed my eyebrow. "I can't believe I'm about to suggest this, but if you're serious, you need to call Caro."

"Your sneaky cousin?" Betty slipped Raider another treat.

I nodded. "She can help you."

"You're okay with me hanging out with your archenemy?"

Raider had left about a cup of slobber on the kitchen tile. Good grief, Betty could slip and fall if she didn't keep on top of his drool. "Where do you get this stuff? Caro and I are not archenemies. We're family. We're just not speaking."

"It's the same thing, Cookie. But don't you worry. I won't spill your secrets."

I found the roll of paper towels next to the kitchen sink. I grabbed a handful and mopped up the mess. "Where's the garbage?"

Betty pointed to the cabinet under the sink.

"I don't have any secrets from Caro."

"I thought you were a smart one. We all have secrets."

I wanted to argue with her, but I did have a secret, or two. Talking about secrets brought to mind Grey. I needed to get back to the dog park; I had a date in a few hours.

"We need to get back to the park and gather our merchandise. I'll need a jump, too." Shoot, I might need a new battery. "Forget the kennel—get a baby gate and close him in the kitchen."

"Great idea. Do you think the final race is over?" she asked.

"It's likely. I think the participants are impatient with all the delays."

"I can't believe you left our merchandise alone. Someone could take everything and wipe us out."

I glanced at her incredulously. "Excuse me, but I wasn't the only one who left the premises."

"It's your shop."

I sighed. There was no way to win. "Line up the chairs and trap him in the kitchen. Hopefully he'll only gnaw on the legs until you get back."

IT WAS TOUCH AND go, but we made it back to the dog park alive. Hell would have to freeze over before I'd let her drive me again. I shuddered, reliving the terrifying journey. In an effort to keep my sanity on the drive back, I'd blathered on about how Darby and I had followed Gia, and how Malone had dragged her in for questioning.

By the time we reached the park, it was five o'clock. The area wasn't deserted, but it wasn't brimming with people either. We missed the last race by thirty minutes. Darby had barely made it back in time to take pictures.

An unknown racer named Lucky Lacey had won the heavyweight race. Barney had finished a respectable third place. Not bad for his first year. Luis immediately started to make plans for next year's race.

Most of the vendors had already packed up and evacuated. Quinn, the pet bakery owner, had left a note. Bless her heart she had instructed my customers to stop by my shop. Betty and I were packing the merchandise when we saw Fallon and her picket sign head toward the exit. I asked Betty to hold down the fort.

"Hey, Fallon. Hold up," I called out, running to catch up to her.

She turned around and glared at me through slitted eyes. "What do you want?"

I sucked in a breath. If at all possible, she looked worse than Gia. I guess I shouldn't have been surprised; Fallon had been on the losing end of the fight. "Do you need to go to the clinic?"

"Where do you think I've been?" She pointed to the bandage stuck to her temple. "Did you want something specific or to just gawk at me? I've had enough people staring at me today."

I excused her cranky attitude. "I heard Richard knew about a secret Hagan was keeping. I wondered if you knew what it was."

"I have no idea." She turned and walked away.

I chased after her. I had more questions, and I wasn't sure when I'd have another opportunity to ask. "Did you know Gia was feeding Zippy energy drinks?"

She froze, then whipped around.

I skidded to a stop.

"I told Richard she was up to no good." She shook her poster in front of my face. "It's because of irresponsible people like her that Doxie Lovers exists. She selfishly risked the life of her dog to win a race. Completely reckless. Zippy isn't safe with her."

I backed up. No surprise here, I agreed with her about Gia needlessly risking her dog's life, but that didn't mean I wanted Fallon to knock me out with her sign. "Is it possible Richard knew what his wife was doing?"

"No," she stated adamantly.

"Think about it for a second. Could that be why he intended to retire Zippy after this race?"

"If he'd known, he would have left sooner. Zippy meant everything to him. Richard talked about retiring while they were on top. Yesterday he had decided it was time."

"Why yesterday?" I asked.

Fallon looked at me confused. "I don't understand."

"What had changed? What made him decide yesterday was Zippy's last race?"

She blinked rapidly. "I—I—I don't know. I was so relived he was leaving that banshee and the racing circuit, I didn't question why." She blushed. "I guess I wanted him to leave for me."

Hey, we've all been there at some point. Although most of us got over it in high school.

Her statement about Gia risking Zippy's life brought to mind a new question. "Do the Eriksens have some type of insurance policy on the dog?"

She shrugged. "Sure. Most of the owners do. That's not uncommon."

"Do you know if Richard had a personal life insurance policy?" Money was a great motivator. Especially if you have an expensive shopping habit.

Her lips puckered like she'd sucked on a rancid lemon. "We didn't talk about his finances."

She didn't have a problem having sex with a married man, but she drew the line at money discussions. Some people had an interesting moral compass.

Tired of waiting for me, Betty sailed across the field and anchored herself next to me. "You're taking too long. What are you talking about?"

I suspected my lovely assistant was not only bored, but snoopy. "I was asking Fallon a couple of questions."

Betty planted her hands on her hips. "I got a question. If Gia killed Richard, are you going to take Zippy?"

I lobbed a meaningful glare at Betty. "I didn't mention any of that."

My looked went heeded. "Well, why not? She'll find out eventually," Betty said.

"What is she talking about?" Fallon asked.

"Detective Hottie arrested Gia," Betty charged on.

"No, he did not. Gia is at the police station answering questions. Fallon, I'm curious, where were you when Richard was shot?"

Her eyes lit up with indignation. "After visiting the ATM for some cash, I stood in line for a fish taco. But the wait was too long so I left. Not that it's any of your business."

The ATM would have taken a picture if she really had been there. The rest of her story wasn't so easy to verify. Either way she had the opportunity to kill him, but my gut said she didn't do it. I believed she really loved him.

"What were you and Richard fighting about?"

She looked away. "He was superstitious. He had to chew Juicy Fruit gum during each race." She shrugged with a soft laugh. "Richard was out of gum and wanted me to buy him packet. I told him that was an errand for his wife." She struggled to keep her composure.

For those who aren't paying attention, their argument wasn't really about a package of gum.

She took a deep breath. "I've answered your questions; now I have one for you." Fallon turned her attention to yours truly. "Where's Zippy?"

Funny how some people were hardwired to be concerned about an animal's welfare. "Last I knew he was still with Gia, on the way to the police station."

"Not for long." Fallon spun around, and with her "Save Our Wieners" picket sign, she marched off into the evening.

"Where'd she go in such a hurry?" Betty asked.

"Where do you think?" I glared at her. "Next time, I'm not telling you anything."

She huffed. "How was I supposed to know you didn't tell her about Gia?"

I pointed at her mouth. "You've got loose lips."

Betty puckered. "Nope. These are smooching lips." She mimicked noisy kissing sounds.

I rolled my eyes. "Let's load up and get out of here."

"THE NEXT TIME you beg me to set up a vendor booth, remember this experience because my answer will be no." I lifted the last plastic storage container off the table and headed toward the Jeep. Again. Betty tagged behind, jabbering about her plans with Raider.

"I think the first trick I'm going to teach Raider is to play dead."

"I think he needs to learn to sit. Stay. Down would be a good idea. Call Caro first thing tomorrow."

My fondness for Betty was the only reason I suggested she reach out to Caro. Sure there were other pet behaviorists in the area, but Caro was the best.

"Hey, there's that sexy reporter." Betty whistled to get his attention. "Mr. MacAvoy, yoo hoo," she sang out at the top of her lungs.

I looked to my left. Sure enough, Mr. TV was heading our way, with his cameraman. "Seriously, would you leave him alone?"

"But what if he wants to interview us for the late night news? Don't you want to be on TV?'

"No." I heard someone, probably MacAvoy, call out my name. I picked up my pace.

"Slow down, Cookie. I can't keep up."

Liar. Against my better judgment, I slowed down anyway.

"Melinda, do you have a minute?" MacAvoy raced up next to me and quickly fell into step.

"Where's your cameraman?" I didn't slow down. The Jeep was within view.

"I sent him to wait in the van. With your aversion to cameras, I thought it was best."

I sighed. I stopped and set the tote on the grass. I was so close to a clean getaway. "I have somewhere to be so make it snappy."

"I'm sorry you had to find Stephanie dead." Betty lunged for a hug. I could tell by her soft moan she was enjoying herself. Watching Mr. TV's discomfort suddenly made the delay tolerable.

He cautiously patted Betty's back and then stepped away. "Who?"

"The filmmaker. We didn't know her name so we gave her one," I explained.

His flashy smile was conspicuously missing. "Olivia. Her name was Olivia Benedict," he said softly.

Odd. Malone mentioned no one knew her name. "Did you know her?"

He nodded. "We worked together many years ago. She was a freelance journalist back then."

Well, well, well. Someone was keeping secrets. Look who was withholding information now? The pieces started to come together. "You knew who she was and what she was doing the entire time."

Betty glared at me. "Cookie, if you had been nicer to him, he could have gotten my gun back."

"Your gun?" he asked.

I covered Betty's mouth with my hand, keeping her quiet momentarily. "This is all off the record. You can't use anything she says. Your word as a journalist." Not that I held much stock in that, but he seemed to.

He threw his hands in the air. "That seems to be the theme of the day. Agreed. What gun?"

"You already know about Betty's public argument with Richard? She may have pulled out a gun as protection. Stephanie—Olivia—snatched the gun."

"She said I could get into trouble waving a gun in public." Betty pouted.

We caught a glimpse of a real MacAvoy smile. "That doesn't surprise me."

"What will happen to her movie?" Betty asked.

I still wasn't convinced there ever was a dogumentary. "Was there a movie?"

He nodded. "She'd been working on it for a while. She traveled from race to race throughout California. It was during the filming here that she uncovered an illegal gambling ring. She was using the film to gather evidence. For the authorities."

"And now she's dead."

"And her camera is missing." MacAvoy had to have the last word. Not that a missing camera is more important than a murder, but if that camera happened to contain evidence that might help solve the crime . . . well, it trumps the dead body every time.

"Do you think whoever killed her took the camera?" I asked.

He nodded.

That's what I thought too. "How do you know all this?"

"Olivia and I had dinner last night."

Since he was in a chatty mood, I continued my questions. I tried to keep my tone and phrasing conversational. "Is Hagan really behind the gambling ring?"

"I have my theories, but no evidence."

He was singing a familiar tune. How many times had I felt that way when dealing with Malone? More than I should.

"If Hagan was making money on Zippy, he'd have motive to kill Richard. And if Olivia had captured people actually placing bets, that would have blown up his entire operation."

"Like I've said, he's not a small-time hoodlum." I heard the warning in his voice.

It was a strong possibility Malone had the wrong person in for questioning. "Where is Hagan?" I figured if anyone knew, it would be MacAvoy.

"He disappeared immediately after the trophies were awarded. Where were you? I thought you of all people would have been here for the presentation."

I eyed Betty. For once she kept quiet. "We were taking care of a personal matter," I said.

His weight shifted in Betty's direction. "Where were you when Olivia was killed?"

"You think I'm a suspect? Again?" Betty whined. "I thought we had something."

I smiled. "Since I haven't heard the time of death, she can't answer that." He looked at me with raised eyebrows. "And neither can I." I finished.

I picked up the storage container and motioned with my head to Betty. "Let's go. I still need a jump."

Betty bid farewell to Mr. TV. As soon as we were out of earshot she said, "I'd rather jump Callum MacAvoy."

I'm sure she would.

Chapter Twenty-Eight

TURNED OUT, THE Jeep didn't need a jump after all. One of the battery cables had come loose. I made a mental note to take the Jeep in for a checkup. A simple fix and I was on the road.

I raced home in ten minutes. I may have broken a few speed-limit laws in the process. Missy was excited to see me. After much love and a belly rub, I took her for a quick walk around the block so she could relieve herself.

The sun had never really broken free from the clouds, Now that it was the end of the day, the temperature dropped quickly. Keep in mind, it was still above seventy degrees.

I fed Missy her dinner. While she ate, I took a quick shower. I didn't have as much time as I'd have liked to get ready for my date with Grey. I figured it was probably better that I was rushed. I had less time to think and just act. Have I mentioned I work better when I shoot from the hip?

One thing I did make sure of—well two things actually—I was wearing my engagement ring. And two, I grabbed Grandma Tillie's brooch.

Grey arrived on time. As always, he looked amazing in his dark charcoal Tom Ford suit. He'd decided against the tie, which I knew was in deference to my taste and not his. There's nothing sexier than Grey in his suit, sans tie, and a couple of buttons undone on his shirt. He looked a little dangerous. Reckless.

I'd also chosen my dress with Grey in mind. He was a leg man. I wore a butterfly-sleeve, silk mini-dress. Paired with my Louboutin glitter slingbacks, it showcased my toned legs. I was also eye level with my dashing G-man. Part happenstance. Part strategy.

Grey's Mercedes SUV floated down PCH, comfortably taking the turns as we followed the shoreline to Newport. Inside the car was a different story. The tension was so thick I felt like I couldn't take a full breath. It was like we were on our first date. A blind date. Our conversation was forced and stilted. As if we knew we were walking a relationship tightrope. One wrong step and we'd lose our balance.

I tightened my hold on my handbag. After the day's events, I decided my relationship with Grey was my number-one priority. I'd come up with a plan, a grand gesture so to speak, to show him that he came first in every aspect. Since I'm not exactly the grand gesture type, I'm sure most of my nerves were a by-product of wanting to get the delivery right. Don't get me wrong. I still had questions about the real reason he'd been at the wiener race. I was certain he'd be more forthcoming now that we were alone.

Once we arrived, I waited on the sidewalk while Grey handed over his keys to the valet. He concluded his instructions and joined me in front of the exclusive restaurant.

Grey's hand pressed onto the small of my back above the low scoop of my dress. The heat of his hand on my skin sent a rush of warmth through my body. We strolled into 401 Chop Oceanside. The hostess greeted us with a warm smile that immediately made me feel like we were being included in her small, exclusive group of friends. She whisked us past two gold-flecked white marble columns standing guard to the floor-level dining area. The old money-feel made me think of Texas, and, for a moment, I missed home.

The dining room was thoughtfully dim, the minimal lighting casting a romantic ambiance on the room. She led us to our table with a view of the ocean that would melt even the harshest cynic's heart. I slipped into the dark leather booth. Grey sat across from me. A long stem red rose lay across my plate.

I smiled shakily. "You're very handsome tonight."

His blue eyes reminded me of the morning low tide—clear and calm. I was glad one of us was calm. "Not that I'm not appreciative, but that's the third time you've told me that. Why are you so nervous?"

"Maybe you look really good for a change." I smiled. "Let's order some wine." I was counting on the alcohol to ease my nerves.

Grey ordered a bottle of DuMol, Russian River Pinot Noir. We sat in a semi-comfortable silence as we watched the brilliant sunset hues spread over the pristine azure waters of the Pacific Ocean. The maître d' arrived with our wine and presented it, the label facing Grey. He nodded, and they continued the dance of a proper wine presentation until Grey finally tasted the Pinot and pronounced it perfect. The ritual complete, I finally got my glass of wine.

Grey was right; it was perfect. Black cherry and toasty oak. Nothing compared to a good Pinot.

I fingered the glass. "Betty finally confessed her secret. She has a dog. A Saint Bernard."

His grin spread across his face. "You're kidding."

I shook my head. "Nope. I've met Raider. He's a stray. His name fits him. She did have enough common sense to have Daniel look him over."

"That explains the fall, the scratches—"

"The missing dog treats." I laughed. "He needs obedience training. He also has separation anxiety. I told her to call Caro."

He reached across the table and held my left hand. "Will she do it? Betty's as protective of you as you are of her." He fingered my engagement ring, adjusting it back and forth. Maybe he wasn't as relaxed as he looked.

"She has to. I'm not sure her house will survive if she doesn't." I took a fortifying gulp of wine. "Speaking of Caro, I have something for you."

A half smile eased onto his face. "Something I can open here?"

I felt my face warm. "Yes." I pulled my hand away and opened my clutch handbag. "When I apologized, I meant it. I also know that for you, actions speak louder than words." I inhaled deeply. I pulled out the white jewelry box and set it on the table. "This is the only way I know to show you how much I regret my impulsive decision. I want to make it right between us. I know we can't go back, but we can move forward."

I slid the box across the table.

He didn't reach for it.

"You don't have to do this." He said, slow and deliberate.

I felt sick and immediately had second thoughts. I sat on my hands, worried I might grab it back, and swallowed hard. "I know."

I didn't know what else to do. I wanted to show him I was serious, and, in my way, I was putting him first. If giving him the brooch to return to the FBI would make it right between us, I was willing to do it.

It hurt like the devil. But there would be other opportunities to repossess my brooch from Caro. It wasn't as if either of us were leaving town.

He looked at me, his eyes serious. "I know this is difficult for you."

He had no idea. I just handed him my heritage with the knowledge he would turn it over to my lovely, but pain-in-the-butt cousin. "You're more important. I love you."

He picked up the box, and, without opening it, slid it into his jacket pocket.

"I love—" He stopped abruptly. Something or someone had caught his eye. And from the strained look on his face, it wasn't good. "I'll be right back. Stay here." He slipped out of the booth and walked away.

I was stunned. I had my back to the room so I couldn't see where he'd gone or what had captured his attention. I fell back against the seat. I'd just given him my Grandma Tillie's brooch. Laid my heart on the table, literally, and he left me sitting alone. He'd left me.

What the hell?

I scooted across the booth and got up to find out what was more important than my peace offering. I didn't have to go far. He was at the bar, a gin and tonic in his hand, yucking it up with none other than Hagan Stone. My eyes narrowed. He hadn't had time to order that drink, he had to have swiped it from someone else. He was in undercover mode.

I adjusted my dress and smoothed my hair, which I'd left down the way Grey preferred. I moved toward the bar with laser focus.

I called up my best beauty pageant smile and pinned it to my mouth. "Why, Hagan Stone, imagine seeing you here. Celebrating the success of the Dachshund Dash?"

Hagan set down his Scotch and stood. "Melinda, it's so nice to see you. May I say, you look ravishing. Surely you're not here alone." He clasped my hands in his and squeezed.

I maintained eye contact with Hagan. Apparently, Grey hadn't told him we knew each other, let alone that we were engaged. "Oh, no. I'm here with my fiancé."

I could feel Grey squirm next to Hagan. My eyes narrowed slightly. Grey was a dead man. How in the world he thought he'd get away with pretending he didn't know me was ridiculous. I looked forward to making him squirm.

"I'm sorry, have you met Grey Donovan? Grey, this is Melinda Langston. She owns the Bow Wow Boutique in Laguna." Hagan made the unnecessary introductions.

"It's nice to meet you." Grey held out his hand. I ignored it.

I smiled slyly. "I must not have made a very good impression on you. We've met before. I believe you own an art gallery."

He pretended to think about when that might have been. "Yes, of course. You attended the ARL benefit I held a couple of months ago."

I tilted my head to the side. "So you do remember me?"

Grey's brow rose a fraction. "You'd be hard to forget."

Obviously not.

"I'm sure your fiancé is wondering where you are." Hagan said, an obvious attempt to get rid of me.

"Oh, he knows exactly where I am," I said with a silly, girly laugh. I rested my hand on his arm. "I did want to apologize for not being at the final race. I heard it was thrilling."

Hagan puffed out his chest like a strutting peacock. "It was a real nail-biter. Great entertainment."

I dropped my hand to my side. I could feel Grey's anxiety level rise the longer I stayed. Good. "It's too bad about the filmmaker. I heard the TV reporter found her murdered at the chili truck."

"I heard that. Yes, it's too bad." His tone was as tight as his expression.

"I guess that works out well for you. You know, since she had accused you of illegal gambling and all."

Grey shifted on his stool, "accidently" stepping on my foot. I ignored him and forged ahead.

"Are you implying I had anything to do with her unfortunate death?" Hagan sputtered.

I shook my head. "No, not at all. Did you know her camera is missing?"

"I did not."

"I'm curious, where were you, Hagan, when she was killed?"

"I don't believe I'm obligated to answer your questions." Hagan's face darkened, the muscles under the shadow of dark stubble twitched.

If you Googled "killer" I imagined that was the face you'd find.

"He was with me," Grey stated, cutting me off at the knees.

My eyes widened as my gaze swiveled between the two of them. "I didn't realize you two were so friendly."

Hagan shot me a smarmy grin. "We were talking about business. A possible partnership."

"I see." I managed to maintain my composure. "Well, I've kept you gentleman distracted long enough. Do you know which way to the ladies' room?"

Grey stood and pointed past the bar. "I believe it's in that direction."

I couldn't look at him. I was an emotional volcano. I headed to the bathroom to pull myself together before I blew Grey's cover. I splashed my face with cold water. After I refreshed my makeup, and paced until I was no longer furious but just pissed off, I returned to our table. I managed to avoid the bar on the way.

Grey was already at the table. His face a mask, but I saw the fire in his eyes. He was just as pissed off as I was. Good.

"You lied." I came out swinging. I thought he was going to deny it or at least lay out some type of FBI excuse. I was wrong.

"I did."

"Why? To get back at me?"

"You know I can't talk to you about the case I'm on." His even tone kept me off-balance.

I leaned against the table, pushing my face closer to him, wanting—no, needing—him to show his emotions. "You're not only lying to me; you're lying to yourself. All you had to say was that he had something to do with a case. I'd have dropped it."

"No. No, you wouldn't have. You don't know how. You're like a dog with a bone—relentless. You just proved you're impulsive and reckless." A thin chill hung on his words. I wanted his emotion, and I got it.

I sat back, feeling lightheaded. I breathed as deeply as I could. I thought about Betty's new dog and wondered if Betty had called Caro yet. Anything to momentarily distract myself from what was happening.

I twisted my ring. "I have never interfered in your cases."

"Until tonight," he bit out.

"I've never lied to you. Even when I knew you'd be mad and we'd fight."

"You knew about my job. I've always been honest about that."

"But this was different. You told me you were going to DC. Was that true?"

He shook his head.

I gritted my teeth. He'd been lying the whole time. He'd never intended to travel to DC There was no out-of-state case. He'd always been looking at Hagan, ringleader of the undercover gambling ring. He'd tried to protect Betty.

I pushed out a sad smile. What was I going to tell Betty?

I drank my wine with a shaky hand. "You were always planning on coming to the race to meet Hagan?"

He remained silent.

"I see." And suddenly I did see. Olivia Benedict was his informant. The one piece MacAvoy hadn't been able to put together. "You used me and Betty. You could have gotten her gun back at any time. I can't believe it. I would have helped you in a heartbeat. But instead you lied. All the while I'm feeling horrible about one moment of bad judgment, *you're lying to me.*"

He sat across from me, stone-faced. His eyes shifted slightly. He was formulating a response.

It felt like my heart was trying to claw its way out of my chest. I never thought I'd be one to back down from a confrontation, but I just didn't have the energy to fight. Nor the desire. I tried to laugh dismissively; instead it came out a cross between a hiccup and a sob. I took off my ring and laid it next to him. "I hope you have a great life, Grey."

"Melinda."

I shook my head. I could see him through the tears pressing against my eyes. "It's not working. I'm done. You're done. I crossed a line you can't forgive. I get it. Well, now you've crossed a line I'm not sure I can forgive."

"Mel." I heard the anger, hurt, and vulnerability all in the one word. My name. My heart wedged in my throat. Feeling my own vulnerability just fired my anger.

"Good God. Be honest with yourself. If you weren't still ticked off at me, you would have told me you were going to be at the race for a case. You wouldn't have needed to give me details. I wouldn't have asked." I hiccupped. "Okay, I would have asked. But I would have accepted that you couldn't have shared specifics."

He didn't say anything. He couldn't. I was right. I grabbed my purse and stood.

"Mel, I drove," he said quietly.

I shook my head. "I can't be with you right now. I'll call a taxi."

With my head held high, and my Montgomery pride on full display, it was my turn to walk away and leave him alone. Forgetting about Grandma Tillie's brooch tucked safely in Grey's pocket.

I stepped outside. The crisp salt air slapped my face, shaking me out of my pity party. I narrowed my eyes in determination. I'd show him "impulsive." For my last reckless move of the night, I cozied up to the valet and talked him into bringing me Grey's SUV.

Mr. Undercover FBI Man could take the taxi home.

Damn him for breaking my heart.

Chapter Twenty-Nine

AN HOUR LATER, I was cuddled up in bed with Missy.

This wasn't the first time Grey and I had called it quits. He and I had broken up before, but it had been different. The last time we'd split up had been due to my inability to stop worrying about his safety. And also due to Grey's refusal to talk about his work. But in the past two years, he'd never lied to me. At least not that I knew about. His blatant deceit caused me to question everything he'd ever told me.

No, this breakup was different. I wasn't being dramatic. I knew in my heart, this was the end. What a fool I'd been. I'd stupidly believed his undercover life hadn't applied to me.

My cell rang. My heart tightened. It was probably Grey. I'd left his car on the street and the keys in the visor. If he was smart he would have had the taxi drop him off here so he could pick up his car.

I let the phone ring. Grey knew how to take a hint. He'd respected that I didn't want to talk to him anymore tonight. Within seconds the phone rang again. The demanding sound refused to be ignored.

I sighed in exasperation and swiped my phone off the nightstand. I looked at the caller ID. It wasn't Grey. It was my mama.

How did she know? I was at one of my lowest points in my life, and somehow she knew it. Unlike Grey, my mother did not know how to take a hint.

I cleared my throat. "Hey, Mama." I tucked the blankets around my body, creating a mummy effect.

"Finally. I've called you twenty times."

Why couldn't she say "hello" like a civilized person? "Twice, Mama. You've called me two times. I'm really not in the mood to talk tonight. Did you need anything in particular?"

"You tell me. You're the one hiding something, Melinda. I could tell the last couple of times we talked."

I stroked Missy's head as I pictured the hurt look I knew she was crafting. A wasted effort since I was two thousand miles away. "I'm afraid your imagination is working overtime."

"A mother knows her child. Is it work? You don't have to waste the best years of your life rising before nine."

"No. There's nothing wrong," I lied.

"Then it has to be Grey. What did you do?" Her accusing tone was the last straw.

"Thank you for your support and vote of confidence, Mama." I could hear her revving up to argue, but I talked right over her. "I'm so tired of your constant assumptions that I'm the one who's going to screw up that relationship. You know, Grey's not perfect either."

For once she had nothing to say. "If you must know, there was another death at the Doxie Dash. I've had a long day, and I'm tired."

"I-I am sorry, sugar."

I closed my eyes suddenly exhausted. "I know you are. Mama, I really am tired. I'll call you later."

I shut down my phone. If it rang again tonight, I didn't want to know. It was bad enough I'd have to tell Betty and Darby about the demise of my relationship with Grey. I released a jagged sigh. I couldn't think about that now.

I snapped off the tableside lamp. Darkness enveloped the room. Strangely, it was somehow comforting. I wasn't the cry-herself-to-sleep kinda gal. Although tonight I might make an exception.

Chapter Thirty

I WOKE UP THE next morning with one thing on my mind—I wanted my brooch back.

Sunshine burst through my window like a floodlight. I closed my eyes and rolled to my side, keeping my back to the dawn. Sleep had been elusive. I'd tossed and turned so often, I'd kicked Missy off the bed more than once. My mind had refused to shut down.

The whole mess sucked.

On the plus side, a fitful night provided plenty of time to rehearse what I'd say to Grey the next time I saw him. I vacillated between demanding a clear explanation for the past two years together, and insisting on knowing exactly what his relationship with Hagan Stone was. I was smart enough to know that neither of those were viable options.

Insomnia also afforded an opportunity to mull over *The Doxie Dash Murders*. Lame, but that's what the media called them now.

With nothing but time on my hands in the wee hours of the morning, here's the suspect list I'd formed for Richard Eriksen's murder:

Gia Eriksen. Betrayed spouse. Key question: when did she know about her husband's infidelity? A cheating husband was a great motive for murder. Shopaholic and hoarder. If her husband was leaving her and retiring Zippy, Gia had just lost her income to buy, buy, buy. Financial problems. A life insurance policy ensured a renewed cash flow and a second motive for murder.

There was proof she'd doped her dog at least once. According to Fallon, Richard didn't have a clue about his wife's scandalous activities. Gia knew Hagan Stone's secret. Darby and I caught her red-handed with a gun that may or may not be the murder weapon. As for an alibi, she didn't have one. She claimed to be looking for her husband. Easy enough to discredit.

Fallon Keller. Richard's mistress. She said Richard was leaving his wife. Per Fallon, she and Richard had argued about Juicy Fruit gum. If he was really leaving his wife, why would Fallon refuse to buy the man of her dreams a measly pack a gum? She had a partial alibi, taking cash from the ATM, which is smart if you're planning to kill someone and you don't want to be fingered as the murderer.

Hagan Stone. The Chairman of the Board for the Laguna Beach Dachshund Dash. Where do I start? Illegal gambling ring. Supposedly, Richard was blackmailing him. Did that have anything to do with betting? Grey had been assigned to watch him. If the FBI was monitoring Hagan, he had to be into something deeper than small-time wiener race gambling. My best guess: money laundering. Grey offered himself as Hagan's alibi. Fact? Only Grey and Hagan know for sure. If Hagan did kill anyone, Grey knew all about it.

Lenny Santucci. Rabid competitor. Lives in his car with his dog. Hates the Eriksens. Tried to pass off Pickles as a descendant of Chip Ahoy. Richard threatened to expose him. For the past year, Lenny had been trying to prove they were cheaters. Probably an alcoholic. Lenny knew about the gambling. He loved his depressed dog. Did he love him enough to kill his competition's owner? What was Lenny's alibi?

As for Olivia, the filmmaker, all I had was a guess as to why she'd been killed. Her film had been uncovering everyone's closely guarded secrets.

Like I said, I'd had a lot of time to think. Unfortunately, even with all that time, I still didn't have a clue as to who killed either of the victims.

With a determined sigh, I rolled out of bed. Today, I'd concentrate on retrieving my brooch.

MISSY AND I STARTED the day as we did most days—a quick breakfast after a short run on the beach, a shower for me, and a thorough wrinkle-cleaning for Missy. As I moved about the bedroom, my trusted sidekick jumped on the bed. She watched as I pulled on my jeans and a T-shirt that read, "Sit Happens." What can I say? It seemed like an appropriate shirt for the mood I was in. My comfy motorcycle boots were the perfect finishing touch for the day's outfit.

Missy settled in with a sigh. I rubbed her back and planted a quick kiss on her head. She licked my cheek.

"I love you too, girlfriend."

I'm sure you're wondering about my emotional status. Honestly, I felt like a contestant on "Wheel of Emotion." I wanted optimism, yet landed on anything but that. Heaven help us all if I ever landed on "bankrupt."

For now, I decided to concentrate on the day's tasks, putting one foot in front of the other, and running on Texas grit.

I headed to the bathroom to brush my hair. Missy jumped off the bed and dutifully followed. She stretched out, blocking the doorway; her soulful eyes surveyed my every move. I firmly believed animals felt their humans' emotions.

I sighed. "I'm not foolin' ya, am I?"

I pulled my hair into a ponytail and swiped on some mascara. "Alrighty then. I guess you and I are hanging out today. Let's go for a ride."

Missy stood and shook, slapping ropes of drool against the bathroom door. I quickly wiped her mess with a washcloth.

"Are you always going to do that?" I laughed lightly. She snorted and wagged her stubby tail.

Ready to hit the road, I collected my purse and Missy's leash, and we headed for the Jeep. As we backed out of the driveway, I rolled down the windows so we could enjoy the fresh air. Blue sky, bright sun, and a soft ocean breeze. A direct contrast to my mood.

First errand of the morning was to drive by Grey's gallery on the off-chance his vehicle was out front. No, I wasn't stalking him. I was eager to take back what was mine.

It was only ten, and, like most of the art galleries downtown, Grey didn't open until eleven. Some days he didn't open at all. But I wasn't leaving anything to chance. Unfortunately, my reconnaissance proved what I'd already known—the gallery was closed. Couldn't blame a girl for trying.

I hung a U-turn and headed toward the boutique. Time to unload the merchandise from the doxie race for the last time. Thank goodness.

My eyes were dry from the lack of sleep the night before so I decided on a quick detour to the drugstore. I was also out of hand sanitizer at the boutique. Not planning to be long, I found a spot along the street. I shoved a couple of quarters in the meter, then grabbed Missy's leash, and we headed inside.

We ambled toward the back of the store. I'd snagged a box of eye drops when I spotted Lenny and Pickles in the oral hygiene aisle. Odd, I would have thought after Pickles's loss yesterday they would have left town with their tails tucked between their legs.

Lenny looked like he was on the back end of a weekend bender with a bad case of bed-head, wrinkled clothes, and a puffy, red face. He was so busy filling his handheld shopping basket with mouthwash, he didn't notice our approach.

"Hey there, Lenny."

He jumped at the sound of my voice like a package of pop rocks dropped into a glass of soda.

"Are you following me?" he groused.

I held up the eye drops. "Nope." I wanted to ask him why he was so paranoid. "What's with all the mouthwash?" I asked instead.

He pulled the basket to his side, out of my direct line of vision. "It's on sale. I like to stock up."

Wow. *Six* containers' worth? Who did he think he was kidding?

I'd read an article once about a recovering alcoholic who drank mouthwash to get smashed. I had a strong suspicion Lenny might fall into that category. That sure would explain his behavior, the minty fresh breath, and lack of alcohol bottles in his car.

Missy stretched her thick neck sniffing the air toward Pickles who sat next to Lenny's feet. Pickles tilted his head and returned her greeting.

"Sit, girl." Missy looked up at me as if I was punishing her. She just wanted to sniff her friend close up. I pointed to the floor. She obeyed, but I could tell she was miffed.

"How's he doing?" I asked.

Lenny frowned at his pooch. "He's depressed."

I hated to break it to him, but he didn't appear any better. "I'm sorry to hear that. Look, I hope you don't mind but I talked to Dr. Darling about Pickles's possible condition."

"What condition?" He asked with all the warmth of a junkyard dog.

"His depression. It's the real deal. The doctor gave me a pamphlet explaining treatment options. I have the brochure at the boutique if you're interested. I thought you might find it helpful."

"I don't need your help," he barked.

I held up my hand. "I'll let you get back to your . . . shopping."

If he wasn't drunk yet, he was about to be.

Missy and I skedaddled to the next aisle. As I reached for a container of hand sanitizer, the hair on the back of my neck bristled. I felt someone behind me. I turned around to find Lenny sneering at me.

A little unnerved to find him following me, I said the first thing that came to mind. "I'm surprised you're still in town. I thought everyone left yesterday." Antagonizing him wasn't the smartest plan.

"The police arrested Gia. I thought I'd stop by the station and tell them what I know."

He didn't fool me for a minute with that phony, helpful smile plastered to his broad face. He was truly giddy about Gia's plight.

"I thought she'd been taken in for questioning. That's not the same as being arrested."

He shrugged. "It's only a matter of time."

"Didn't you already give a statement at the dog park?"

"Sure. But they didn't ask what I knew about Gia and Richard." He brushed past me harder than he needed to as he moved down the aisle toward the cold remedies.

"So, where were you when Richard was shot?" I know, I know. The smart move was to walk away. But today I was living on the edge. He was the only suspect I didn't have an alibi for.

He stopped and slowly faced me. He glowered with squinty eyes. "You know, you keep asking me questions like you're investigating. You sure you're not with the cops?"

I forced a laugh. "Nope. Just curious. I found him, you know."

"I heard."

"One more thing. I don't remember seeing you after the argument between you and Gia."

"Unless you were standing in the line for the men's john, you wouldn't have." His offhanded tone didn't ring true.

I whistled. "That must have been some line." There were two areas with portable bathrooms—by the spectator section, and the other in the food area adjacent to the parking lot. I wondered which line he'd been in.

"You know, I passed the bathrooms by the racetrack a number of times. I don't remember seeing you."

He dropped a bottle of cold medicine into his basket. "I was in the line by the food."

Which was closer to where Richard was shot. Another flimsy alibi that was all too easy to shoot down.

Suddenly, Lenny's bloodshot eyes lit up. "I'm not the only one still in town," he chirped, pointing over my shoulder. "There's Richard's girlfriend."

Not surprisingly, Fallon Keller made a beeline to the first aid section. Her face was still rockin' a number of cuts and bruises. She looked in our direction and froze. A weak smile tugged at the corners of her mouth.

I smiled back and waved. She lowered her head and then ducked behind an endcap of sunscreen.

"What do you think she's still doing here?" Lenny asked.

Other than buying bandages? "I think she's worried about Zippy."

"Why would she care?"

"She doesn't believe he's safe with Gia."

Speaking of safe. It dawned on me as Lenny and I watched Fallon sneak around the drugstore that it was possible they were both still in town for reasons altogether different.

The filmmaker's camera.

I PAID FOR MY items and left Lenny and Fallon in the store. After my sparring match with Lenny, I felt positively energetic. I parked in front of the boutique and unloaded Missy. Since it was Monday, Betty wasn't scheduled to come in until one.

I unlocked the shop then propped open the front door. Missy waddled inside. She turned, double-checking I was right behind her.

"I'm coming. Go lay down."

She headed to her bed behind the counter.

I moved as quickly as possible. In a matter of minutes, I tugged the last tote out of the Jeep. That's when I saw Fallon a block away, heading in my direction. I tried to get her attention, but she slipped inside the bank without noticing me.

I stood smack-dab in the middle of the sidewalk and weighed my options. As much as I wanted to pepper her with questions, it was time to get my behind in gear and restock the merchandise. I trudged inside the store and kicked the door shut behind me.

I lined up the totes against the wall across from the register. I removed the lids and tossed them in a pile.

I grabbed an armful of dog sweaters to hang on the sale rack in the back. I was absorbed in the task when the door opened. Mr. TV strolled inside. He wore perfectly pressed chinos and a green button-up shirt. No blazer. No cameraman. Interesting.

I stepped out from behind the rack. "Hello."

He removed his aviator sunglasses. "Good morning." His cheerful tone caught me off guard. He examined a couture dog dress prominently displayed toward the front window. "Are all of the clothes made by local designers?"

"Some of them. If you're looking for something specific, I'd be happy to help you find it." It dawned on me that I didn't know if he had a pet.

A half smile tugged at his mouth. "Nice shirt."

"I like to make a statement."

"I noticed." He tucked his glasses in his shirt pocket. "I didn't realize until I'd arrived, Laguna Beach is very dog-friendly."

You'd think a guy like him wouldn't need small talk before getting to the point. "More registered dogs than kids. But as the king of research, I'm sure you already knew that."

I returned to unpacking and pulled out the last of the dog clothes from the storage container. One down, three more to go.

"How long have you been in town?" I asked.

"Not long. Have you heard from Detective Malone today?" he asked.

I guess small talk was over and we'd moved on to the main event.

"Nope. Contrary to what you may believe, we're not in each other's back pockets."

"That's good. Otherwise your fiancé might find that objectionable."

I carried the tote full of chew toys, balls, and other play items to the display baskets up front. "I guess he would."

I dropped to one knee and made quick work of unloading the storage container. He stood nearby, watching quietly. I tossed the last stuffed animal in its appropriate basket.

"Where's the rock you were wearing yesterday?"

My heart skipped a beat. He was observant; I'd give him that.

I looked up and lied through my teeth. "I dropped it off for its annual inspection and cleaning." I stood. "I'm sure you didn't stop by to talk about my engagement ring."

He nodded. "I wanted to give you a courtesy heads-up. I'm picking up the story where Olivia left off."

"Okey dokey." I picked up the tote and carried it back to where the other empty containers sat.

MacAvoy followed me. "You don't seem to understand what that means."

I sucked in a breath well aware of what it meant, but I knew there wasn't anything I could do about it. Most of all, there was no way in hell I was about to confess to someone I hardly knew that Grey and I had broken up last night.

I stacked the empty totes inside one another. "Am I supposed to be surprised that you're taking up the charge to end illegal gambling at wiener races?" I asked with more than a hint of impatience in my voice.

I knew I was being awful, but I didn't know any other way to get him to leave.

His jaw tightened. I'd struck a nerve. "That includes Hagan Stone."

I shrugged. "Congratulations. The story has Pulitzer written all over it."

He crossed his arms. Frown lines edged the corners of his eyes. "Your boyfriend is up to his elbows in this mess."

He had no idea. "Look, I get it. You have a job to do. Like I told you yesterday, Grey is a big boy. He can take care of himself."

"What about you?"

I squared my shoulders. "What about me?"

"If your name comes up, I can't overlook it."

I blinked. I had to have heard him wrong. He thought I was involved somehow?

I side-stepped the lids on the floor and stood in front of MacAvoy. I locked eyes with him. "I wouldn't expect you to. But let me be perfectly clear. It won't."

An adversarial silence filled the air. Missy must have noticed the coldness in my tone. She waddled out from behind the counter to check out what was happening. I motioned for her to come to me.

"If you've gotten everything off your chest, I'd like to get back to work."

Without a word, he slipped on his glasses and left.

I squatted next to Missy and absently scratched her back. "That man is a pain in the butt. I wish he'd go back to wherever he came from."

I pushed out a frustrated sigh. I'd basically declared war on MacAvoy. Stupid move on my part. A sensible person would apologize. I could be sensible. It just wasn't going to happen today.

Chapter Thirty-One

I NEEDED A DISTRACTION. Who better to distract me than Darby? I retrieved my purse from behind the counter and pulled out my cell. I paused. Why call when she was probably right next door? I shoved my phone in my back pocket and popped outside to see if her studio lights were on.

From the sidewalk, I could see the closed sign hanging on her door. "Darn."

I spun around and bumped into Fallon Keller, knocking her drink out of her hand. Pink lemonade flowed down the sidewalk.

"Geez, I'm sorry. I keep running into you don't I?"

Fallon held out her hands to protect herself from further abuse. "You don't seem to watch where you're going."

I cringed. She was right. "Did that spill on you?" I quickly snatched up the cup, lid, and straw.

She inspected her purple knit blouse and white capri pants. "I don't think so."

I grabbed her by the elbow, ushering her toward the boutique. "Let me replace that. I have bottled water and soft drinks."

She allowed me to lead her inside the shop. I left her up front by the interactive toys.

"What would you like?" I tossed the garbage in the trash behind the counter. Missy lifted her head long enough to confirm I was back.

"Water is fine." Fallon tucked her purse under her arm. "I saw that reporter leave your shop."

"He was checking out the store," I fibbed. I break up with Grey, and suddenly I'm a proficient liar. The irony wasn't lost on me.

I hurried toward the office, grabbed a cold bottle of water from the mini-fridge, and returned with her drink. "Feel free to look around. Watch out for the storage containers. I'm still unpacking from the weekend."

She gripped the bottle with one hand, but didn't open it. "I saw you at the drugstore. You were talking to Lenny."

I glanced at her and said, "We were discussing Pickles." A half-truth. I had questions of my own and didn't want to scare her off before I got the chance to ask them.

Her eyes darted around the shop. "He was really mad after the race."

I smiled. That was an understatement. "Were you able to see Zippy yesterday?"

She nodded. "He was with the ladies at the front desk. They promised to watch out for him."

Sally and Lorraine worked the information desk at the police station. Not only were they missing a sense of humor, they carried guns. If they said they'd look after Zippy, they meant it.

Fallon moved thoughtfully around the front of the shop. "I checked out your booth at the race. I saw a medium-sized animal-print pet carrier. Do you still have it?"

I tilted my head to the side. "I haven't unpacked it yet. Are you interested?"

She nodded. "I'd like to buy it."

I motioned at the display of dog carriers less than a foot from where she stood. "I have one exactly like it up front by the window. To your left."

"No," she snapped.

I blinked in surprised at her sudden hostility.

She regained her composure and smiled shakily. "I want the one that was at the booth."

Okay. This was interesting. What was so important that she had to have the one she saw at the Dachshund Dash? I refrained from pointing out how strange she was acting.

"Are you sure it has to be that one? It's been in the storage bin. The carrier is soft-sided so it might be damaged." I didn't believe for a second there was anything wrong with that carrier.

She shook her head adamantly. "I'd rather buy the one from the race."

It was clear from her tone she was not budging. "Whatever you say."

I gingerly made my way to the last two full storage containers and dragged the one with the dog beds and carriers behind the counter.

I coaxed her back to a topic of my choice. "So do you and Lenny know each other well? He was surprised you were still in town."

"I'm sure he was." She pressed her lips together and didn't elaborate.

I pulled out the carrier and surreptitiously looked it over. I didn't notice anything unusual about it. I had no idea why she was so emphatic that she had this specific one.

She sidled up to the counter and placed her unopened water bottle on the glass. "Can you hurry? I'm sort of in a rush."

Since when? I returned to the counter, but didn't hand it to her right away. Fallon's gaze was fixated on the carrier like a cat stalking a flashlight beam. I wouldn't have been surprised if she suddenly pounced on me and yanked the item out of my hand.

It occurred to me she could be plotting a dognapping and the carrier was how she planned to smuggle Zippy out from under Gia's nose.

"Wasn't there a blanket with it?" she asked.

"That's sold separately." I had to admit that was one of Betty's excellent ideas—stick matching blankets inside all the carriers.

"I'd like that too."

"The same one from the race?"

She nodded.

I don't know why I bothered to ask; I knew the answer.

Something wasn't adding up. If she was scheming to steal Zippy, it wouldn't matter which carrier she purchased. No, I was definitely missing a piece of the puzzle.

I set the dog carrier next to her bottle. I turned slowly, keeping my eye on Fallon for as long as I could before turning my back to her. I dug though the plastic tote and found the blanket at the bottom. I also noticed a memory card. I tucked it in my front pocket. It had to be Darby's. She was the only one—

Oh. My. Gosh. I knew who killed the girl with the dachshund tattoo. I froze, bent at the waist, breathing in the heady aroma of my own fear.

"Did you find it?" she asked.

My heart raced as I straightened. "I sure did."

I took measured steps back to the register. All I had to do was sell her the items and lock the door behind her. Then I could call Malone.

I passed the blanket to her. "Is this what you wanted?"

Missy snored at my feet. One more reminder to keep calm and my head clear.

Her terse nod was all the confirmation I needed. I rang up the two items. "Your total is one-sixty-eight."

She blinked. "One hundred and sixty-eight dollars?"

"I take all major credit cards." If I could get her to pay with credit, it could be helpful to Malone.

She pulled out a card from her purse and handed it to me. The door swung open, and Lenny stumbled inside.

"You got a lot of crap in your store." He staggered toward us.

I reined in my annoyance at his ill-timing. He was just drunk enough to get us both killed. I'd never look at mouthwash the same again. "Did you come by for that pamphlet?"

"Yeah."

I gripped the credit card tightly in my hand, the edges pressed deep into my palm. "Just give me a minute and I'll be right with you."

"I've got plenty of time."

Lenny stared at Fallon. She returned his stare with one equally intense. I heard Fallon's sharp intake. I noticed her grip tightened on the soft handle of the carrier. Lenny's gaze followed her hand.

He stomped toward us. "I want to buy that." Once again his breath smelled minty fresh.

Fallon yanked the carrier away from him. "It's mine." Her voice sounded really small and frightened.

Clearly not a happy camper, he grabbed for the dog carrier, managing to latch on to the edge. "I don't know what game you're playing, lady, but you'd be wise to let go of that. Betty said it was mine."

Um, no. Betty had been around less than I had yesterday. I stepped back and shoved my hand in my front pocket. I felt for the memory card, making sure it was still here. Reassured it was safe and that it hadn't managed to fall out, I knew I had to act fast.

While Fallon and Lenny stared at each other, I eased my cell phone out of my back pocket.

"Drop it," Lenny ordered.

I jumped. He was talking to Fallon, but I flinched all the same. There were suddenly too many things happening at one.

Missy jumped out of her comfy bed and barked. I motioned for her to lie down, but she refused to move. Fallon and Lenny played a heated game of tug-of-war with merchandise neither had paid for.

"I was here first," she shouted.

"I'm here now," he bellowed.

At this point I wasn't sure which one of them I was supposed to be afraid of. I secretly dialed Malone.

I turned down the volume, then set the phone on the shelf under the register. I prayed he answered and didn't hang up. My shop was less than ten blocks from the police station. If Malone was there he'd arrive in minutes. If he wasn't there . . . Well, I didn't want to think about that yet.

"I'm so glad you both love shopping at Bow Wow Boutique," I spoke brightly, sounding like an infomercial host. If Malone was listening, he had to know where to find me.

I continued talking as loudly as I could without making either of them suspicious. "Lenny, I have a second carrier just like the one Fallon has. I'd be happy to sell it to you."

"I want this one. And she's gonna give it to me." He reached behind his back and whipped out a gun from somewhere. Fallon faltered but refused to let go.

"Don't shoot us Lenny," I shouted. That wasn't just for Malone's benefit. I really was scared.

"Let go, Fallon, and I won't have to kill either of you." He was lying, but there was no sense in provoking the guy.

"Don't be an idiot; let him have the dog carrier," I said.

She shook her head. "No."

I wanted to reach across the counter and slap some sense into her. "It will be okay. Trust me."

"But he killed Richard." She started to cry.

I sighed. "I figured that out. I'd rather not be shot too. Let the man have the carrier."

She dropped the handle so quickly Lenny staggered backward. Now with the carrier in his possession, he searched for the memory card he'd never find.

I mouthed for Fallon to back away from Lenny but she was too busy bawling her eyes out. I backed away from the hothead with the gun.

His head jerked up. "Where is it?" He waved the gun at her.

"It's in there. I saw you hide it," Fallon said through her tears.

"No it's not." He looked at me. Redirecting his gun at me, he said, "Where is it?"

I managed a shrug. It was hard to think with a weapon aimed at my head. "I don't know what you mean."

"The memory card from the filmmaker's camera. I hid it in here. It was perfect. You and your nosy assistant were so busy playing mystery detectives you were never at your booth. Why'd you even bother to come?"

I rolled my eyes. "Trust me I won't make that mistake again. What's on the card that's so important?" Again, that wasn't just for Malone's benefit.

"You know exactly what's on it. That stupid filmmaker was everywhere. She caught me following Richard to his car." At the sound of Richard's name, Fallon wailed even louder. "Shut up," Lenny roared. "He wasn't worth all the tears."

I agreed with him.

Fallon hissed. "I knew you were a horrible person."

"I asked her nicely to hand over the camera, but she refused. I didn't mean to break her neck, but she wouldn't stop fighting me."

I gasped as I remembered talking to Lenny in front of the chili truck that afternoon. He'd been sweaty, and his shirt had been ripped.

A sick smile spread across his mouth. "You remember now, don't ya? He asked, soft-voiced and crazy-eyed.

I swallowed hard. "You'd already killed her."

"But she was shot," Fallon said.

"Melinda had seen me. I had to cover my tracks, so I shot the filmmaker with the gun I found in her camera bag. I needed to frame someone. The owner of that gun was the perfect patsy."

Betty's gun. Great. I'd probably heard the gun fire, but chalked it up to the starting gun. Just like everyone else at the race.

"Get out from behind the counter," he demanded with a wave of his weapon.

I ordered Missy to stay. She didn't want to, but she sat, growling at Lenny.

"Don't be a hero, girlfriend. Please, stay." I bent down and shoved her back under the counter where she was safer.

That gave me an idea. During my college days, I was a bartender. I'd dealt with plenty of functioning drunks. Many of whom were jocks. One thing I'd learned, the bigger they were the harder they fell.

I came out from behind the counter, my back to the door. Lenny hadn't thought his instructions through very well because now he was sandwiched between Fallon and me. Not that crybaby Fallon would be much help anyway.

"Please don't hurt us," I pleaded. I eyed the three empty plastic totes.

"I want the memory card. Now," he bellowed, pointing the gun at me.

It was now or never. I dropped to a tight ball at Lenny's feet. "Don't hurt me. Please don't hurt me." I told myself not to panic. Breathe. Wait for the right moment.

"Get up," he shouted.

I could sense him leaning down to grab me. With every ounce of strength I had, I popped up as fast, and as hard, as I could, clipping him under the chin.

He stumbled backward and tripped over the storage container. He lost his balance, collapsing to the floor like a passed-out drunk. The gun fell from his hand.

Seeing double, I scurried on my hands and knees toward the gun, grabbing it before he could stand up.

I aimed the weapon at him. "Don't move."

My eyes watered. My head felt like it was about to explode. I could hear Missy barking and Fallon yelling. I felt lightheaded. I would not pass out.

"Fallon, call 911," I said, barely above a whisper.

"No need." She pointed a shaky finger toward the front door behind me.

"Police. Don't move." Detective Judd Malone.

I lowered the gun and sat down. Malone and Officer Salinas stood behind me, firearms drawn on Lenny.

Salinas cuffed Lenny, who started to blubber about Pickles alone in the car. He wanted someone to check on him. An officer I didn't recognize ushered Fallon to my office for privacy.

"Are you okay?" Malone asked.

I thought he looked worried, but with double vision, it was hard to tell. I closed my eyes. "I'm going to have one hell of a headache."

"The EMTs will be here in a minute."

I assured him I'd be fine. He assured me that for once I'd do as I was told without arguing. I called for Missy. She ran over to me and immediately assessed my situation.

"You did a good job, Melinda."

I smiled up at him. "There's something to be said for having a homicide detective on speed dial."

Chapter Thirty-Two

ONCE LENNY STARTED talking, he couldn't stop. Due to his addiction to mouthwash, he'd lost his job as a personal trainer two months earlier. He'd been living out of his car ever since. Around the same time, Pickles had been diagnosed with arthritis. With his racing days numbered, Lenny was desperate for his beloved dog to experience one win before he had to hobble away.

Fallon had seen Lenny lurking around my booth at the race. She didn't know what he'd put in the carrier, but she believed it was important. Maybe next time she'll call the police before taking matters into her own hands.

Gia planned to file for bankruptcy and have an estate sale. After having an unauthorized preview of what would be up for grabs, I made a mental note to keep an eye out for the announcement.

Richard did have a life insurance policy, but neither Gia nor Fallon were the beneficiaries. Being the superstitious fellow that he was, he left all five hundred thousand to charity—Save Our Doxies. Fallon was moved; Gia was honked off.

As for Hagan Stone, the official story was that he'd been arrested at LAX for tax evasion before he could jet off to his bar in the Florida Keys. I knew the real story. Grey had been responsible for the take-down of Hagan. I'd never know the details, but I was okay with that. Grey was safe, and Hagan was out of all of our lives. It was time for new beginnings.

IT HAD BEEN THREE days since Lenny had been arrested. The bump on my noggin from where I'd slammed my head into Lenny's chin was finally starting to heal. My heart, well it would take a little longer.

It was noon. My heart raced as I pulled into Grey's driveway. I'd rehearsed my speech for what seemed the one-thousandth time. Each time I said something different. Each time the ending was the same.

With stubborn single-mindedness, I opened the door and slid out of the Jeep. I was halfway up the walkway when a white Audi Roadster raced into the driveway like a superhero ready to save the day. The sun shined on the driver's side front window, making it impossible to see who had parked behind me, subsequently blocking me in.

The white door flung open. I couldn't believe what I was seeing. The bump on my head had to be far worse than what the paramedics had thought, because that looked like my Mama, Barbra Langston, gliding up the driveway in her favorite Carolina Herrera chiffon lace dress.

I rubbed my eyes. No such luck. She was the real deal.

"How did you get here?" I demanded.

Her natural charming smile shone as bright as the California sun. "The private jet. You know I don't fly on those public planes. With the delays these days, and all those germs." She shuddered.

"That's not what I meant. How did you find me here?"

"You weren't at your house, which we will talk about later because that is not a house. It's barely suitable for a weekend vacation home. Anyway, you weren't at your little business either, so I came to Grey's house. And here you are."

"You have got to be kidding me. How did you know where he lived?"

She smiled mischievously. "Darlin', don't you know? We exchange birthday and Christmas cards. I have his return address."

Of course. "Go home, Mama. I'm fine."

"I will not. That is no way to greet your mother. I've come a long way to see you. You need me." I wasn't fooled by her soft feminine voice.

She glided toward me. I braced myself for the perfunctory air kiss. What I wasn't expecting was a hug. Not just any hug, but a real one, with warmth and concern. It was almost my undoing.

I pulled out of her embrace. I dragged my hand through my hair. "I'm sorry, Mama. I didn't mean to be rude."

She pursed her lips. "I've obviously surprised you."

"You could say that again," I muttered. "How about you go back to my place and I'll meet you there in a few minutes. I won't be long. We can catch up then." And find out why she really left Dallas.

Mama didn't travel domestically. If she wanted to vacation at a beach, she headed for Barbados, St. Barts, or the Dominican Republic. Not Laguna. Mama hadn't set foot here since I was a teenager, which was one of the many deciding factors of why I chose to live here.

"I'd rather catch up now. Why are you loitering outside Grey's house?"

I didn't move. I couldn't do this with her here, watching my every move. I knew from experience, her judgment was deafening when she didn't agree with my choices.

"Melinda, I'm not leaving. Not when my baby needs me. How could I stay at home knowing you needed your mama?"

And suddenly it was about her. I knew a losing battle when I was in it. "Fine. Stay outside until I tell you to come in."

She followed me up the walkway, her Jimmy Choo heels clicking a rhythm I hadn't heard in years. I pulled out my key to Grey's place and unlocked the door.

"Give me a minute to turn off the alarm." I said.

For once, she did as she was asked without debate. I slipped inside and punched in the code to deactivate the security system. "Okay, come on."

My mother followed me inside and smiled satisfied. "This is a house," she pronounced.

I rolled my eyes. "Well, he makes a lot more money than I do."

"Melinda, you have plenty of money. You could buy ten of these—"

"Mama. Stop." I cut her off. I exhaled. It was hard enough concentrating on what I needed to do without her babbling on about my, in her opinion, lackluster living conditions and how I spent the family war chest.

I took the stairs two at a time to the master bedroom. I heard my mother right behind me. I kept my emotions at bay and concentrated on retrieving my brooch.

I crossed the room to the walk-in closet. Grey always kept the door open. I assumed it was part of his training: never allow an enemy a hiding spot where he could get the jump on him.

Grey's suits hung on the right side of the closet. I pushed jackets aside, looking for the one he'd worn our last night together. I found it quickly enough. I shoved my hand in the pocket and pulled out a folded note.

Melinda. My name in his handwriting.

My heart beat so fast I thought it would explode right out of my chest.

I unfolded the paper. *I'm sorry.*

Two simple words. Sorry for what? Lying? Keeping my brooch?

Giving it back to Caro? That my mother had shown up for a visit and he wouldn't be around to run interference?

I crumbled the note in my fist.

"Bad news?" my mother asked softly.

I looked up. "You could say that."

"Tell me what happened."

I shook my head and looked away. "It doesn't matter."

"Yes, it does."

"Grey and I broke up," I stated matter-of-factly.

"I guessed that much. What did he do?"

My jerked my head around and stared at her. I narrowed my eyes. "What did you say?"

She sighed the exasperated sigh I'd heard my entire life. "It's times like this when I wish I still smoked." She paced around the room nervously.

I raised an eyebrow. I couldn't recall a time I'd ever seen her nervous. "You smoked? When?"

She waved her hand dismissively, yet managed to make it look graceful. "Years ago. Before you and Mitchell were born."

I smiled. "That's scandalous."

"I've had my moments. What did Grey do?"

I sighed. "We, Mama. *We* stopped trusting each other."

She didn't say a word for a full minute. We stood in silence with only the clock ticking in the background.

"What was supposed to be in the jacket?" she asked.

I pressed my lips together, warring with myself if I should tell her or not. In for a penny, in for a pound. "Grandma Tillie's brooch."

She expertly arched a dark brown eyebrow. "I see. And where is it now?"

Yeah, this was the sticky part. "I'm not sure. Probably with Caro."

"Why in Sam Hill would he give your brooch to Carolina?"

I shrugged. "Because he thinks I stole it from her unfairly."

"Did you?"

I thought about it for a second. "No, Mama, I didn't. However, my covert actions hurt Grey because I didn't trust him."

"So you tried to fix the situation by giving your brooch to Grey?"

I nodded.

"Melinda, why would you close the barn door when the horses are already out?"

"I was tryin' to do the right thing," I said exasperated. I knew it would become my fault.

Mama shook her head. "You know what your daddy would say about all of this?"

I rolled my eyes so hard it took me back to my teenage years. "Good judgment comes from experience, and a lot of that comes from bad judgment." I quoted. I'd heard that sayin' for most of my doggone life. Unfortunately, it was accurate.

"No. He'd tell you to keep your saddle oiled and your gun greased."

The gratitude and love I felt for Mama at the moment was evident by the humongous smile on my face. I guess sometimes a girl did need her mama. I heard what she was telling me loud and clear.

Always be prepared so when opportunity came knocking, you were ready to invite her inside.

Look out, Caro. Here I come.

The End

Fifty Shades of Greyhound

(excerpt)

Mel's cousin Caro, a Laguna Beach pet therapist, has the same knack for finding trouble among the town's pampered pets and their equally pampered owners.

The crime was doggone sinister. Soon, the police would be barking up the wrong tree.

"Catnip for mystery fans!"
—*Maggie, the cat of Donald Bain* (Murder She Wrote *Series)*

Chapter One

IT WAS A KILLER party.

Blanche LeRue, CEO of Greys Matter, barked orders for more seating, more native California bubbly, and more gourmet shrimp appetizers. I'm sure Blanche hoped the overflow crowd translated to big donations for the Greyhound rescue.

Her dress was a formal length charcoal satin that complemented her tall, reed-like figure. A commanding woman, she wore her chin-length silver hair in a way that framed her narrow face yet still managed to look more regal than severe. But make no mistake, Blanche LeRue was a regal with a cause. And that cause was Greyhound rescue.

I know it must seem to y'all that I'm always at some big fancy schmancy party. You've probably also noted that it's usually an animal-related fancy schmancy deal. You'd be right. That's me, Caro Lamont, pet therapist and big-time subscriber to the there-are-no-bad-pets-just-uneducated-pet-parents philosophy.

My Laguna Beach pet therapy business is called PAWS, which stands for Professional Animal Wellness Specialist, but, in truth, I work more with problem people than problem pets.

Invitations to charity events abound in this pet-friendly southern California haven, but tonight's gala was a special one, the Fifty Shades of Greyhound Charity Ball, at *D'Orange Maison*, a gorgeous historic ranch estate just outside of Laguna Beach. The main house had recently been spiffed up, the huge rooms used for wedding receptions, political affairs, celebrity functions, and events such as this five- thousand-dollar-a-ticket fund-raiser.

The room was shades of gray everywhere. Pale gray skirting and deep gray brocade tablecloths, slate-colored vases filled with silver floral arrangements.

I know what you're thinking: they were playing off the mega success of a book that started with the same phrase. Well, you'd probably be right, but you have to admit it was for a great cause. And there were truly fifty, count them, *fifty* real live Greyhounds of varying shades staged at strategic places around the room. Most sat at attention at the feet of their owners or handlers. Though all the dogs were not gray—some white, some black, and still others fawn or brindle—all were adorned with gray leather collars. Blanche LeRue was nothing if not a detail person.

There were many wonderful Greyhound rescue groups in California, but Greys Matter was, in my opinion, one of the best. I hoped the clink and clatter of the crystal and china as waiters refilled champagne glasses and people filled their plates was echoed by the *cha-ching* of hefty contributions to the rescue group.

Speaking of details, Blanche and her event committee had come up with the idea of silver-framed signs around the room printed with factoids about Greyhounds. It was a superb idea. What a great way to convey important information to attendees without some talking head standing at a microphone. I'd seen it time and time again—people who'd paid a pricey admission impatiently waiting for a speaker to be done so they could resume their conversations. People were still waiting, but they were waiting in line to pile gourmet food on their china. And the Greys Matter crew had made sure the buffet tables were placed strategically close to the framed signs. Brilliant.

Part of the fun of attending events like this one was the people-watching. There's always more to people than what you first noticed. Ever a student of human behavior, I loved the opportunity to observe.

Which was why I stood watching people while Sam Gallanos, my— well heck, what was Sam?

My friend? No, we're more than friends. My lover? No, less than that one? My escort? Now that just sounds wrong, doesn't it? My man? My main squeeze? Hmmm. What we were to each other was complicated. So for now, let's just call him my date for the evening.

Sam, my "date" was off fighting the crowd for a plate of food. While I enjoyed the people-watching, I hoped he'd be back soon. Partly because I enjoyed his fabulous company, and partly because I'd begun to get hungry.

I looked around the spectacular ballroom. Several of my PAWS clients were in attendance. I spotted retired news tycoon Davis Pinter standing near a sign that said, "The origin of the Greyhound name has nothing to do with color. In fact, gray is not a common color among Greyhounds." That was true.

Davis is a lovely man, always well-dressed, and he looked snappy tonight in his gray tux. Davis has an adorable Cavalier King Charles Spaniel named Huntley. A smart man and a smart dog, but sometimes there ensued a battle of wills between the two, which was how we'd become acquainted.

Each of the signs had an artistic outline of a Greyhound at the top. The one closest to me said, "Before the 1980s, many racing Greyhounds were put down at the end of their careers. Now, thanks to rescue groups like Greys Matter, more than 20,000 are adopted each year."

I knew the stats, but still seeing them in black and white was sobering. I could understand why Blanche and the other volunteers were so passionate about Greyhound rescue.

I saw my friend, Diana Knight, across the way and a smile welled up inside me. Her elegant, perfectly-coiffed, blond head bobbed up and down as she talked. She'd cornered a California congressman near another sign which stated, "Most Greyhounds are at the end of their racing careers at two to five years of age, but they still have a lot of life to live. The average lifespan is twelve to fourteen years." Diana pointed at the words on the sign and pointed at the congressman.

What Diana Knight is to me isn't at all complicated. Diana is my very best friend in the world. She's eighty-something and old-school Hollywood at its best, having starred in a number of golden age romantic comedies as the perky heroine who always got the best of the guy.

Well, perky had morphed into feisty. Based on the distance of her perfectly manicured finger from said congressman's nose, Diana was definitely getting the best of the politician. I couldn't hear the conversation because of all the chatter in the room, but I was willing to bet it had something to do with animal rights. With Diana it was always about the animals. You always knew where you stood with her and she unapologetically lived her passion. I aspired to be Diana Knight when I grew up.

Diana was dressed in gray like the rest of us, though her dress was a soft, silvery-gray chiffon, the perfect foil for her delicate coloring. I knew she'd want to do lunch soon so we could dish on who was with whom, and which designers made the best show.

The main door opened and the last few arrivals hurried inside, victims of a steady rainfall. We could use the rain, but maybe *D'Orange Maison* should think about a covered portico.

Tova Randall sashayed into the ballroom with the new man in her life. I'd heard she'd been out of the country. Tonight, all eyes were on her as she made an entrance in a gray-toned sheath that hugged her silicone-enhanced curves. Tova was sprinkled with raindrops which looked good on her flawless skin. She'd been a very successful lingerie model and, on her, the rain almost looked like an accessory in a photo shoot. I was thankful I'd arrived before the rain as the moisture would not have been as kind to my naturally-curly red locks.

Tova's previous significant-other relationship had met with an unfortunate end. I'd not been much of a fan of the woman, but no one deserved what she'd been through. I was glad to see Tova was getting out.

My cousin, Melinda Langston, who owned the Bow Wow Boutique, an über-fancy pet shop in downtown Laguna Beach, had been involved in solving the murder of Tova's boyfriend and plastic surgeon, Dr. O'Doggle.

Speaking of Melinda—where was she?

I scanned the room of high-steppers. They were all tricked out in gray and black and silver fashions, but dark-haired Mel with her striking good looks would be easy to spot. I didn't see her.

It wasn't like her to miss a rescue event. I'd heard she and Grey Donovan, local art gallery owner and her on-again-off-again fiancé, had been seen around town. So the current future wedding status must be "on." I think it was a sure bet I could count myself out as a bridesmaid.

Mel's mama and my mama were sisters. We'd been childhood best friends, even up through our teen years and into our twenties. We shared a background of over-achieving high-competition mothers. We shared a love of critters. We shared a loathing of the pageant circuit.

But then things had happened, words were said, and, well, it's beyond complicated and partly involves the brooch I wore tonight.

You see, our Grandma Tillie had left the bejeweled basket of fruit pin to her "favorite granddaughter." She only had two granddaughters. Clearly, only one could be the favorite. That would be me. I'd recently retrieved the brooch from Mel's possession and I sure as shootin' did not want her to miss seeing me wear it tonight.

"Hello, Caro." Alana Benda appeared at my side. "Isn't this awesome?" Her voice was a little too bright. A little too loud. Either too much excitement or her champagne glass had been refilled a few too many times.

"It is," I agreed. "A great turnout, and the venue is absolutely stunning."

"Speaking of stunning, is your dress a Jenny Packman?" Alana tapped the peplum skirt of my silver-gray satin gown, her heavy diamond tennis bracelet winking in the lights.

"It is." I could have worn something I had, but I didn't really own anything formal in gray. Not a great color for a redhead. Besides, why pass up an excuse to buy a new dress? Right? Especially something from the newest hot designer. I loved the simplicity of her designs, although I'd worried the delicate beading would be damaged by the brooch prominently pinned to my left shoulder.

"I thought so." Alana looked like she thought there might be a prize involved for the correct guess.

Also, I got the impression I'd suddenly been raised a few notches in her who-might-possibly-be-important list. Leave it to Alana to be into the haute couture label on what everyone was wearing. Not that Diana and I wouldn't be doing a designer debrief when we got together for lunch, but we weren't picking our friends based the status on their closet.

Alana had picked a silver and black Roberto Cavalli animal print that accented her toned-to-the-max body. I didn't know Alana all that well except for talking to her at functions like this.

She was married to Dave, the accountant who had an office in the group where PAWS was located, but come to think of it, I didn't really know Dave that well either. He wasn't around the place a lot and when he was, it seemed he was always busy. During tax season, there was a steady stream of wealthy Laguna residents coming through the office. I imagined the guy needed to work long hours if his wife had a penchant for designer dresses and diamond bracelets.

I glanced over Alana's shoulder at the silver-framed placard behind her. "Greyhounds are bred and built for speed but they are often referred to as 40 MPH couch potatoes. They are exceptionally calm dogs."

That was true. Greyhounds were great family dogs. Gentle and good-natured.

I clearly didn't know much about Dave because I hadn't realized he and his wife were interested in Greyhound rescue.

"Do you and Dave have Greyhounds?" It didn't necessarily follow, though many attendees at the event did.

"We do." She flipped bleached blond bangs out of her eyes. "We have two Italian Greyhounds, Louie and Lexie."

Italian Greyhounds are extremely slender and the smallest of the sighthounds. They looked like miniature Greyhounds, but a lot of IG owners didn't care for the term. The American Kennel Club sees them as true genetic Greyhounds, with a bloodline going back more than two thousand years.

The main thing as far as my PAWS clients go is, while they're incredibly sweet and well-behaved, an Italian Greyhound, like any Greyhound, should not be trusted off leash because they have an extremely high predator drive. That means, you may be walking with your dog and suddenly he takes off after a small animal. Not good at the dog park.

"They're great dogs." I waited, expecting her to pull out pictures of her fur kids, or point them out if they were in the room. Most of the pet owners I'd talked to did once the topic came up.

Not Alana.

Her fake eyelashes fluttered. "And David is the CFO for Greys Matter." She gestured with her champagne glass toward the corner of the room where Dave stood talking to Alice Tiburon and her husband, Robert.

I knew CFO meant Chief Financial Officer, but Alana's tone implied it meant Dave and Warren Buffett were pals.

I glanced over at the trio. Alice Tiburon was the chair of the board of Greys Matter and she definitely was no trophy wife. In fact, she was the one with the money in that pairing. She was a very successful businesswoman. The Tiburons had recently moved from their mansion in Ruby Point to a bigger mansion in the even more exclusive gated community of Diamond Cove. On the coast, and in Laguna in particular, it's all about the view, and this Diamond Cove property was purported to have the best view in Orange County. Certainly it was one of the most expensive.

Dave and Robert wore gray tuxes like the rest of the men. Alice was striking in a gray crepe ribbon-striped gown that perfectly accented her slender height and her shoulder-length dark hair. I wondered if Alana had asked her who the designer was.

I should say hello to Dave and the couple. I'd known the Tiburons had Greyhounds, but apparently not problem ones. Or, if so, they used a different pet therapist. Alice and Robert Tiburon were regulars at Laguna Beach events and a solid supporter of pet causes. I knew the latter because she was often on Diana's donor list.

I turned back to speak to Alana, but she had moved away, obviously spotting another potentially important person in designer dress. I looked around once again for Sam, and my glance caught Blanche LeRue's silver head as she surveyed the crowd and the lavishly decorated *D'Orange Maison* ballroom. I could see a slight frown form as she noted the gaps in the sumptuous platters of food surrounding the towering

Greyhound dog ice sculpture.

She waved over Dino Riccio. The dapper Italian caterer hurried to her side and, in turn, motioned to Eugene, the latest addition to his catering team. Dino owned the popular Riccio's Italian restaurant and was also the current leading man in Diana Knight's life.

Eugene, the new foodie recruit, was the twin brother of Verdi, an über multitasker who'd we'd recently hired as a part-time receptionist for our shared office group. She'd been recruited after an unfortunate series of ill-suited temps.

Scanning the room again, I finally spotted Sam making his way toward me through the crowd with two plates of food. Thank heavens! I was famished.

He caught my attention, and I felt a little answering kick in my gut from the warmth of his gaze across the distance.

Even in this crush of people, the guy stood out. It hardly seemed fair. It was a gray-tie affair so it was a level playing field. Every man in the room was pretty much dressed the same, yet still, Sam's air of relaxed assurance along with his Greek heritage added up to something that turned heads. At least female ones. Call it charisma or sex appeal or whatever you want, Sam had it in spades.

There was a sudden break in the chatter around me and I turned away from the sight of Sam and my food to see what had drawn everyone's attention. There was some sort of a commotion over by the room's service door.

I stood on tiptoes to see over heads. No small feat, let me tell you, in my new silver-strappy Jimmy Choos. Eugene and one of the guests were in a heated exchange. There was a collective gasp as one of the Greyhound signs fell into a stack of used silverware which hit the floor with a clatter. Both men were red-faced.

I'd vouched for Eugene to Dino, who'd needed extra help for the party, but I knew him only in passing. I knew Verdi and I'd figured if they were related, he had some of her work ethic and multitasking skills. And Dino had been in a tight spot.

I hoped Eugene hadn't spilled something on the guy.

The man was bigger and towered over Eugene, but the young man did not back down. At least his body language said so. Finally with a shove to Eugene's shoulder, the ruddy-faced fellow stalked off and Eugene continued through the service door.

After a slight pause, we all went back to our conversations. I worried about the argument and if there'd been damage, but not overly.

According to Dino, there are always mishaps and disgruntled guests at every function. Dino was a pro—he'd sort things out.

I'd turned to look for Sam and those plates of food, when Blanche suddenly appeared beside me. I'm tall, but the woman had to be at least six feet, and she practically vibrated with energy. She was in her element and having the time of her life.

"Hi, hon, how's the event going?" I asked.

"Great. Just great." Blanche's blue eyes snapped with excitement. "I think we'll hit our goal before the night is over."

"Everything looks wonderful. The signs were a brilliant idea. And I can't believe the ice sculpture of the Greyhound." I pointed toward the banquet table. "And the rabbit looks so lifelike."

"Rabbit?" She frowned and turned toward the table. "There's no—"

Just then the rabbit moved.

"Well, for cryin' in a bucket." The rabbit looked like a real bunny rabbit because it *was* a real bunny.

The furry floppy-eared critter scampered the length of the loaded feast, honey-glazed carrot clamped in its teeth, leaving a trail of shrimp cocktail bunny tracks across the buffet. Then the rabbit went airborne onto the closest guest table.

Which was all it took. It was like the starting gun had been fired.

The Greyhound stationed near the table sighted the hare and began the chase. Instantly, chaos reigned.

Hound chased rabbit, hound chased hound, humans chased hounds. Leashes trailed, tables tipped, trays of glasses tumbled.

I could still see Sam, but he was carried backward by the wave of people and Greyhounds. Complete and utter pandemonium.

I surveyed the bedlam to see what I could do to help.

I decided one Greyhound at a time was the best tactic. I started toward the closest dog, a beautiful jet-black hound.

All at once, a man popped up in front of me. It was the big ruddy-faced man Eugene had fought with earlier. His face was now pale as he tried to speak, but he gasped for air instead.

Thinking perhaps he had claustrophobia or was having a panic attack of some sort, I laid my hand on his arm and asked, "Are you okay? What's wrong?"

He opened his mouth, but still nothing.

The man reached out to me and grabbed my shoulder. I winced as his hand leaned on Grandma Tillie's brooch and pushed it into my flesh.

He lunged forward against me knocking me off balance.

"Sir? Sir, what's the problem?"

As he fell at my feet, my question was answered.

The problem was there was a very large carving knife sticking out of his back.

Acknowledgements

We are indebted to the countless dachshund lovers who shared stories and photos of their beloved dogs. Your passion for your low-rider pooches is contagious. Thank you for entrusting us with your memories and tales of adventure. Or in some cases, misadventure.

To the compassionate staff at MacRae Park Animal Hospital, thank you for answering our numerous questions about the risks of dogs ingesting caffeine. Your knowledge and insight ensured that we weren't endangering any animals with our storyline idea. You certainly didn't need to call us with new information while you were on vacation, but we appreciated it! The education on canine depression and pet grief was eye-opening. If we all cared as deeply for each other as you care about our pets, the world would be a better place. Thank you!

To our fabulous editor, Deborah Smith, who pushed us to dig a little deeper. Thank you for believing in our ability to create an entertaining story when we present you with nothing more than a "punny" title. Your faith in our storytelling abilities is inspiring.

Christine Wittholm, our agent, at Book Cents Literary Agency, thank you for believing in us. Your enthusiasm is a great motivator for us to be our best.

Christine, Cindy, and Tami, thank you for telling us when we've gotten off track and when we've made you laugh. But most of all, thank you for the words of encouragement at the perfect moment. You are the best.

We couldn't do this without the support of our amazing families who don't bat an eye when we ask to schedule special family events around deadlines and book signings. Thank you for understanding. We love you all.

Once again, to the residents of Laguna Beach. Please forgive the creative license we've taken with your community, especially with your dog park.

As always, a huge thank-you to our readers. You rock! We are overwhelmed by your love of Caro, Mel, and "Pajama Betty." We love to hear from you. If you'd like to join our street team, Sparkle Abbey's Pack, and get the lowdown on future projects, you can sign up at our website: sparkleabbey.com

About the Authors

Sparkle Abbey is the pseudonym of two mystery authors (Mary Lee Woods and Anita Carter). They are friends and neighbors as well as co-writers of the Pampered Pets Mystery Series. The pen name was created by combining the names of their rescue pets—Sparkle (Mary Lee's cat) and Abbey (Anita's dog). They reside in central Iowa, but if they could write anywhere, you would find them on the beach with their laptops and, depending on the time of day, with either an iced tea or a margarita.

Mary Lee

Mary Lee Salsbury Woods is the "Sparkle" half of Sparkle Abbey. She is past-president of Sisters in Crime—Iowa and a member of Mystery Writers of America, Romance Writers of America, Kiss of Death, the RWA Mystery Suspense Chapter, Sisters in Crime, and the SinC internet group Guppies.

Prior to publishing the Pampered Pets Mystery Series with Bell Bridge Books, Mary Lee won first place in the Daphne du Maurier contest, sponsored by the Kiss of Death chapter of RWA, and was a finalist in Murder in the Grove's mystery contest, as well as Killer Nashville's Claymore Dagger contest.

Mary Lee is an avid reader and supporter of public libraries. She lives in

Central Iowa with her husband, Tim, and Sparkle, the rescue cat namesake of Sparkle Abbey. In her day job, she is the non-techie in the IT Department. Any spare time she spends reading and enjoying her sons and daughter-in-laws, and five grandchildren.

Anita

Anita Carter is the "Abbey" half of Sparkle Abbey. She is a member of Sisters in Crime—Iowa and a member of Mystery Writers of America, Romance Writers of America, Kiss of Death, the RWA Mystery Suspense chapter, and Sisters in Crime.

She grew up reading Trixie Belden, Nancy Drew, and the Margo Mystery series by Jerry B. Jenkins (years before his popular Left Behind series.) Her family is grateful all the years of "fending for yourself" dinners of spaghetti and frozen pizza have finally paid off, even though they haven't exactly stopped.

In Anita's day job, she works for a staffing company. She also lives in Central Iowa with her husband and four children, son-in-law, grandchild, and two rescue dogs, Chewy and Sophie.

3-19-20

CPSIA information can be obtained
at www.ICGtesting.com
Printed in the USA
LVHW091544200220
647643LV00005B/934